The Magic Mirror
of the
Mermaid Queen

Also by Delia Sherman

Through a Brazen Mirror
The Porcelain Dove
The Fall of the Kings (with Ellen Kushner)
Changeling

The Magic Mirror of the Mermaid Queen

Delia Sherman

VIKING

VIKING

Published by Penguin Group

Penguin Group (USA) Inc., 345 Hudson Street, New York, New York 10014, U.S.A.

Penguin Group (Canada), 90 Eglinton Avenue East, Suite 700, Toronto,
Ontario, Canada M4P 2Y3 (a division of Pearson Penguin Canada Inc.)

Penguin Books Ltd., 80 Strand, London WC2R 0RL, England

Penguin Ireland, 25 St Stephen's Green, Dublin 2, Ireland
(a division of Penguin Books Ltd.)

Penguin Group (Australia), 250 Camberwell Road, Camberwell, Victoria 3124, Australia
(a division of Pearson Australia Group Pty Ltd.)

Penguin Books India Pvt Ltd., 11 Community Centre, Panchsheel Park,
New Delhi – 110 017, India

Penguin Group (NZ), 67 Apollo Drive, Rosedale, North Shore 0632, New Zealand
(a division of Pearson New Zealand Ltd.)

Penguin Books (South Africa) (Pty) Ltd, 24 Sturdee Avenue,
Rosebank, Johannesburg 2196, South Africa

Penguin Books Ltd., Registered Offices: 80 Strand, London WC2R 0RL, England

First published in 2009 by Viking, a member of Penguin Group (USA) Inc.

1   3   5   7   9   10   8   6   4   2

Text copyright © Delia Sherman, 2009
Map copyright © Sam Kim, 2009

Lines from "The Adventures of Isabel" copyright © 1936 by Ogden Nash.
Reprinted by permission of Curtis Brown, Ltd.

LIBRARY OF CONGRESS CATALOGING-IN-PUBLICATION DATA IS AVAILABLE
ISBN: 978-0-670-01089-9

Printed in U.S.A.
Set in New Aster
Book design by Kate Renner

To Liran, Aliza, and Caleb Bromberg, who provide me
with good advice, inspiration, and enthusiasm.

NEEF'S NEW YORK BETWEEN

HUDSON RIVER

NEW YORK HARBOR

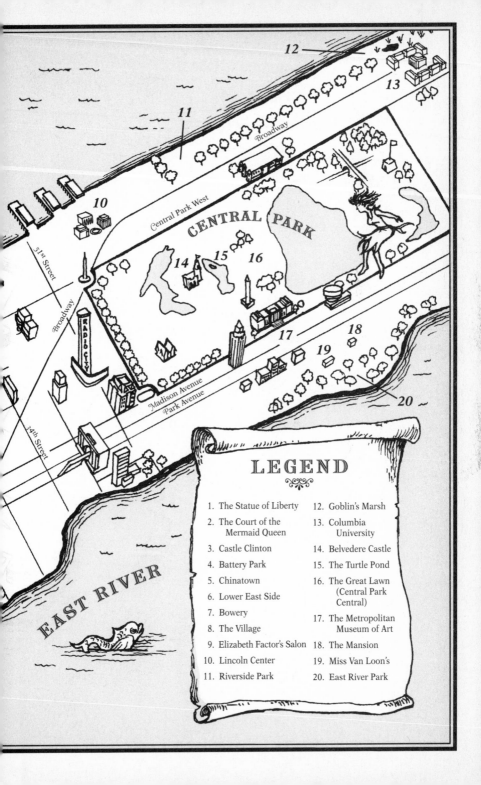

LEGEND

1. The Statue of Liberty
2. The Court of the Mermaid Queen
3. Castle Clinton
4. Battery Park
5. Chinatown
6. Lower East Side
7. Bowery
8. The Village
9. Elizabeth Factor's Salon
10. Lincoln Center
11. Riverside Park
12. Goblin's Marsh
13. Columbia University
14. Belvedere Castle
15. The Turtle Pond
16. The Great Lawn (Central Park Central)
17. The Metropolitan Museum of Art
18. The Mansion
19. Miss Van Loon's
20. East River Park

The Magic Mirror of the Mermaid Queen

RULE 10: STUDENTS MUST NOT COMPLAIN ABOUT THE RULES.

Miss Van Loon's Big Book of Rules

"Set the table, Neef," my fairy godmother said. "White cloth, the china with the blue flowers. And get out the extra-large teapot. The Pooka's coming to tea."

I dropped the white cloth on the kitchen floor. "The Pooka? You're putting out the good china for the Pooka?"

"He's your fairy godfather, pet. Why shouldn't I?" Astris leapt onto a high stool and opened the oven door carefully. A delicious scent of falling leaves and frost curled around my nose.

"And autumn cookies!" I exclaimed. "Okay, Astris. What's up?"

Astris pulled a tray of leaf-shaped cookies from the oven. "What kind of a question is that?" she asked sternly.

"Well, it's not officially autumn yet. And the Pooka broke a plate last time, remember? You said you'd never use the china for him again. Something's got to be up."

Astris sat up on her haunches. It's hard for a large white rat with pink paws and powder-puff fur to look stern, but she did her best. "I need fewer questions and more work here, young lady. Your godfather will be along any moment."

The Pooka arrived just as I was getting out the teapot. He had the bright look of a trickster who is just about to drop you into a heap of trouble, and a bunch of roses from the Shakespeare Garden, slightly brown around the edges. My suspicions, already roused, jumped up and danced.

He handed me the roses with a flourish. "Sweets for the sweet." He sniffed the air. "Autumn cookies? Astris, it's the wonder of the world you are."

I put the roses in a plastic jar and set them on the table while Astris poured tea. We sat down. Cups were handed around. The Pooka dipped a leaf-shaped cookie into his tea and stuffed it, dripping, into his mouth. Astris glared at him. I ate one cookie and reached for a second.

"You'll be starting school tomorrow, Neef," Astris said brightly.

My hand fell to the table.

"Miss Van Loon's School for Mortal Changelings," the Pooka added helpfully.

I looked from one to the other. "School for *Mortal Changelings*?" I repeated stupidly.

Astris nodded. "Mortal as butterflies, pet."

A school for mortal changelings. A school for me. When I was little, Astris brought me to live with her in New York Between, leaving a fairy twin to take my place Outside. I'm the only mortal changeling in Central Park. I used to think I was the only changeling in New York Between, but last summer I'd met my friend Fleet, and she told me there were plenty of other changelings. I'd been wanting to meet some of them ever since. And now I was going to.

I whooped happily. The Pooka laughed. Astris covered her pink-leaf ears with her paws. A white rat can't smile or frown, but if you pay attention, a wrinkled nose or a whisker twitch can give you a lot of information. What Astris's whiskers were saying right now was, "Mortals are so emotional."

"Well, I *feel* emotional! I'm going to *school* tomorrow!" I hesitated. "Astris . . . what's school?"

It wasn't that I hadn't seen the word before. Mortals are always leaving magazines and books in Central Park, so I know about lots of things I've never actually seen. But a school in New York Between probably wouldn't be the same as a school in New York Outside.

The Pooka swallowed a gulp of tea. "Well, that's the thing of it. We're not entirely certain what a school might be." He hesitated. "I've heard tell you learn things there."

"I learn things *here*, in the Park," I pointed out. "Astris teaches me Folk lore. Mr. Rat teaches me fishing and rowing, Stuart Little teaches me sailing, and the Water Folk teach me swimming and water sports. The Shakespeare Fairies teach me poetry. The Old Market Woman at the Metropolitan Museum teaches me ancient languages and art appreciation, Iolanthe teaches me dancing, and you teach me questing and trickery. What else is there to learn?"

Astris fixed me with a stern ruby eye. "We don't know. And that's why you have to go to school." She hesitated. "You're growing up, Neef. You're changing every day. I'm used to mortals growing from little to medium-sized, but—" She stopped, her whiskers twitching unhappily.

"None of them grew up," I finished for her. "Yeah, I know."

Last summer, I'd found out that none of the Central Park changelings who came before me lived very long. They'd drowned in the Harlem Meer or fallen off a cliff or done something stupid and been eaten by the Wild Hunt. I did something stupid, too, but I didn't get eaten. I got sent on a quest instead.

"But you *are* growing up," Astris said. "And school is part of it. Think of it as your reward for surviving your quest."

The Pooka picked up the last cookie. "The truth is," he said, waving it at me, "you're the official Central Park changeling. When you get big, you'll do whatever it is official changelings do. Which we haven't a notion of, not having had one since before the Genius Wars. And that's why you must go to school—to learn official changelinging."

I looked at the Pooka and Astris and my cooling tea and the empty plate. I got up. "I'm hot," I said. "I'm going for a swim."

I took off before they could react. When I reached the courtyard, I heard Astris chittering behind me. I speeded up. I needed to move, I needed to think, I needed to get away from the Pooka's eyebrows and Astris's anxious whiskers.

And I *was* hot.

Astris and I live in Belvedere Castle, high on a rocky cliff between the wooded hill of the Ramble and Central Park Central, the big field where all the Fairy Gatherings are. I swim in the Turtle Pond, which is at the foot of the cliff. The only way down is to follow the path through the Shakespeare Garden to the stair cut into the cliffside.

It was a hot, muggy afternoon, all white sky and dust and sticky sweat down my back. The shadows of the Shakespeare Garden looked cool, but weren't. I slowed down and pulled up the hem of my T-shirt to wipe the sweat out of my eyes. As I passed the big mulberry tree, a voice floated down from the branches: "I know something you don't know."

I looked up, and saw the hobgoblin Puck, grinning slyly at me through the leaves.

My life is full of tricksters. I know how to deal with them.

"Don't you always?" I said. "Well, guess what? I don't care who the Willow weeps for or where the Squirrel King hides his nuts."

Puck grinned wider and started to chant. "*School days, school days, dear old Golden Rule days.*"

I groaned. "Am I the only person in Central Park who didn't know I'm going to school tomorrow?"

"Lord, what fools these mortals be."

"All right, Puck. If you know so much, tell me. What's school like?"

Puck made a wry face. "*Readin' and 'ritin' and 'rithmetic, taught to the tune of a hick'ry stick.*" He shrugged. "What know I of mortal ignorance, Neef, save that it is boundless?"

He stuck out his tongue, long and red and pointed, then disappeared among the mulberry leaves, leaving me feeling like an idiot, as usual.

At least nobody at school could tease me about being a mortal.

At the Pond, I shed my jeans and cannonballed into

the water, splashing the ducks who'd been dabbling, tail-up, in the shallows.

They popped upright, sputtering and coughing. "Why don'tcha watch where you're goin'?" they quacked angrily.

I dove into the water and frogged my way through the cool, green dimness, scattering fish and upsetting the turtles. I didn't care. I had to move, or I'd jump out of my skin.

It wasn't just having school sprung on me and the Pooka eating all the cookies. I'd been crabby and restless ever since I came home from my quest.

The thing was, I'd learned there was more to New York Between than just Central Park. I'd been to Broadway. I'd played the Riddle Game with the Mermaid Queen of New York Harbor and done a deal with the Dragon of Wall Street and lived to tell about it. I'd even met my fairy twin, which was a trip all by itself. I'd had a real Fairy-tale Adventure.

After that, Central Park felt kind of tame. Here I was, officially the hero and champion of Central Park, and I still had to keep my room clean and go to bed when Astris told me to. It was enough to make a tree scream.

When I got tired of swimming, I floated on my back, looked up into the hazy white sky, and wondered what school would be like. Would there be a lot of rules, like the Folk had, about who you could speak to and how and when? Would they make us learn long lists of Folk and their ways?

Would they teach us magic? I really wanted to learn magic.

The shadow of Castle Rock crept out over me. I paddled to the shore and climbed out onto the bank.

And that was when I realized that I'd forgotten to bring a towel or anything dry to put on over my wet T-shirt.

The ducks laughed like loons, and I thought I could hear the turtles sniggering. I picked up my jeans and dripped all the way up the steps and across the courtyard to the Castle.

I peeked in the kitchen door. The entire contents of my clothes chest was draped over the furniture, with the Pooka standing in the middle of it, holding my Demon Dance T-shirt by one sleeve and shaking his head.

"What are you *doing*?" I squealed.

Astris snatched up a kitchen towel. "You're as wet as a fish, pet. Come by the stove and have a cup of tea. You'll catch your death."

I ignored her. "Why are my clothes all over the kitchen?"

"Your godfather and I were discussing what you should wear to school tomorrow. Do dry yourself, pet. You're dripping all over the floor."

"There's nothing to discuss." I took the towel and

rubbed at my hair. "I'll wear jeans and a T-shirt. It doesn't have to be the Demon Dance one."

The Pooka dropped the shirt and nudged it to one side with his toe. "My heart," he said, "you will not so. Your jeans are out at the knees, and each and every one of your shirts is a crying and a shame. Mortals care about such things."

"I'm a mortal," I said. "I don't care."

"You should." To my surprise, he was totally serious. "The pride and honor of the Park are at stake." He pointed to a chair piled with black and white. "Put those on, and let's have a look at you."

It was the black pants and white top Honey the vampire had given me last summer so I'd fit in on Wall Street. I took them upstairs, changed, and came down again, tugging at my top and wishing my waistband wasn't cutting me in half.

The Pooka walked around me. "The britches are a bit snug."

"I've grown," I said defensively. "There's no rule against that, is there?"

The Pooka *tsk*ed. "With your leave," he said, and laid his hands on my shoulders. Immediately, my clothes began to squirm unpleasantly against my skin.

I squealed and wriggled. "Be still," the Pooka said severely, and I bit my lip and endured until everything settled down.

"Better," the Pooka said, "but it's lacking something." He took off his own coat. It was black, with a nipped-in waist and full skirts and wide sleeves with turned-back cuffs and big silver buttons. He helped me into it. It snuggled across my shoulders, smelling faintly, like the Pooka, of animal.

"There," he said. "They'll all be inquiring after your tailor, so they will, and never mind your worn jeans. Mind you take care of it, now. Coats like that don't grow on trees."

I spun around, making the skirts whirl, and grinned at him gratefully.

"One thing I do know about school," Astris said, "is that you must get there bright and early in the morning."

I hate getting up early. I sighed. "Is there a Between-ways stop nearby?"

The Pooka shoved a pile of clothes off a chair and sat down. "Will I let a godchild of mine take the Betweenways her first day of school? I will not so. See you're waiting for me in the courtyard—shall we say dawnish?—and I'll take you there myself."

Since Folk don't like being touched unless they ask, I didn't hug him.

Astris announced it was time for dinner and I must tidy everything away. Because of the coat, I did not point out that I wasn't the one who had spread my clothes all over the kitchen. I gathered them up and headed to my room at the top of the tower.

On the second-floor landing, I passed the full-length mirror hanging outside Astris's room.

Mirrors are rare in New York Between. Astris's mirror is the only one in Central Park, if you don't count the Magic Magnifying Mirror I won from the Mermaid Queen, which now belonged to the Green Lady of Central Park. As magic mirrors go, Astris's mirror is pretty lame: it shows things exactly the way they are.

I dropped the clothes on a step and studied my reflection.

Now that everything fit, my outfit looked super-cool— a lot cooler than I did. My hair was okay, a slightly tamer version of the twiggy mass the moss women in the Ramble sported, but my face was just medium. I wasn't extra-beautiful or extra-ugly, I didn't have horns or warts or feathers or scales or green skin or anything to make me stand out in a crowd. Which was good, right?

I stuck out my tongue. My reflection returned the gesture. Then I picked up my clothes and went upstairs.

Chapter
2

RULE 2: FOLK ARE NOT ALLOWED TO SET FOOT INSIDE MISS
VAN LOON'S, NOT EVEN FAIRY GODPARENTS.

Miss Van Loon's Big Book of Rules

Early next morning, a black pony with flaming yel-
low eyes clattered into the courtyard of Belvedere
Castle, ready to take me across the City to Miss Van Loon's
School for Mortal Changelings.

Astris was one big twitch of nerves. "Did you brush
your hair? Eat your breakfast? Drink your orange juice?
I know you don't like orange juice, but it's good for you.
Do you have Satchel? What about a scarf? Are you sure
you'll be warm enough?"

Satchel is my magic bag. It's old and beat up and
smells of damp leather, but I never go anywhere without it. It gives me mortal food and holds everything
I put in it without getting any heavier. "Satchel's
right here. And it's still summer—I don't need a scarf.

Stop fussing, Astris. I went on a whole quest by myself."

Astris patted my knee with pink paws. "I know, pet. It's just . . . well, I worry, you know. It's a fairy godmother's job to worry."

"I know," I said impatiently. "I'll see you tonight."

I didn't say good-bye. It's against the rules to say good-bye.

It's also against the rules to ride black ponies with flaming yellow eyes, because they might buck you off into a bottomless lake and drown you. But since the black pony in question is my fairy godfather, it's one rule I can safely ignore.

The Pooka and I trotted east until we got to the low granite wall that marks the boundary between the Park and Fifth Avenue.

I've lived next door to Fifth all my life, but I've actually never been there. It's all buildings, vaguely fortresslike, guarded by door wardens dressed up in ceremonial armor with elf swords at their hips—not very appealing to someone used to trees and grass. The Pooka leapt lightly over the wall; the nearest wardens glared and fingered their swords. I waved cheerfully to them as we trotted east toward Park Avenue.

Astris had told me that the strip of trees and flowers down the middle of Park Avenue was under the care of the Green Lady. She hadn't mentioned that the trees were imprisoned in stone pots and the flowers were barricaded behind iron fences. I wanted to stop and find out if they minded, but the Pooka trotted on into Yorkville, where the German Folk live in narrow brownstone houses with white lace curtains at the windows.

"East River Park ahead," the Pooka remarked.

Up to now, I'd been feeling pretty good. I was seeing the City, the Pooka was with me, I was going to meet mortals, everything was fine—except maybe Park Avenue. Now I panicked. "You'll come in with me, won't you, Pooka?"

"With the red curiosity burning my heart like a bonfire at Samhain? You couldn't keep me out."

A breeze sprang up, carrying a bitter, salty, unfamiliar smell. "That'll be the East River," the Pooka said. "Miss Van Loon's is down a bit on the right, in case you're interested." ·

I was interested. First, I saw a wide, paved courtyard. Then, as we got closer, a solid red building, like a giant brick with windows and a door. The door was black; the windows were barred.

My heart sank.

I clung to the Pooka's mane, more nervous than a champion and hero had any business being.

He stopped in front of the front steps, shook me off briskly, and shifted into his man shape. "Go on, knock," he said. "They'll hardly eat you with me looking on."

I climbed to the door and knocked.

A long, brown, wrinkled face appeared, very like a brownie's. It was kind of oversized, but maybe brownies grew bigger out in the City. "No Folk allowed," the face said. "No godparents, no guardians, no magic animals. No exceptions."

Not a brownie, then. A mortal.

The Pooka put his foot on the bottom step. The face's owner came outside and crossed her arms over her black silk bosom. In the sunlight, she looked a lot more solid than the Pooka. Of course, she was wider than he was, and much better padded. But that wasn't it. If I had to describe it, I'd say he was air and she was earth.

I wondered if all mortals were like that.

The Pooka flashed her his most charming smile.

The mortal door keeper frowned. "No exceptions," she repeated firmly.

The Pooka turned to me helplessly. "I've little choice, it seems, but to leave you to face your fate alone. Never fret, my heart. You've faced dragons worse than this."

He shifted into a black dog, lifted his leg on the steps of Miss Van Loon's, and trotted off across the courtyard into the friendly green oasis of East River Park.

The door keeper *tsk*ed. "Tricksters. Well, are you coming in or aren't you?"

The front hall of Miss Van Loon's School for Mortal Changelings was long and low and echoing. The ceiling was curved, the floor was a black-and-white checker-board. A flight of black steps led upward. On the landing stood a tall wooden box with a metal disc stuck into it, ringed with numbers from 1 to 12. A short metal arrow pointed at 9; a longer one hovered just before 12. Below the disk, a long metal rod swung gently back and forth. As I watched, the long arrow jerked forward onto the 12. The box bonged nine times.

I jumped.

"Never seen a clock before?" The door lady was amused. "Well, you'll learn—that's what you're here for. Follow me."

The door lady led me to a room furnished with more books than I'd ever seen, a big wooden desk, and an uncomfortable-looking chair. Behind the desk sat a mortal woman (I could tell right away, this time) with skin the color of tree bark and gray hair in little coils, like sleeping snails. Despite the heat, she wore a scarlet sweater zipped up to her throat.

"I'm the Schooljuffrouw," she said briskly. It sounded like "*school*-you-for-now." "That's Dutch for school mistress. You're late."

"I got here as soon as I could."

The Schooljuffrouw pointed to a gray bundle on the chair. "That's your Inside Sweater. Hurry, now. Tester is waiting for you."

So school was going to be all about following orders

I didn't understand. Fine, I could do that—I'd been doing it all my life. Still, I was disappointed. I'd hoped mortals would be different.

I took the bundle, bowed to the Schooljuffrouw, and went back into the hall, where the door lady was waiting. "Got your Inside Sweater?" she asked, sounding comfortingly like Astris. "Good. Put it on."

The last thing I needed on a warm late summer's day was a sweater. I took off the Pooka's coat, tucked it into Satchel, and unfolded the bundle. The Inside Sweater had two pockets and a little collar and a zipper. It was wool, scratchy, and made me even hotter than I'd been before. I pushed up the sleeves. The door lady pulled them down. "Against the rules," she said. "You'll get used to it."

We passed the clock, its arrows pointing to 9 and 2, on our way up the stairs. The door lady led me to the second floor, where double doors opened onto a low hall lined with more doors. She pointed at one of them.

"In there," she said kindly. "It's time to start getting educated."

I took a deep breath and went in.

The room contained four other mortal changelings about my size. They were sitting at little tables, looking as hot and nervous as I felt. A tall woman stood between a big desk piled with paper and a piece of black slate with TESTER written on it in white.

"Welcome to Miss Van Loon's, Neef," the woman said. She pronounced it *Van Lo-ens*. "You're late."

The desks had chairs attached. I slid into one, catching the pocket of my sweater on the chair back. The other mortals giggled. I kept my eyes on my desk. There were words scribbled on it: "I hat sppelin" and "Phone likes gnomes."

This was worse than meeting vampires on Broadway. At least with vampires, I knew what the rules were.

Something big and heavy hit my desk with a crack. I jumped. The other mortals snickered.

"Do pay attention, Neef," Tester said. "This is school, not a fairy revel. And stop playing with your hair."

I jerked my hand away from the curl I didn't even know I was tugging. It was a habit I thought I'd broken last summer. Apparently, I was wrong.

She raised her voice. "Listen, children. You all know that Folk have lots of rules. You also know that they don't usually tell you what they are until you've broken one. Here at Miss Van Loon's, we tell you all our rules right at the beginning, along with the consequences of breaking one. That way, you can concentrate on lessons without worrying about doing something you didn't know was wrong."

I looked at the book in front of me. It was square and thick, with stiff red covers.

"You have until the next full moon to learn them," Tester went on. "We call this the Honeymoon. Just remember, it's a grace period, not permission to do whatever you want. You may open your books now."

The first page was a drawing, in profile, of a very pretty woman with a lacy collar and her hair in ringlets. It was labeled "Miss Wilhelmina Loes Van Loon."

The second page looked like this:

RULE 0:

RULE 1: STUDENTS MUST NEVER FIGHT OR QUARREL AMONG THEMSELVES.

RULE 2: FOLK ARE NOT ALLOWED TO SET FOOT INSIDE MISS VAN LOON'S, NOT EVEN FAIRY GODPARENTS.

RULE 3: STUDENTS MUST NEVER SPEAK OF WHAT HAPPENS INSIDE THE WALLS OF MISS VAN LOON'S TO ANY SUPERNATURAL BEING WHATSOEVER, INCLUDING THEIR FAIRY GODPARENTS.

RULE 4: STUDENTS MUST NEVER VISIT ONE ANOTHER'S NEIGHBORHOODS WITHOUT PERMISSION OF ALL RELEVANT GENIUSES, THE SCHOOLJUFFROUW, AND A NATIVE GUIDE.

This was worse than the lists of treasure guardians and fictional bogeymen Astris had made me memorize. I flipped through the pages with growing horror.

RULE 50: STUDENTS MUST BE EXACTLY ON TIME TO ALL LESSONS.

RULE 76: STUDENTS MUST NEVER RUN UPSTAIRS TWO

STEPS AT A TIME. ONE STEP IS USUAL. THREE IS
ACCEPTABLE. IF THEY ARE SEEN TAKING FOUR, THEY
MUST REPORT TO THE TALISMAN ROOM TO HAVE THEIR
SHOES CHECKED FOR UNAUTHORIZED SPELLS.

RULE 103: STUDENTS MUST NOT USE ANY MAGIC
TALISMAN WITHOUT SUPERVISION.

RULE 242: STUDENTS MUST NOT PLAY WITH THEIR HAIR.

I was sunk.

There were two hundred pages in all, with five rules on a page: one thousand rules to learn and follow. At the bottom of each page, in big, black letters was printed:

ANY STUDENT CAUGHT BREAKING ANY OF THESE RULES
MAY BE:

1) BANISHED

2) DEPRIVED OF GOLD STAR POINTS

3) OTHERWISE PUNISHED AT THE TUTOR'S
   DISCRETION

A boy at the front of the room waved his hand, black as night against the pale green walls.

"Yes, Fortran," Tester said. "You have a question?"

"What's Rule Zero?"

"Zero is not a number," Tester said. "Any other questions?"

We all shook our heads gloomily.

"Good," said Tester. "Now I'm going to tell you something about our founder, Miss Van Loon."

If I'd listened carefully, I would have learned exactly when Miss Van Loon had come to New York Between and why she'd founded a school for mortal changelings and a lot of other things it might have been interesting to know. As it was, I didn't hear a thing. I was too busy hating everything around me.

It wasn't the *Book of Rules*. I was used to rules. There are rules for everything in New York Between: words to say, rituals to follow, things not to do or else. Astris and Pooka had been teaching them to me ever since I could remember. Why you should never look behind you. (Something might be gaining on you.) When to say "thank you." (When you want to get rid of a brownie.) What to take on a quest. (A magic bag. Jellybeans. Your five wits.)

They'd never taught me how to deal with mortals.

"Neef," said Tester. "Have you heard a word I said?"

I stiffened. "Um."

"I didn't think so," said Tester. "You're the Central Park changeling, aren't you?" She consulted a piece of paper. "Geas, quest, godparents a magic animal and a trickster. It's a wonder you survived! Well, don't worry. You're with your own kind now."

If Astris hadn't taught me to be polite to anybody I didn't trust, I would have thrown Tester's stupid rule book at her. As it was, I bared my teeth in what I hoped looked like a smile.

My own kind? I'd never felt more out of place in my life.

I examined the other changelings: Fortran, the dark-skinned boy who'd asked about Rule 0; a girl no bigger than a faun, with sleek brown hair and smooth brown skin; a tiny blond boy; a red-haired girl who looked like an oversized leprechaun with round ears. Were they my kind? Was anybody?

"Now I'm going to ask all of you some questions," Tester was saying, "to get an idea of your strengths and weaknesses so we know what classes to put you in." She picked up a pencil and a pile of papers and sorted through them. "Espresso?"

The leprechaun girl sat up straighter.

"Name six storm spirits, please, with their countries of origin."

The girl called Espresso blinked slowly. It was perfectly obvious that she didn't know there even were storm spirits, much less their names, and was wondering whether she'd get in less trouble admitting that or whether she should take a shot at making them up.

Invention won. "There's Buffy the Wind Queen from Transylvania, and Windy Witch from England, and—"

"Very creative, Espresso," Tester interrupted. "But this isn't Story Telling. I take it you don't know any Folk lore?"

Espresso shrugged.

Tester made a note on the paper. "Tosca, you meet an old woman at a crossroads. What do you say to her?"

The little seal girl stuck her thumb in her mouth.

Tester made another note. "Peel, what's a Genius?"

The little boy, who'd been looking frightened, perked up. "*Everybody* knows what a Genius is," he said. "It's the spirit of the Neighborhood, who runs everything and protects all the Folk and the changelings. Mine's the Burgher of Yorkville."

"Very good, Peel," Tester said. "Fortran, tell me about Little Red Baseball Cap."

"Isn't that a Boston question?"

They were pitiful. Tosca knew how to say "I am under the protection of the Genius of Lincoln Center" only in French, German, and Italian. I could say the Words of Protection in a hundred languages, including an obscure Slavic dialect spoken only by the kazna peri that lived in the ravine. I not only knew "Little Red Baseball Cap," but also "Jack and the Extension Ladder" and "Sooty Slush and the Seven Dwarfs." By the time Tester got around to me, I was convinced that school was going to be a complete waste of time.

"Neef. Tell me what the first mortal changeling was called."

My mouth dropped open. "Why would I want to know that?"

Everybody snickered.

Tester sighed. "I suppose I shouldn't be surprised. And yet . . . Fortran, would you like to tell her why?"

Fortran wanted to tell me so badly he could hardly sit still. "You know how Folk are always getting into stupid feuds? Well, it's worse with Geniuses, and more dangerous for everybody because they're so powerful and everything. So the Folk steal mortals from Outside to make alliances 'cause we're flexible and know how to lie and stuff. I'm really good at the lying part," he said modestly. "I'm the best liar at Columbia University."

Tester's mouth twitched. "In Diplomacy, it's called Being Tactful, and it does not necessarily involve lying. Mortal changelings are also Champions and Questers, of course—that's been going on since Folk were Folk. In this modern age, we can also be Organizers, Personal Assistants, and Secretaries to Geniuses and Business Folk. And there are the arts: Storyteller, Composer, Artist, Magic Tech. Espresso here is going to be a Poet. She's from the Village."

We all looked at Espresso, who made a face. "That's my fairy godmother's bag," she said. "I want to be a hero. Questing's where the action's at, man."

Espresso, I decided, was probably my kind, even if she didn't know about storm spirits and talked funny.

After about a million more questions, Tester made a few more notes, reshuffled the papers, then handed them around.

"These are the lessons you'll be taking. Neef, it wasn't easy to decide where to place you. You've a very unusual combination of strengths and weaknesses. I've decided to assign you to Basic Manners, even if you are a bit old for it, as well as Diplomacy for Ambassadors, even though you're a bit young."

I wanted to tell her that Astris had been teaching me manners since I could walk, but I could tell, even without whiskers, that Tester's mind was made up.

I studied the list of lessons.

Talismans. Fair enough. I knew how to turn on the Mermaid Queen's Magic Magnifying Mirror, but that was about it. History of New York Between and Mortal History and Customs all sounded interesting. But Questing? *Diplomacy*? After I'd been on an actual quest, dodging giants and outwitting Geniuses and coming home in triumph?

The boy Fortran was having a similar experience. "Arabic?" he burst out. "Urdu? What do I need foreign languages for? I already know DOS and HTML and Java. I'm learning to be a Magic Tech, not a Diplomat."

"There are a lot of new supernaturals coming into the City," Tester said. "Some of them may be Tech Folk. You need to know how to talk to them. Any other questions?"

Espresso held up her hand. "I'm not grokking the sweaters, man."

Tester smiled. "I'm glad you brought that up, Espresso. The sweaters are a beautiful tradition established by our last Schooljuffrouw, who remembered some things from her life Outside. There's a school song, too: 'It's a Beautiful Day in the Neighborhood.' We sing it at assembly every morning."

A horn blew, loud enough to make us all jump.

"That signals the end of this lesson," Tester said. "Soon you'll hear another. It means the beginning of the next lesson. Each of you has a guide waiting outside to lead you until you learn your way around." We got up uncertainly. "Get moving. And don't forget your Rule Books."

Chapter 3

RULE 1: STUDENTS MUST NEVER FIGHT AMONG THEMSELVES.

Miss Van Loon's Big Book of Rules

O ut in the hall, a small crowd of changelings was leaning against a wall, talking. When they saw us trooping out of Tester's room in our new Inside Sweaters, they smiled.

I'd seen smiles like that before, on members of the Wild Hunt: a little too wide and much too full of teeth.

The toothiest of them looked like a dryad, tall and smoothly beautiful, with arms and legs as long and skinny as branches. Her Inside Sweater had a pattern of gold stars swirling from her right shoulder down across her chest to the hem. Under it were blue jeans, extra-skinny. Her blue eyes examined me from top to toe, widening when they got to my bare feet.

"Don't tell me," she said. "You're the Wild Child."

I'm used to teasing. The Folk love to make mortals cry. Even the moss women, who are all about helping unhappy mortals, let them wander around and moan for a while first. The moss women say it's to find out whether the mortals are really and truly unhappy and not just pretending. But I've heard them giggling in the Ramble while some poor tourist stumbles around the paths looking for the way out.

I gave the beautiful mortal the same once-over she'd given me, ending at her high-heeled glass slippers. "Pretty. What'll you do if you meet an ogre? Break your shoe over his head?"

"Ooh!" The blonde turned to her friends. "Listen to the spunky heroine! Maybe she'll challenge me to a duel." The friends giggled like squirrels. They had gold stars on their sweaters, too, laid out in different patterns.

"If I did, I'd win," I said.

"*I* have a gold star in combat."

"Good for you."

Another dryad wannabe peeled herself away from the wall. She wasn't quite as blonde or blue-eyed or willowy as the first one, but her stars were laid out in exactly the same swirling pattern.

"Obviously," she said, "you don't know who you're talking to. This is Tiffany, Debutante of the Court of the Dowager of Park Avenue. She's going to be the Dowager's Voice some day? Which, since you obviously don't know anything at all, is gigantically important. The Dowager

is constantly making alliances with all the most powerful Geniuses. Tiffany's going to be presented to the
Dragon of Wall Street at the Solstice Ball this winter."

"As what?" I asked curiously. "Dinner?"

Tiffany flipped back her shining hair. "Is that the best
you can do, Wild Child? Because, I have to say, I'm so not
impressed."

One of the boys said, "Um, Tiffany. Rule 386?"

"I *am* being polite," Tiffany said. "I'm just showing
the Wild Child what life is like out here in the real City."

Before, I'd been playing. Now I was mad. "Oh, is this
the real City? I thought it was just a place to store mortal
changelings who are too stupid to survive outside their
own Neighborhood without their fairy godmothers holding their hands."

Tiffany turned a deep rose color that unfairly made
her eyes look even bluer.

"Stupid?" she hissed. "For your information, I have a
hundred and twenty gold stars. All I need is Urban Leg-
ends, Diplomacy, and Advanced Talismans, and I'll be
ready to leave school. How many gold stars do *you* have,
Wild Child?"

"Tiffany," a new voice said sternly. "Would you please
recite Rule One for me?"

Like magic, Tiffany went from scarlet Queen of the
May to little white lamb. All in one smooth movement,
she backed away from me and sank into a deep curtsy.
I wasn't surprised. Except for her mortal solidity, the

newcomer looked like one of the Daanan sidhe—long, pale face, high-bridged nose, finely cut lips, eyes as dark and hard as asphalt. Beside her, Tiffany looked gawky and unfinished.

"Rule One," Tiffany said primly. "Students must never fight among themselves." She came up again without a wobble, which was pretty impressive, considering how tight her jeans were. "We weren't fighting, Diplomat. We were simply sharing observations on the customs of our respective Neighborhoods."

"I see," said the Diplomat. "You do realize that if the new student had any magic at her disposal, you would most probably now be a frog, a snake, or a sheep-headed freak?"

At the thought of Tiffany with a sheep's head, a tiny giggle bubbled out my nose. This was a mistake. The Diplomat pinned me with her granite eyes.

Heart beating like a drum, I curtsied—not as gracefully as Tiffany. "I'm Neef of Central Park."

"Charmed. Bergdorf?" The Diplomat turned to the second blonde girl. "Shouldn't you be taking Neef to her next lesson?"

The horn blew again, and Bergdorf grabbed my arm. I shook her off. "You are such a fairy," she said. "And I totally mean that in a bad way. Come *on*."

She barreled through the double doors and pulled me up the steps three at a time.

"Where are we going?" I panted.

"You're going to Talismans," Bergdorf said. "I'm going to Organizing Fairies. And if you don't move it, I'm going to be gigantically late, and that would be just so *human*."

Two floors up was another hall lined with doors. Bergdorf pointed me at one, then sped back the way we'd come.

When I entered the room, a Chinese man with a long gray braid down his back turned from writing MAGIC TECH on the big slate. "Welcome," he said. "Come in and sit down. I've got an exciting lesson planned."

The Magic Tech loved talismans like ravens love shiny things; he wanted us to love them, too. He opened the nine times nine magic locks on the talisman cabinet and brought out three pairs of boots, taught us how to tell which ones were seven-leaguers, and how to put them on without transporting ourselves out of state.

All the changelings in Talismans had gold stars on their sweaters, too, but not as many as Tiffany and Bergdorf. I was glad to see that almost all of them wore jeans, though there was one girl in a long skirt with a scarf over her hair and another in a saffron-colored sari. They seemed pretty friendly, too. While we were waiting our turn with the boots, a boy about my size asked me where I was from.

"Central Park," I said.

Suddenly there was a little circle of emptiness around me, and the boy was talking to someone who wasn't me.

Folk try and kill you when they don't like you. Being ignored was way better than that. Still, I was relieved when the horn blew again and everybody boiled out into the hall, where Bergdorf was waiting impatiently.

"Where to now?" I asked.

"Lunch."

Later, I found out there were two hundred pupils (give or take) at Miss Van Loon's, which was about one-fifth of the total New York Between population of maybe one thousand mortal changelings. Two hundred isn't really very many mortals when they're separated. But when they're all smooshed together in a long, narrow room with no windows and a hard floor, laughing and eating and gabbing, it's like a Full Moon Gathering without the music.

Bergdorf abandoned me at the door. I was about to slink off to find somewhere quiet to eat when a dark head popped out of the crowd, grinning excitedly: Fortran, the best liar in Columbia. I pointed at myself. He nodded and waved some more.

Feeling more cheerful, I shoved through the crowd toward the long table he was sharing with the leprechaun girl—Espresso, from the Village. I sat down next to her. Even though the dining hall was packed, we had a whole table to ourselves.

Espresso pulled a steaming cup out of a brightly striped woolen pouch. A dark, rich smell tickled my nose.

"Is that *coffee*?"

Espresso made a face. "It's mostly moo juice, man. But there's a lick of java in there somewhere."

It sounded like English, but I didn't have a clue what she'd said. "Huh?"

"Moo juice," Espresso said. "Milk. Java is coffee. Haven't you ever heard anybody talk Village before?"

I shook my head.

"It's easy," Fortran said kindly. "You'll pick it up in no time."

"Right," I said. "Um. Isn't coffee just for Folk?"

Espresso laughed. "You're jiving me. Every mortal in the whole City drinks java."

"Not me."

Silence. We set our magic bags on the table. Fortran's was blue and lumpy and rich in straps. Espresso's was a brightly striped woolen sack.

Fortran sighed. "I thought for sure some of the Columbia guys would come sit with me, but no. They're all over there, talking about amulets." He pulled a floppy slice of very thin bread with red sauce on it out of his bag and stuffed the pointy end into his mouth.

"So why aren't you sitting with them?"

Fortran's dark eyes slid toward Espresso, whose sack had produced a bowl of something that looked like green-flecked sand. "Oh, you know," he said. "I see those guys all the time. The whole point of school is meeting new people, right? So I'm meeting you."

I opened Satchel and wished, as usual, for a hamburger and French fries. I got a cold chicken leg, a chunk of brown bread, an apple, and cider.

"Wizard!" Fortran said as I tore into the chicken with my teeth. "That's the real deal. Super-trad, right from the Old Country, I bet."

"Isn't that where all magic bags come from?"

"No way." Fortran patted his lumpy blue bag, its zipper open on enchanted emptiness. "I got Backpack here at Talisman Town."

I put down my chicken. "Are you telling me you can just go out and buy a bag like Satchel?"

Fortran shook his head. "Not just like Satchel—it's too old-fashioned. But you could get a bag that *looked* just like it. Plus, it would give you whatever food you wanted—even burritos and hot dogs and pizza." He waved the remains of his tomato-smeared slice.

I thought it might be nice to have a Satchel I could boss around. But then it wouldn't be Satchel. I clutched the old, worn, stubborn leather strap. "I'll stick to this one, thanks."

We talked for a while longer. Fortran told us his fairy godfather was a geek in Columbia's Magic Lab. Espresso's godmother was a hippie chick called Earth Mother.

"What about your fairy godmother?" Fortran asked. "She's a wood nymph, right?"

I thought about lying, then decided that if Fortran and Espresso were going to hate me because of my Park-related weirdness, I might as well get it over with as soon as possible. "Astris is a giant white rat," I said. "She bakes really good cookies."

Two pairs of eyes stared at me, round as marbles. I closed Satchel and got ready to move to the empty end of the table.

"Wizard!" Fortran said.

"Groovy!" Espresso said.

I looked up. They were smiling. "You don't mind?"

"A giant white rat is cool from Coolsville, man."

That sounded pretty positive. "Thanks," I said shyly. "I think being a Poet is pretty cool, too."

Espresso blushed an uncomfortable red that clashed with her coppery hair. "That's jive, man. I'd rather groove on giant-slaying."

I looked at her with surprise. "You've slain a giant?"

Espresso shrugged. "I know a poem about one. You want to hear?"

Fortran nodded eagerly. Espresso folded her hands and began to recite.

"Isabel met a hideous giant,
Isabel continued self reliant.

The giant was hairy, the giant was horrid,
He had one eye in the middle of his forehead.
Good morning, Isabel, the giant said,
I'll grind your bones to make my bread.
Isabel, Isabel, didn't worry,
Isabel didn't scream or scurry.
She nibbled the zwieback that she always fed off,
And when it was gone, she cut the giant's head off."

I thought this through. "I don't quite get it," I said. "What did she cut his head off with?"

Espresso gave me a look. "It's a joke, man."

"I knew that," I said hastily, and laughed. "Funny."

"Did you make that up?" Fortran asked.

Espresso shook her head. "That would be a mortal named Ogden Nash. I told you, I'm not a Poet."

Bergdorf didn't show up after lunch, so Fortran's guide, Abercrombie, took both of us to Basic Manners. He was one of Tiffany's gang—tall, blond, heavily starred, and as snooty as an elf lord. He led us upstairs to a door that looked like every other door. "Welcome to the nursery," he said, and went away.

Fortran opened the door. "Oh, nuts," he said. "He's brought us to the wrong room."

Looking at the fifteen round, rosy-cheeked little faces turned to stare at us, I had to agree. Except for the gray sweaters and no wings, they looked like a nest of Victorian fairies.

"Eyes front!" We all snapped to attention. It was the tutor I'd met in the hall earlier, the Diplomat. "Clearly," she went on, "we all need more practice on focus and cultivating a pleasant expression. Neef, Fortran, welcome to Basic Manners. Fortran, you may be seated." Fortran slipped hastily into an empty desk. "Neef, if you could step to the front of the class?"

I stepped, doing my best to look cool, and bobbed the Diplomat a curtsy.

"Please face the class, Neef. I wish to present you to the other students."

I turned and watched everyone work on their pleasant expressions. They weren't very good at it.

The Diplomat folded her hands at her waist. "Neef is a new student," she announced. "She comes from Central Park."

Everyone's eyes bulged with the effort of not reacting. I curved my lips in what I hoped was a friendly smile.

"You've all heard about Central Park Folk," the Diplomat went on. "They're primitive, backwards, stubborn, uneducated, and violent. Their music is old-fashioned, and they all hate City Folk."

My smile became a frown. "That's not fair," I exclaimed. "How would you like it if I said that City Folk are stuck-up, snotty, stupid, and prejudiced?"

The Diplomat didn't even blink. "I'd say that snotty and stuck-up are essentially the same thing, and that you've left out impractical, self-centered, and unreliable, but you've hit most of the high points. I'd also say you need to work on keeping your temper. Thank you, Neef. You may sit down now."

Seething, I started for the back of the room. "Stop." I stopped. The Diplomat turned to the class. "Peony, would you like to tell Neef the proper response to a formal dismissal?"

Peony looked like a doll, with golden ringlets tumbling over the shoulders of her Inside Sweater. "You say, 'Diplomat.' Or 'my lady,' or 'my lord Genius,' or whatever. And you nod a little." She inclined her head a few respectful degrees.

"Gracefully done, Peony," the Diplomat said graciously. "That is worth a gold star point."

"Diplomat." Peony nodded briskly and sat down, grinning.

If I'd screamed or stomped out, I'd just have convinced everybody that everything they'd heard about the Park was true. So I nodded curtly, and retreated to the back of the room.

"What's a gold star point?" Fortran muttered as I sat down beside him.

"Something we'll never get," I muttered back. "Now shut up, okay?"

Basic Manners lasted forever. We practiced making formal introductions and polite conversation. Fortran made a blatting noise on Tosca's hand instead of kissing it. The Diplomat sent him to the corner to sort a jar of mixed dry rice and beans into separate bowls as punishment. While he was still sorting, the horn blew, and the Diplomat excused us.

My first day of school was over.

Out in the courtyard, I stopped to take off my Inside Sweater, which I stuffed into Satchel with the *Big Book of Rules*. All around me, changelings were chasing each other, huddling in groups, and playing mortal games with twirling ropes and bouncing balls. Over near East River Park, a magic swing hung from the sky by ropes of ivy. I thought I saw the horrible Tiffany in a crowd of blonde heads and skinny, jean-clad bodies, but the East Siders all looked so much alike it was hard to tell.

The Pooka came bounding up to me, black tail whipping the air, yellow eyes aflame with welcome, barking out questions about how I was liking education and what had I been after learning and were there any mortal boys as handsome as my fairy godfather at all.

I wanted to throw my arms around his furry neck and tell him just how horrible it all had been and how much I hated Tiffany and Bergdorf and how Fortran and Espresso were okay, for City mortals. Then I remembered Rule 3.

I shook my head.

The Pooka stopped bouncing and sat at my feet. "Are you telling me there are none? Or there are, and you're sparing my vanity?"

I shrugged. His ears drooped. "Well, if you won't tell me, you will not. It's beneath my dignity to ask twice, as I'd think it was beneath yours to deny your fairy godfather an answer to a civil question."

"I can't, Pooka. There's a rule against talking about school stuff to Folk."

"They can't be meaning your fairy godfather, surely?"

"It mentioned godparents particularly. Don't be mad, Pooka. I've had kind of a complicated day."

His ears returned to normal. "No harm in asking."

"I want to go home," I said, trying not to sound as pathetic as I felt.

"Right," he said. "Step into the Park with me, then, and I'll be shifting into something more practical for traveling."

Chapter

4

RULE 160: STUDENTS MUST NOT BULLY, INTIMIDATE, TEASE, OR OTHERWISE PROVOKE OTHER STUDENTS.

Miss Van Loon's Big Book of Rules

The second morning, the Pooka didn't show up.

Astris fixed a silver clip in my hair. "He's a trickster, pet. He comes and goes. You'll be fine on the Betweenways." She surveyed my slightly ragged Green Man T-shirt disapprovingly. "Are you sure that shirt's appropriate?"

"It's what everyone else is wearing," I protested. I didn't say that the green man's faded, leafy face painted across the back was like a little bit of the Park I could carry with me. I also had my jade frog amulet around my neck, for luck.

The frog was from last summer, when Fleet and I had spent an afternoon shopping in Chinatown. It reminded me of strange smells and bright colors, of meeting my first genuine mortal changeling (apart from myself), of making my first mortal friend. She'd given it to me because it winked at me. I was still waiting for it to wink again.

"Well, pet. If you're sure." Astris twitched the T-shirt straight. "You be good, now."

My second day of school wasn't any better than the first. I totally forgot to put on my Inside Sweater until some snotty East Sider reminded me. I didn't know the words to the school song. I couldn't find Bergdorf to take me to my morning lesson and had to ask the door lady where it was. I got to Mortal History and Customs just as the second horn blew, very out of breath.

"Knowing about time," the Historian said as I sat down, "is important. Think of it as a kind of mortal magic—something we have that the Folk don't understand. It helps us tell the difference between yesterday and today, which is how we know that things change."

Then he explained that mortals Outside divide days into hours and minutes and seconds. He showed us a small clock and told us what the arrows and numbers meant. He told us what an hour was. He told us that morning and afternoon lessons lasted between two and three hours. Lunch was one hour, more or less, depending on what kind of mood the Horn Blower was in.

Two or three hours is a long time, even when the lesson is interesting.

Lunch, on the other hand, didn't seem very long at all.

I joined Fortran and Espresso at what already felt like our table. They were arguing about whether there were boy flower fairies. Fortran said a real boy wouldn't be caught dead dancing on roses, and Espresso said it was different for fairies, and what was wrong with dancing on roses anyway?

"Espresso, sister-girl!" a new voice broke in. "A thousand apologies for not catching you yesterday, but you know how it is on opening day."

Espresso lit up happily. "Stonewall! What's happening, man?"

Great. Another new mortal to deal with.

The newcomer was as colorful as a garuda, with rosy brown skin and bright blue hair gelled straight up like grass. His Inside Sweater shone with gold stars sewed on with colored thread. He grinned at Espresso and gestured to another changeling standing next to him.

"Danskin's happening. He's going to be a Costume Designer at Lincoln Center when he's earned his galaxy and left Miss Van Loon's behind. Danskin, this is Espresso. Earth Mother's her fairy godmother, too."

Danskin looked a lot like my friend Fleet—dark coppery skin, tiny black braids, big soft brown eyes. He smiled at Espresso. "Any god-sister of Stoney's is a friend of mine." His voice was coppery, too.

Espresso treated him to a measuring stare, then smiled. "Groovy, man. Grab a pen."

As soon as they sat down and opened their magic bags, Stonewall started to ask questions. He was the nosiest person I'd ever met, Folk or mortal, and strangely hard to lie to. He even got Fortran to admit that he wasn't really twelve, like he'd told us, but ten last full moon, and he did it so nicely that Fortran didn't even sulk very much afterward.

"And you, Neef. How old are you?" Stonewall asked brightly.

After watching him deal with Fortran, I didn't want to make any mistakes. "I don't really know."

Stonewall narrowed his eyes thoughtfully. "Twelve," he said at last. "Coming up on thirteen, maybe. Could even be older. You know that changelings age slower than Outside mortals, right?"

I didn't, but nodded anyway. There are only so many explanations a girl can stand in one day.

"So you're the famous Neef," Danskin said. "I hear you've been giving Tiffany a taste of her own medicine."

"I didn't even do anything," I protested. "It's like she hated me before she even saw me."

Stonewall rolled his eyes. "Wild Child. I heard. East Siders are like that."

"Folk wannabes," Danskin said.

"Total idiots," they said together, and smiled at each other.

"And *you* don't want to be gorgeous and immortal and magic?" I asked. "You're worse liars than Fortran."

Stonewall laughed. He had a nice, bubbly laugh. "I like you," he said. "Gimme five." He held up a hand, like he was saying hello. There was a slightly embarrassing moment where Espresso realized I didn't know what he meant and explained.

"Of course we wanna be Folk," he said, after I'd slapped his hand. "But we know it's not going to happen. The East Siders, now, they won't accept that. They're like Folk without the magic. They love power and beauty and gold. They don't like change. They pitch fairy fits when they're irritated. They never give anything away. They like playing nasty tricks."

Espresso stared over my shoulder. "I hear you, god-brother. Dig that evil cat over there."

I turned around. Abercrombie was creeping up on a boy hunched over a plate of raw fish at the end of a table. The boy was skinny and small and so pale that the dark fuzz on his head looked like ink spilled on white paper.

Abercrombie brushed his hand across the top of the boy's head. The boy jerked and gasped in a huge gulp of air. Then he sat still, cheeks slightly bulged, lips pinched tight, narrow chest puffed and unmoving.

Abercrombie laughed nastily.

Without even deciding to, I was on my feet and in Abercrombie's face. "What did you do that for?" I asked furiously.

Abercrombie squinted down his nose at me. "I'm just

admiring my friend Fish Boy's breath control. He doesn't mind, do you, Fish Boy?" The boy stared straight ahead, breathless and pop-eyed. "Why don't you mind your own business, Wild Child?"

"Why don't you?" I said.

"You going to make me?" Abercrombie sneered.

"Sure. I'm from Central Park, remember? I know Folk who would eat your head if I told them to."

"Of course you do," Abercrombie sneered.

Espresso appeared beside me. "You wanna bet on that, Jack?"

Abercrombie hesitated, then shrugged. "Betting's against the rules. But you wouldn't care about that, would you, Wild Child?"

He sauntered off. I turned to the kid he'd called Fish Boy. "It's okay. He's gone now."

Heavy-lidded dark eyes glanced at me and away.

The lunchroom had gotten very quiet. I didn't have to look around to know that everyone was staring at us. Whatever had made me take on Abercrombie drained away, leaving only embarrassment.

Stonewall came up. "He holds his breath when he's startled," he said. "Better hit him on the back, or he'll pass out."

I whacked Fish Boy sharply between the shoulder blades. He whooshed out the breath he'd been holding, then dragged in a new one.

"Everything copacetic?" Espresso asked kindly.

Fish Boy didn't answer. Somebody behind me made a smart crack. There was a ripple of laughter and everybody started talking again. I shrugged and turned away.

Stonewall stopped me. "Where are my manners? Airboy, this is Neef of Central Park. Neef, this is Airboy of New York Harbor."

Now I was really embarrassed.

I'd been to New York Harbor last summer, to get the Magic Magnifying Mirror of the Mermaid Queen for the Green Lady. It had not been fun. I'd been imprisoned in a magic bubble full of air and towed through murky water by mermaids with spiked hair and pierced fins. Who'd almost drowned me. Twice. The Mermaid Queen was a sore loser.

Which wasn't Airboy's fault.

"Pleased to make your acquaintance," I said, showing off my basic manners.

Airboy picked up a piece of raw fish, popped it into his mouth, and chewed. Stonewall rolled his eyes and led us back to the table.

As we sat down, Espresso punched my arm.

"Ow," I said. "What was that for?"

"Isabel met a horrible jerk, Isabel, Isabel didn't lurk.
Isabel faced him, Isabel spaced him,
Isabel turned him to grass and grazed him."

It took me a minute to figure out that she was talking about Abercrombie and another to realize she was being complimentary. I felt my ears burn. "He'd have grazed *me* if you hadn't backed me up."

Espresso shrugged. "You're the front man, I play bass. Everything's copacetic."

This must have been a good thing, because she was grinning.

Over the next few days, I learned how Miss Van Loon's worked.

The gold stars, for instance. When you did anything really smart in class, you earned a gold star point. When you did something really stupid, you lost one. Once you'd earned enough points, you got an actual gold star to sew on your Inside Sweater and could stop going to that lesson.

When you'd earned enough gold stars, you could leave Miss Van Loon's. Starting as late as I was, I'd probably be there until I was as old as the Diplomat.

There were one or two lessons every day, with a lunch break in the middle. Every day was different. Sometimes a whole day would be devoted to Talismans or History of New York Between, sometimes just a half. Sometimes Diplomacy for Ambassadors came two days in a row, but never on the same day as Basic Manners.

Every morning, we checked a board in the front hall

for our schedules. The Schooljuffrouw announced any changes in assembly, after the school song and a reading from *Miss Van Loon's Big Book of Rules*. She read five rules a day. Fortran, Number Man, calculated that it would take about a year to read through the whole book, with days off for full moons, Solstices and Equinoxes, Hallowe'en, and weekends.

Weekends fell whenever the Schooljuffrouw felt like announcing one.

My first weekend came nine days after school started. Because of Rule Three, it took some fancy talking to explain to Astris why I didn't have to go to school for two days. When she finally got it, her whiskers perked up. "Good," she said. "Then you can clean your room. It's getting to look like a hooraw's nest."

I did that. I also had a game of lily polo with the nixies in the Reservoir, played hunt-the-acorn with some squirrels, and had a picnic with Mr. Rat and Stuart Little by the Turtle Pond. When the third morning dawned hot and bright, it was really hard to get myself to the Betweenways station.

My first lesson that day was Questing.

Everybody had to take Questing. You couldn't get a gold star in it, no matter how good you were or how long you'd been at Miss Van Loon's. You never knew, the theory was, when you might have to climb a building or a tree, wrestle a kappa, or outrun an ogre. You always had to keep in practice. The students were mixed, little kids and kids who'd earned almost enough gold stars to graduate, East Side, West Side, Up, Down, and Midtown, twenty of us at a time in different combinations, at least once a week. I never knew who I'd be racing or facing for wrestling or karate practice.

When I got to the Questing Room, I saw the far wall had been transformed into the fronts of two ordinary brownstone buildings with steep stoops and flat roofs. The space between them was spanned by an iron beam.

The Quester had us form a long line. I caught sight of someone tall and blonde and willowy and hoped it wasn't Tiffany or Abercrombie or Bergdorf. They gave me the willies.

"Listen up," the Quester said. "Today, we're climbing brownstones. Count off by twos. Even numbers climb the West Side building; odd numbers climb the East Side. If you meet another student on the beam, cooperate to pass. Slide down the drainpipe on the other side, and you're done."

She gave us all a serious look. "You all get fairy dust. I don't care if you live in the Empire State Building. No arguments. There's being a hero, and there's being stupid. If you fall, it's a long way down. Of course, it's better if you don't fall. Got that? Good. Now count off."

I was a two. I couldn't tell what the blonde was.

Central Park isn't exactly packed with brownstones. While I waited my turn, I watched the others scramble up the stoop, swing themselves to the nearest window-sill, and work their way upward, using window frames and decorative friezes, jamming toes and fingers into the spaces between brownstone blocks. Some of them looked like they were having fun, but only Airboy made it look easy. He might be skinny, but he was strong. I could see his muscles bunch as he pulled himself up the building, sure as a lizard, darting his head back and forth look-ing for handholds. When he got to the top, some kids cheered. I thought I saw him blush.

The line moved me closer to the building.

A little kid—Tosca, who hadn't known what to say to old women at crossroads—climbed up the stoop and clung to the wall while the Quester sprinkled her with fairy dust, instructed her to think happy thoughts, and gave her a boost. Tosca clambered to the windowsill and stayed there, whimpering.

The next kid in line helped her climb to the top of the window. She looked down, freaked out, and wrapped herself around his neck, tumbling both of them off the building. The helpful kid drifted gently to the floor and detached her, howling like a thunderstorm. Obviously trying very hard not to break Rule 98 (Students must never laugh at another mortal's tears), he patted her on the shoulder.

I heard a lot of suppressed sniggering from the East Side. To be fair, I heard it from the West Side, too. I couldn't help smiling myself, even though I knew how much I'd hate it if it was me they were laughing at.

Mortal tears are funny. That's all there is to it.

Soon, it was my turn.

"Your first time, right?" The Quester reached into her bag of fairy dust. "Remember: happy thoughts. And don't look down."

I'd climbed plenty of trees in Central Park, but that didn't help me now. Trees aren't flat and hard. They have broad branches where you can sit and rest. They usually slope, and they provide little intermediate steps in the shape of small branches set close together. Buildings have none of these things. By the time I hauled myself onto the roof, I was sweating and panting, my arms and legs were burning, and I couldn't make a fist. But I hadn't fallen, which was pretty good for my first time, I thought. All I had to do now was cross the beam to the next building and slide down the drainpipe, and I'd be done. Piece of cake.

I wiped sweat out of my eyes, shoved back my hair, and stepped onto the beam.

At the other end was Tiffany, the Debutante Terror.

She wasn't sweating, not that I could see. Her grin said that in a minute I was going to be floating with my butt in the air, a stupid expression on my face, and everybody in the room laughing at me because there's no rule against laughing when somebody takes a fall. It was a Wild Hunt grin, a troll grin. It made me mad.

Iron beams are a whole lot easier to walk on than log bridges. I felt pretty stable as I walked toward Tiffany, who was walking toward me. Neither one of us held our arms out for balance.

We met somewhere around the middle.

"Back up, Wild Child."

"No way."

Tiffany gave me her best menacing stare. It was like being hit with ice balls. "Don't tell me you expect *me* to back up?"

I shrugged. "We could cooperate. Everybody else seems to have managed. I'm sure we could think of something."

"You could jump."

"So could you."

The Quester shouted up at us. "Move it, you guys. Time's a-wasting."

"You heard the Quester," Tiffany said.

"I heard."

Faintly, I heard the Easts and Wests who'd made it up to the roof yelling at us to hurry. Tiffany grinned evilly.

"You're holding everybody up," she said. "That's selfish, you know. Nobody likes a selfish mortal. Everybody's going to hate you even more than they already do."

"I don't care," I said, and took a step toward her.

I intended to take her hands and swing around as I'd seen the other kids do, but Tiffany must have thought I was going to push her off. She flailed her arms wildly and fell off the iron beam.

I was so surprised, I nearly followed her, but managed to wobble over to the other building, where I sat down and put my head between my knees. I heard a few muttered "good work"s and a "right on" or two, along with several variations on "you're in big trouble now."

From down below, I heard laughter, and somebody, probably Tiffany, pitching a fairy fit.

After I'd slid down the drainpipe, the Quester lectured me about fair play and cooperation and made me spend lunchtime scrubbing the West brownstone's steps with salt. Tiffany had to wash the East brownstone's windows. Every once in a while, I'd look over and see her glaring at me.

I hadn't been at Miss Van Loon's a full cycle of the moon, and already I had a mortal enemy.

Chapter 5

RULE 968: STUDENTS MUST PAY ATTENTION AT ALL TIMES.

Miss Van Loon's Big Book of Rules

Six days later, I wore my spidersilk dress to the Full Moon Gathering.

The dress was soft and silver-gray, with leaves woven into it. I'd found it in the Shakespeare Garden last summer, right before the Solstice Dance. I loved it. I thought it made me look like a wood elf, or maybe a hawthorn dryad—something bushy, anyway. Astris had hinted, more than once, that it was far too magic for a mortal, but I'd worn it on my quest, so she couldn't tell me not to, even with her whiskers.

It's always confused me, how the Folk can consider mortals important enough to steal, take care of, play with, and even use as heroes and champions, and still treat us like inferior beings. But that's Folk for you. Not even Astris really understands that mortals have feelings, just like trolls and magical animals do.

The Autumn Equinox was only a week away. Even though the weather was still hot and humid, summer was definitely dying. The grass was brown, the dryads were getting sleepy, the days were growing shorter. During my before-Gathering swim in the Turtle Pond, I overheard the ducks arguing about the best routes south. The field mice were already moving their nests to the Castle cellar, and the resident ghosts were already grumbling about the noise.

At sunset, the trees clacked their branches to summon Folk to the Gathering. Astris and I crossed the courtyard and joined the crowd of moss women and flower fairies, were-bears and fox-wives from the Zoo, peris and corn-spirits and fauns all flying and lumbering and rolling and scampering toward Central Park Central.

A roiling fog at the edge of the field hung over the demons and water-horses and vodyanoi, the trolls and ogres and hags who ride the air with the Wild Hunt.

Astris and I joined Mr. Rat and Stuart Little at our usual Gathering spot beside a grove of pin oaks. It was close enough to the great lawn of Central Park Central to let us see what was going on, but sheltered enough to keep us from getting trampled if the Wild Hunt got out of hand. They're not supposed to rampage at a Gathering, but you don't want to get too close in case they forget.

As the sky darkened, the windows of the buildings around the Park began to light up like constellations of low-hanging stars. The trees gave a woody flourish, and the crowd of Folk parted to make way for the Lady's Court.

At the head of the procession, dryads and nymphs trailing late summer draperies of dusty green and brown scattered dry leaves and twigs on the grass. The Lady's scouts scampered after—squirrels and rats and a few big black crows flying above, cawing raucously. Next came the Lady's Councilors, one from each of the different kinds of Park Folk: Nutter the Squirrel King, Chiron the centaur, Iolanthe the fairy, Pondscum the ondine, Snuggles the werewolf, the Huddlestone Bridge troll, and Herne of the Wild Hunt.

And at the end of the procession, surrounded by lantern-carrying fairies and fireflies, came the Green Lady of Central Park.

When I haven't seen the Lady for a while—or have only seen her when she's in a temper—I'm always surprised by how beautiful she can be when she wants. Tonight, her long greeny-brown hair bounced on her shoulders in a million ropy dreadlocks, and her browny-green face glowed. Her fringed leather miniskirt and jacket were the color of fading leaves, and her high boots were bright green. She looked tall and queenly and proud, and not even a little bit mortal.

She walked past us to the exact middle of Central Park Central, which is the heart of New York Between, and held out her hands over the grass. The earth groaned and a granite boulder appeared, slowly pushing aside the grass and dirt, rising and rising into a granite throne sparkling with mica.

Everybody cheered, and the Lady sat down. "Moon's up," she said in a voice as clear as the night sky. "Let's get this show on the road. Who's got a beef?"

Officially, Gatherings are for business. Folk complain about their neighbors, ask for favors, brag about adventures, pay tribute. In Neighborhoods whose Geniuses have alliances with other Geniuses, mortal Ambassadors visit between courts, planning street fairs and trading mortal changelings and minor amulets and other precious things. The Lady doesn't have any alliances, of course. She hasn't had a mortal Voice to talk to the other Geniuses for her, not for a very long time. When I was finished being educated, I guess she'd have me.

This was a scary thought.

Across the lawn, I saw a forest of claws and talons shoot skyward: the Wild Hunt.

"Fuggedaboutdit," the Lady said. "I ain't in the mood for the Hunt's bellyaching tonight." She pointed to a leprechaun jigging impatiently in the front row. "Seamus, you got something on your mind, or do you need to go find a bush?"

The Lady was in a hurry. In short order, she disposed of Seamus's complaint that the Glen Span Bridge troll was trying to steal his gold, the troll's complaint that the flint sandals Seamus made him had rubbed a crack in his right foot, and a petition by the flower fairies for more autumn-blooming flowers in the Conservatory Garden. My old enemy Peg Powler of the Wild Hunt had just stepped forward to argue, as she always did, that the Hunt needed more fresh meat, when a crow blundered out of the sky and landed on the Lady's knee in a flurry of black feathers.

"Dwarfs," he cawed. "Dwarfs, dwarfs, dwarfs."

The air quivered with tension as three dwarfs marched into Central Park Central. Dwarfs are not popular in the park. The nature spirits don't like their axes, and the animals aren't wild about their taste for exotic fur cloaks. The fairies are nervous around naked iron, even though they're all protected by anti-ironsickness spells.

The dwarfs stopped a little way from the Lady's throne and bowed awkwardly. I noticed their hands were stuck respectfully in their belts. No fur. No iron. No axes. This was obviously a peaceful delegation.

The middle dwarf stepped forward. "It's like this, Lady," he said. "There's a mess on the border between Riverside Park and the Upper West Side. Seepage. Leaking. Water everywhere. The wall's undermined, the sidewalk's a box of dominoes. The trees are upset—leaves all over the place, bark peeling, dryads panicking."

The Lady leaned her elbow on her knee, unbalancing the crow. "And the Riverside dryads ain't telling me all this, why?"

"It's the panic, Lady. Afraid to leave their trees. Anyway. Us dwarfs thought we'd do a little quiet poking around on our own, see what's up, not make a Neighborhood case out of it, if you know what I mean."

The Lady obviously didn't, but I thought I did. The Diplomat had told us about the feud going on between the Provost of Columbia and the Psychiatrist of the Upper West Side. There'd be a horrible fuss if Geniuses got involved. Dwarfs don't like fuss.

The Lady looked thoughtful. "Where in Riverside Park?"

"Up by the marshes," the dwarf said. "We might have to do some damming."

He launched into a speech about water tables and landfill that I did my best to listen to. The Green Lady's booted foot jigged, and the long ropes of her hair braided and unbraided restlessly. Finally, she interrupted the dwarf in the middle of a sentence.

"So the marsh is getting out of hand. Fix it. Just don't go crazy with the digging and don't move any trees. First complaint I get from a dryad, you're landfill. You get my drift?"

The dwarfs groped at their belts where their axes

should be. "You do realize we're trying to do you a favor?" the spokes-dwarf said.

"Yeah, yeah, yeah. You got hearts the size of the Waldorf." The Lady stood up. "Now, get lost. We got real Park business to do. And then we're going to dance. You know what they say: It ain't a Gathering if you don't dance."

The dwarfs marched away, muttering. I wondered if I could have handled things better.

"Listen up, guys. Autumn Equinox is almost here, right? I thought I'd get the fun started early this year. You've heard about scavenger hunts? You run around collecting special things? There's a prize? Okay, here's what you look for. Round things. Shiny things. Things that reflect. Look in any of the Green Places—East River Park, Gramercy, Riverside, Fort Tryon. Anything you find, bring to Councilor Snuggles's den before the Equinox. I'll announce the winner at the revel."

Peg Powler waddled forward like a huge green toad. "If I can ask one small question, Lady dear? As to the prize? Is it warm and crunchable? Will it fill my belly?"

"Talk about your one-track minds! It's a *surprise*, Peg Powler. That means you'll have to wait and see. Any more questions? No? Then let the dancing begin!"

Chapter

6

There is no school the day after a full moon. I danced until moonset and slept until noon, when Astris woke me up to use my negotiating skills on the Castle ghosts. She said she was tired of their moaning and wanted them to stop. I tried to tell her that ghosts moaning is as natural as fairy godmothers worrying. But she insisted, so I went down and told them they were getting on Astris's nerves.

They haunted me out of the cellar. I guess I needed more practice in Diplomacy.

The next morning was the kind of day only Water Folk and ducks could love. By the time I got to school, my sneakers were soggy and squelchy and my black coat smelled like wet dog. For the first time, I didn't mind putting on my Inside Sweater.

Basic Manners was a disaster. Even Peony, who was usually so well behaved I wanted to pinch her to see if she was real, had trouble keeping her pleasant expression cultivated. Fortran, whose manners were pretty basic to begin with, was a total demon. He jittered in his chair and tapped on the desk with his pencil. And when the Diplomat was showing us how to set a table for a formal dinner, he licked a dessert spoon and hung it off his nose.

We all collapsed into helpless giggles. Even Peony.

The Diplomat silenced us with a granite glare. "I'm deeply disappointed in each and every one of you. Lightbulb and Sweater, bring me the beans and rice, if you please."

In Diplomat-speak, deeply disappointed was about as bad as it could get. Lightbulb and Sweater scrambled to the corner cabinet and got the ritual bowls. The Diplomat upended the small, hard kernels of raw rice and dried black beans over the floor, where they spread into a crunchy, slippery carpet.

"Girls take the beans. Boys take the rice. Smile while you work. And meditate on the importance of self-control. Fortran, another peep out of you and I'll send to Talismans for a Cone of Isolation."

Everybody was relieved when the horn blew for lunch.

Our table had been filling up since the beginning

of school. Two other Village changelings had followed Stonewall, plus a couple of Danskin's friends from Lincoln Center. Espresso had made friends with the sari-girl I'd seen in Talismans—Mukuti, from Little India. She had wavy black hair down to her waist and at least three protective amulets around her neck at all times. Her magic bag was made of embroidered silk and produced wonderful spicy-smelling dishes that burned my mouth.

I took a seat next to Espresso. "Hey there, Neeferbear," she said. "What did you do to Tiffany, man? That's some hairy eyeball she's giving you."

I turned. Tiffany narrowed her sapphire eyes at me. I narrowed mine back. Tiffany mouthed "Wild Child" and bared her perfect teeth. Her fellow East Siders burst into giggles.

I lowered my eyes to my lunch. "I'm sick of cheese. Anybody want to trade?"

Espresso offered me a spoonful of what looked like pebbles floating in milk. "Granola?"

I shook my head.

Fortran fished around in Backpack, brought out a glass of thick orange stuff. "Mango batido," he said. "Try it. You'll like it."

It was sweet and cold and creamy. I drank it all.

During talismans, I had to get permission for a trip to the bathroom.

I was disappointed, but not surprised, when I opened the bathroom door to see Tiffany and her sidekicks, Best and Bergdorf, posing in front of the mirror. The girls' bathroom on the third floor boasted the only mirror in Miss Van Loon's. It wasn't magical, but the bigger girls spent a lot of time looking at themselves in it. Especially the East Siders.

Bergdorf was standing sideways and frowning at her skinny reflection in the mirror. ". . . gigantically fat," I heard her say. "If I want an elf lord to dance with me at Midwinter, I'm going to have to do something extreme."

"Stop eating." Tiffany sounded bored.

Bergdorf saw me watching in the mirror and blushed painfully.

Tiffany sneered. "Oh, look. It's the Wild Child. Need a sandbox, Wild Child?"

Best gave me a haughty look. She wasn't as good at it as Tiffany. "Yeah, go find a sandbox. This bathroom is for civilized mortals only."

The diplomatic thing to do was to go to the bathroom downstairs. I wasn't in a diplomatic mood. "Then what are *you* doing here?" I snapped, and headed for the stalls.

Tiffany blocked me. "You heard Best. Get lost, ugly girl."

"Go soak your head in the toilet," I said, and tried to push past her.

Tiffany grabbed my shoulder and shoved me back

into the door. "Temper, temper," she cautioned. "Remember Rule One."

I rubbed my shoulder. "*You* remember it. Why should I pay any attention to the rules if you don't?"

Tiffany looked down her nose at me. "I can break the rules, Wild Child, because I've been at Miss Van Loon's since I could talk. I'm smart and I'm quick and I'm beautiful. The tutors love me. I have a position and a following. You have nothing. Except a frizz-ball head and the lamest coat in the universe."

I resisted the urge to check out my reflection. "And what have you got?" I said. "A bunch of stupid stars and shiny hair? Big deal. You can't do magic. You're still a mortal in a fairy world, just like the rest of us."

Tiffany's face went pink, then white and pinched around the nose. "I can so do magic."

I laughed. "Isn't carrying magic talismans against the rules?"

"I don't need one," she said tightly. "There are spells mortals can do. Or didn't they tell you that in the Park?"

They hadn't, but I wasn't about to say so.

Bergdorf tugged at Tiffany's gray wool sleeve. "Um, Tiff? Don't you think we should be getting back to Urban Myths?"

Tiffany shook her off. "I know what I'm doing, Bergdorf. She's got to learn her place."

I'd been mad before. Now I was furious. "I'm up for

anything you can do, Tiffany of Park Avenue, except maybe sliding down a drain from the inside."

Tiffany lowered her voice ominously. "How about summoning Bloody Mary?"

"Sure," I said. "When and where?"

Best gasped. Bergdorf said, "Tiffany, are you—?"

"Shut up, Bergdorf," Tiffany snapped, her blue gaze unwavering. "Midnight. During the Hallowe'en Revels. In here. Deal?"

I looked from face to face. Bergdorf and Best looked like sheep when the Hunt's riding. Tiffany looked like one of the Hunters. Now that it was too late, I realized I'd just broken Rule 13 (Students must not make or accept dares or challenges while on school property), and thought maybe I should have kept my mouth shut, but I couldn't back out now.

"Deal," I said. Then I turned my back on them and retreated into a stall. Deal or no, I still had to pee.

At the end of the day, Espresso and Fortran and Mukuti and I usually headed for the swing. Espresso and Mukuti taught me hopscotch and jump rope while Fortran tried to see how high he could swing. He said he should be able to go higher than Miss Van Loon's roof, but so far, he'd only gone level with the top of the trees in East River Park. I thought he was scared to go higher.

Playing mortal games in the rain held no appeal, and

nobody was ready to go home yet, so we hung around the front hall, trying to figure out if we could play giant checkers on the squares. While we were talking, Airboy, the changeling from New York Harbor, came downstairs. He sat on the bottom step and watched us with his chin in his hands.

Remembering the scene in the lunchroom, I had to wonder why he was so interested in us all of a sudden. I was about to go right up and ask him when Danskin and Stonewall wandered by.

"Hi, kidlets," Stonewall said cheerfully. "We're going to the Mansion. Wanna come with?"

I immediately forgot about Airboy. The Mansion was a café catering mostly to dwarfs and kobolds and other underground Folk, but the kobold who ran it didn't mind if Van Loonies hung out in the afternoons as long as we ordered milk (which was the only thing on the menu mortals could eat) and didn't complain about the dirt. Mostly, it was the older kids with a lot of stars who went there. It was an honor for newbies like us to be asked.

Fortran played it cool. "I've got an important experiment cooking at home, but I guess I could spare the time."

Mukuti didn't know what cool was. "We'd *love* to."

Espresso jerked her chin toward Airboy. "What about him?"

Stonewall looked startled, then shrugged. "Why not? Hey, Airboy. Want to join us?"

Airboy's eyes, long and black and expressionless,

rested on Stonewall's face for a moment, then moved away.

"I guess not," Stonewall said.

As we walked, we talked about what was up with Airboy. Mukuti said maybe he was under a spell of silence (except during lessons, Fortran pointed out); Stonewall thought he might even be half Folk.

"Maybe he's just a snot," I said. "Like Tiffany. What did you think of Talismans today? Who knew there were so many kinds of magic pins?"

At the Mansion, Danskin led us to an empty booth under a murky picture of dwarfs bowling. Since I was soaking wet, I took off my black coat and spread it over the back of my chair to dry before I sat down.

"Groovy threads, Neefer-girl," Stonewall said approvingly. "Highwayman, with a side of dandy."

Danskin winked at me. "He wants it for himself, you know. Tell him he can't have it."

"Of course he can't. My fairy godfather would kill me."

Stonewall sighed theatrically. "Bummer. A ruffled shirt, a pair of breeches, some silver-buckled shoes, and I'd be the grooviest Headless Horseman in the history of Miss Van Loon's."

"Hello?" Fortran was scornful. "You've got a head? There's a *rule* about wearing glamours to school."

"Three-oh-five," Mukuti quoted helpfully. "Students must not wear glamours or alter their appearance magically."

Danskin looked thoughtful. "How about a black burlap bag with a hat on top?"

"I want them to die screaming, not laughing," Stonewall said.

I gave up trying to deduce what was going on. "What *are* you guys talking about?"

Espresso's green eyes went round. "Hallowe'en, man. You dig? Costume competition, haunted house?" I shook my head. "How about trick or treat?"

"There aren't any treats on Hallowe'en where I come from," I said shortly. "In the Park, the ghosts get solid and the ghouls get frisky. You don't even want to know what the Hunt does."

"Sure I do."

"Shut up, Fortran." Stonewall turned to me. "So what do you do?"

"Astris invites some friends in and we tell stories."

"Boring," Fortran said, then winced. "Ow, Espresso, that hurt! I'm sorry, Neef, but it doesn't sound like a lot of fun."

"It's not supposed to be fun," I said. "It's supposed to be comforting."

Espresso's face took on her poetry-reciting look. *"'From ghoulies and ghosties and long-leggedy beasties and things that go bump in the night, good spirits deliver us.'"*

"At Miss Van Loon's," Stonewall said, "we have a different philosophy. Hallowe'en is the bash of the year. We stay up all night and there's a day off afterward."

"And that helps how?" I asked.

"Well, Folk hate being laughed at. We wear scary costumes and eat too much sugar and play games and scream a lot, but it's all a big joke. And the Folk know it, too."

Danskin laughed. "Either that, or they're more scared of us than we are of them."

"We don't bother with any of that at Columbia University," Fortran announced. "We're too sophisticated." Everybody looked at him. "Okay, we do costumes. But only because it's fun. I always have the best costume. This year, I'm going to be a monkey warrior." He paused. "Or maybe an evil wizard. I haven't decided yet."

Mukuti bounced happily. "Last year I was a demon, with big tusks and everything. Nobody even knew it was me."

"And that's Hallowe'en?" I asked. "A bunch of kids running around dressed up like Folk?"

"Scary Folk," Danskin reminded me. "And there are special rituals. Tricks and games and stuff. *The Big Book of Rules* takes a real beating sometimes."

Light dawned. "I get it!" I said. "Hallowe'en is for getting even. Did you guys challenge anyone?"

Everybody got very quiet. I looked around the ring of startled faces. "No challenges? But Tiffany said . . . "

"Tiffany?" Danskin asked blankly.

"Yeah. She challenged me to summon Bloody Mary with her. At Hallowe'en. In the girls' bathroom."

Espresso laughed doubtfully. "You're busting our chops, right?"

"No-o."

Stonewall said, "You seem awfully calm about this. Do you actually know who you're dealing with?"

"I'm not calm. I'm mad. And I already *know* Tiffany's evil."

"Not Tiffany," Danskin said seriously. "The *other* one."

I wasn't about to admit there was a supernatural somewhere I'd never heard of. "What's to know? She's called Mary and she's all bloody. Standard-issue bogey-woman. No biggie."

Espresso shook her head. "Either you're the Girl Who Didn't Know What Fear Was, or you're out of your ever-loving mind. Possibly both."

"Okay," I said. "Tell me about Bl—"

Espresso's hand clamped over my mouth. "Don't! Just don't."

I wiggled my eyebrows to show I wouldn't. Espresso withdrew her hand. "What's with you guys?"

"We don't want to take any chances," Stonewall explained. "Saying her name might call her up. She usually appears in mirrors, but lots of things reflect. Liquids, picture glass." He glanced up at the bowling dwarfs.

"The changelings from Spanish Harlem call her the Angry One," Mukuti said helpfully.

"Okay, tell me about the Angry One."

Everybody leaned in real close and whispered at me, more or less at once.

"She's a nightmare."

"She comes out of the mirror and rips your face off."

"She scratches you with her long claws."

"She kills you dead."

Most bogeys just hide under your bed and moan. My stomach felt cold. "Why summon her, then?"

Stonewall sat back. "She's supposed to show you your future, if you stay alive long enough to ask."

"If she even shows up in the first place," Danskin added. "She's not exactly predictable."

I took a mouthful of dirty milk and examined my choices. If I backed out of Tiffany's challenge, I'd be safe. And Tiffany would have some new names to call me, like "coward" and "dealbreaker." I'd rather risk having my face ripped off. Especially since I didn't think it would really happen. If Tiffany thought she could handle this Bloody Angry Mary person, then I could, too.

"Fine," I said.

"Fine what?" Danskin asked. "Fine you're going to tell her you changed your mind?"

"Fine, I'm going through with it. If I don't go through with it, Tiffany will get even more unbearable than she already is."

Chapter

7

RULE 653: STUDENTS MUST NOT INVOLVE THEMSELVES IN
INTER-FOLK CONFLICTS WITHOUT A TUTOR'S SUPERVISION.

Miss Van Loon's Big Book of Rules

"Well, you certainly can't wear it to the Equinox
Reel."

Astris smoothed the skirt of my spidersilk dress. It
was ripped where I'd caught it on a branch falling out of
the mulberry tree that morning.

"I thought spidersilk was the strongest cloth there is,"
I complained.

"It was made with summer magic," Astris said. "The
strength's gone out of it."

I fingered the soft material sadly. The dress had survived all the wear and tear of a magical quest without so
much as a rip or a wrinkle. Now, one lousy tumble off a
not-very-high branch and the skirt was in shreds. Plus,
the spidersilk had lost its glow and the leaves and flowers
woven into it had turned brown and brittle.

"Don't worry," Astris said soothingly. "A fairy god-mother can always come up with something to wear to a dance—it's what we *do*, after all."

I ran upstairs, changed into jeans, and ran down again, expecting a ball gown. What I got was dinner. While I was eating roast chicken, mushroom pie, and peas from Satchel, Astris nibbled cheese and told me about her afternoon boating with Mr. Rat. Just as I was about to burst with impatience, she handed me a silver walnut.

"Oh, wow, Astris. A Dress Silver as the Moon!"

Astris's whiskers twitched. "I found that walnut at the back of a drawer. Judging from the state it was in, it's been there a lot longer than a year and a day. There might be nothing inside but dust."

The nut didn't so much crack as disintegrate. One minute, I was holding a nut; the next my hands and arms were overflowing with fabric, heavy, slippery, and cold.

"Well, it's not dust, at any rate," Astris said.

The dress was a kind of dull iridescent pewter color with black streaks, and it smelled sharp and acrid. "It's more like a Dress Gray as Rain."

"Once something magical tarnishes, it's never quite the same," Astris said. "Do you want to try it on?"

We struggled with the mass of slithery fabric, looking for the top and the sleeves and then fitting me into them. The dress rustled and sighed, stretching and shrinking so it would fit me. When it was still, I spun around. The skirt belled out, then slapped heavily shut around my legs.

"Well?" I asked anxiously. "How do I look?"

"It's a dress fit for a debutante," Astris said truthfully, but her whiskers looked amused.

Convinced I looked like a complete troll, I gathered the heavy skirts and ran up the stairs to the landing mirror. My face was framed by two tarnished silver rolls sticking up from my shoulders like sugared doughnuts. The top was cut square right across the middle of my chest and fit like it had been painted on. I smoothed my hands down my silver skirt and shook the liquid folds cautiously. They let out a clear, tinkling chime and a metallic tang of tarnish.

I sucked in my stomach and ran my fingers through my hair. It sprang up again, wild as ever. Then I noticed something.

"Hey, Astris," I shouted. "I have a shape!"

Astris scurried up the steps, grabbed the neck of the dress, and tugged it sharply upward. The magic cloth obediently expanded to reach my collarbone. Then she patted the sleeves into a soft fluff, tore a strip off the hem, and tied it around my head with a bow over one ear.

"That's better," she said. "Come along now. We don't want to be late."

It was almost full dark when Astris and I took our places in the dance, with just a blush of deep blue in the west to remember the day by. At the center of the field, the Lady was a blaze of ruby and deep gold in a dress that fluttered like falling leaves around her bare brown arms and legs.

In the dance of the year, the Spring and Autumn Equinoxes are points of perfect balance. The Folk dance a reel around and around the Park, stepping—or floating, or slithering—behind each other. The trees fiddle on twigs and boughs; the rocks pound time; the grasses rustle. On a clear night, with the windows around the Park twinkling and the stars burning overhead, I can almost feel the world turning under my feet.

The music began. The Lady led and the Park Folk followed her, skipping and swaying over the grass. I closed my eyes and danced with them. Eventually, I'd get tired and drop out. But right now, I felt like I could dance forever.

Suddenly, the music faltered. My feet went on a few steps by themselves before stumbling over Astris, who squealed unhappily. Something was horribly wrong.

I wadded up my skirt and scrambled up the nearest tree.

The Folk milled aimlessly around Central Park Central, dazed and bewildered, bumping into each other, still half entranced. I climbed a little higher. In the center of the field I saw a clear space, and it in, the Lady, her arms crossed, her head thrown back, her crown of leaves blazing on the woven coils of her hair.

She was face-to-face with a mortal.

He stood out against the Folk like a boulder in a flower garden. He moved, and starlight glittered from the silver safety pins on his shiny black vest. I'd seen vests like that last summer on my quest. They were the official uniform of the merguards at the Court of the Mermaid Queen of New York Harbor.

My heart and hands were suddenly as cold as my moon-silver skirt.

The mortal bowed. "My Lady Genius of Central Park," he shouted, loud and deep. "I am the Voice of the Mermaid Queen of New York Harbor. On this day of balance between light and dark, my mistress sends you greetings."

The Lady's hair burst angrily from its neat coil, scattering her crown of leaves. "I'll just bet she does, buster. Let's cut to the chase here. I'm not giving up the Magic Magnifying Mirror. My champion won it fair and square. You can tell old Fish Breath, from me, that she can put that in her water pipe and smoke it."

By now, the Park Folk were listening intently. Those who had hands applauded.

The Voice of the Mermaid Queen ignored them. "My Lady Queen foresaw your answer. And she bade me say this: The Magnifying Mirror is part of New York Harbor, just as the trees and water and grass and stones are part of Central Park. It was given to her by the first mortal changeling at the Council of Inwood, and it cannot be taken from her without upsetting the balance of power. You must return it."

The Green Lady's hair writhed around her head. "*Must*, Fish Boy?"

"My Lady Queen," the Voice went on, "says this: Return the mirror by the Winter Solstice or she will flood all the waters of the Park with salt."

Now would be the time, I knew, for the champion of Central Park (namely, me) to jump in and save the day. Except I couldn't think of any way of saving it. The Diplomat's lessons on negotiating treaties and making conversation flashed through my brain, offering not a single useful clue. If there was a lesson about preventing a disaster, we hadn't got to it yet.

"Winter Solstice, huh?" The Lady's voice was thoughtful. "Okay. Here's the deal. You tell Her Fishyness I'll get back to her. I'm not making any promises here, but I'll think about it. Now, get lost."

The Voice of the Mermaid Queen bowed and walked away.

The Lady clapped her hands. "Dance time! Come on, you guys, whatcha waiting for? Solstice?"

Nobody moved.

"What a bunch of chumps! Look at you, scared of a stupid mortal that smells like three-day-old fish! Old Lady Fish Breath can't make salt from seawater, let alone turn the Reservoir and all the lakes and ponds into brine. She's talking through her hat."

A low murmur of doubt and rebellion swept through the Folk, rising into panic. I clung to my branch. Then a couple of nixies surged forward, weedy hair streaming in distress, and begged the Lady to save them. That did it. Naiads wept, water-horses whinnied, and vodyanoi croaked nervously. Above the hubbub, I heard a banshee shrieking that she'd never get her bloody linen clean if she had to wash it in salt water.

"Shaddup!" the Lady screamed. "Am I or am I not the Genius of Central Park? Would I let anything bad happen to our water? Fuggedaboutdit!"

Slowly, the tumult faded. The nixies and naiads backed off; the water-horses pawed the ground uncertainly. The Lady's hair settled back on her shoulders. "That's better," she said. "Now. Let's have a little music here!"

The trees began to play, raggedly at first, then more enthusiastically. I wasn't surprised when the Folk started to dance. Folk are Folk. They do what they do. When they see gold, they have to take it. When you make a wish, they have to grant it. When music plays, they have to dance until the dance is done.

Not me. I'm mortal. I can't dance all night without stopping. And I can't dance if I don't feel like it.

I climbed down from the tree, careful not to get tangled in my skirt. Then I collapsed on the nearest rock, put my spinning head in my hands, and tried to think.

I'd hardly started when the Pooka appeared in front of me in his man shape. His long black hair was braided in a thick tail between his shoulders, his eyebrows looked like they were about to fly off his forehead, and his narrow eyes shone a bright, wicked yellow.

"You're not dancing!" he cried. "Is it waiting for your old fairy godfather you are?"

"Go away, Pooka. I don't want to dance."

"Don't want to dance? Are you stone mad? Why should you not want to dance, for all love?"

"I'm not in the mood."

He quirked a flying eyebrow at me. "It's the Mermaid Queen, isn't it, with her puffing and blowing threats here, there, and everywhere. Never mind her, my heart. She'll not be salting the waters tonight. There's plenty of time before Midwinter."

"Maybe," I said. "But I still don't feel like dancing."

He pulled me to my feet and toward the reel. I jerked away.

"Stop it, Pooka. I'm worried, okay? The Water Folk are my friends. I don't want them to get all salty and poisoned. Why doesn't the Lady just give the Queen her mirror back? It's not like she knows how to use it or anything."

"You're right," the Pooka said. "The Lady can no more make the mirror work for her than a brownie can fly to the moon."

"Then why not return it?"

"She's a Genius," the Pooka said, "not a sheep. She may be led, but she won't be driven." He grinned. "Which is why you're in school, learning the finer points of Genius-herding."

School, where Tiffany was Queen of the May and I was just a Wild Child slated to get her face scratched off on Hallowe'en night. I made a quick decision. "I'm quitting school, Pooka. Maybe I'll go back later, after I've saved the Park."

The Pooka was amused. "And how will you be doing that thing?"

This seemed obvious. "I'll persuade the Lady to give the Mermaid Queen her mirror back, of course."

"The Lady'd throw you to the Hunt before you'd opened your mouth."

"Well, I'll get the Mermaid Queen to back off."

"Have they taught you underwater breathing, then, in that school of yours?"

I had one last idea. "I could go on a quest?"

"Bah," the Pooka said. "What kind of quest? For what? To where? Herne the Hunter help me, do you know nothing? No," he went on before I could argue, "you'll go to school tomorrow as always, bright and early in the morning, brushed and dressed and ready to learn. In the meantime, tonight is a dancing night, and dance you must, willing or no."

I knew I'd lost the argument, but at least I could have the last word. "Aha," I said triumphantly. "I can't go to school tomorrow. It's a day off."

"All the more reason to dance tonight, then." And the Pooka drew me into the reel.

At dawn, the Pooka carried me up to the Castle. I slept all day, and when I woke up, it was dark out. Disoriented, I got up and tripped over a heap of cold slitheriness that smelled of tarnish.

I remembered everything: the Dress Silver as the Moon, the Equinox Reel, the Voice of the Mermaid Queen. I remembered the threat to the Park. I remembered Miss Van Loon's Hallowe'en Revels and Tiffany's challenge.

It looked like this fall was going to be even more full of adventures than last summer.

Chapter
8

The first lesson the morning after Equinox Break was Talismans.

When we were all seated, the Magic Tech said, "Today we're going to talk about magic mirrors. Anybody here ever used one?"

I didn't raise my hand. Too many explanations I didn't feel like making, too many questions I didn't want to answer. I listened with half an ear while the Magic Tech went on about doors between realities and harmonic resonances and the technical differences between mirrors backed with silver and mirrors backed with mercury.

"It's possible to tune mirrors to each other," the Magic

Tech said. "But it's dangerous, and ultimately unstable. If one mirror goes offline, it weakens all the others."

The only mirror that interested me at the moment was the Mermaid Queen's. I stopped listening.

While I'd been waiting for it to be dawn, I'd done a lot of thinking. Taking the Magnifying Mirror from the Mermaid Queen had made me a hero, but it had also put the Park in danger. Was that my fault? Or was it the Lady's for giving me the quest in the first place? Not that it mattered one way or the other. As official Park changeling, it was my job to fix it.

If I could figure out how. If I survived Hallowe'en and my stupid bet with Tiffany.

At this point, I realized the Magic Tech was standing in front of me. He was holding a ring with a black stone over my head and looking concerned.

"Problems, Neef?"

I cranked up a smile. "Problems?" I said brightly. "No. Just not enough sleep."

He frowned at the ring. "The Mood Ring says Distress. Must be broken." He shook the ring and stuck it in the pocket of his lab coat. "Pull yourself together, Neef. What if you broke a mirror and you'd been woolgathering when we talked about counterspells?"

"I'd be in deep trouble," I said. "I know. I'm focused now."

Which wasn't true, but what else could I say? The ring

was right. On top of everything else, what was I going to tell my friends when they asked how my Equinox had been? The thought of explaining what had happened, of some random East Sider overhearing and telling Tiffany—or, worse yet, that sneaking Airboy . . . No. I'd just keep my head down and my mouth shut and maybe they'd mind their own business for a change.

I'd hardly sat down at lunch when Fortran looked at me. "What's up? You look like ogre spit."

"Thanks," I said. "And you look like an apopa."

"What's that?" Fortran asked.

"An incredibly ugly and misshapen dwarf from Alaska."

Stonewall *tsk*ed. "You're in a *mood*, girl. Did Radiatorella stay too long at the ball?"

Espresso passed me her cup of milky coffee. I took a sip. It tasted almost as good as it smelled. I opened up Satchel and reached inside, too depressed even to make a wish, and pulled out a hamburger.

"Whoa," Fortran said. "Satchel's being nice to you. You must be *really* upset."

"Are you worried about that stupid challenge?" Danskin said. "Because if you want to get out of it, I bet we can come up with a way."

I'd almost forgotten Tiffany's challenge. Now I really wasn't hungry. I laid my hamburger on Satchel's flap. "I don't want to get out of it. I just want to survive."

"We need to know more about the Angry One," Mukuti

said. "You want me to go look her up in the library?"

"You won't find anything," Stonewall said. "She's an urban legend. In Folkish terms, she's just a baby. There's no traditional way to get rid of her. Nobody even knows if she's a ghost or a ghoul or a hungry demon. That's why she's so dangerous."

This was not what I wanted to hear. "Are you telling me that she doesn't follow any rules?"

"Of course she does. We just don't know what they are."

Stonewall opened his magic bag, pulled out a plate of poached eggs in white sauce, and started to eat. Mukuti, Espresso, and Fortran argued about where Folk came from. I didn't listen. I'd just remembered that the Magic Mirror of the Mermaid Queen knew everything.

Relief percolated through me like coffee. I could ask the mirror how to control Bloody Mary. And since the Green Lady never let the mirror out of her sight, I could at least raise the subject of giving it back to the Mermaid Queen at the same time. Of course, I'd have to find the Lady, and then I'd have to think of how to phrase the question so the mirror would answer me, but those were minor details.

Suddenly I was starving. I picked up the hamburger and took a bite. Even cold, it was still good.

The Green Lady is hard to find unless she wants you to find her. The Pooka had taught me that the best way to run into her accidentally on purpose was to get really, really lost. And there's nowhere in Central Park that's as easy to get lost in as the Ramble.

Even when you're used to it, the Ramble is spooky at night. The trees stick their roots in front of your feet and catch their twigs in your hair. There are ghosts, too, shadows that are white or gray instead of black. Some of them are still person-shaped; some are so old that they're nothing but trails of chilly mist or a sudden shiver down the back. I was careful not to look at them too closely, or at the lights that twinkled invitingly between the trees. They were will o' the wisps, *feux follets*, *ignis fatui*. Following them would mean falling into the Lake at the very least.

I don't even like to think about what kind of Folk play in the Lake on a dark night before moonrise.

So there I was, totally and completely lost, groping around in the dark with leaves brushing the back of my neck, ghosts moaning around me, and a fresh wind stirring up a smell of rotting leaves and wet rock, when something swooped at me, chittering.

I ducked, tripped, and fell into a bush.

There was a complicated moment full of scratchy branches. And then I was in a clearing with hard, grainy rock under my knees and the Lady in front of me, lounging on a boulder. At her feet sat Councilor Snuggles. Since the moon wasn't anywhere near full, he had two legs instead of four, but he was still plenty hairy and toothy and sharp-eyed. The Lady's face glowed in the darkness like a lamp, rich amber-green, with the ropes of her bark-brown hair coiled around it.

I scrambled up and bowed with my hand to my chest.

"Snuggles," the Lady said. "Why do I know, whatever she says, I ain't gonna like it?"

Councilor Snuggles cocked his head in a doggy shrug.

All Folk are easier to deal with if they think you're not afraid of them. Ignoring the fluttering in my stomach, I stuck my hands behind my back so I couldn't play with my hair. "I need a boon," I said.

"Mortals," the Lady said. "They never show up unless they need something. What d'ya want?"

I took a deep breath. "I want to ask a question of the Magic Magnifying Mirror."

Apparently, this was exactly the wrong thing to say. The Lady grew taller and incredibly skinnier. Her eyes spun like sparklers. Her head tipped back and started to grow into her neck, and she started to hiss like a kettle boiling over.

Part of me shook like a tanuki's belly. Another part, trained by the Diplomat, noticed that the Lady's fangs stayed folded in her mouth and that Councilor Snuggles didn't bother to move away from her tail. Was it possible that this fairy fit was more for show than for real?

I took a harder grip on my fingers. "Very scary. But I'm not going away until I get my boon."

The Lady-serpent hissed. "I am the Genius of the Green Places of New York. Who are you, to make demands of me?"

At last—a question I could answer. "I'm your champion. I got the mirror for you in the first place. That gives me rights."

To my surprise and relief, the Lady shrank back to her usual size.

"Okay, you're my champion. You got rights. I didn't blast you for getting on my nerves. That's plenty of rights for one day. Now go away."

There was something about her voice and the way she wasn't looking at me that reminded me of Fortran telling the Diplomat that he hadn't put beans down Lightbulb's back. Folk can't lie, but they can mislead.

"Genius of the Green Places," I said formally, "Green Lady of Manhattan Island, Guardian of the City's Heart. As your champion and your Voice, I charge you to answer me: Where is the Magic Magnifying Mirror of the Mermaid Queen?"

Councilor Snuggles winked at me.

The Lady bit her lip. "You're asking as my champion?"

"And your Voice."

The Lady sighed. "All right. I'll tell you. When a Voice asks, a Genius answers. That's the rule."

I waited.

The Green Lady yawned and looked up at the sky, where a nail-clipping moon balanced on the treetops. "What were we talking about again?"

"The Mermaid Queen's mirror."

Emerald eyes gazed into mine. "You're a good kid. Smart. Brave, too. Great Voice material. I always knew it."

"Thank you, Lady. Now tell me about the mirror."

Her dreads gave a slither. "I lost it."

I thought about the Diplomat and kept my eyes steady on the Lady's face.

The Lady's hair retreated into a quivering braid.

"That's too bad." My voice was astonishingly level. "Do you have any idea *where* you might have lost it?"

"Somewhere green?"

Calm. Poise. Pleasant expression. "In Central Park, maybe?"

"I don't think—nah. Definitely not." She lifted her chin defensively. "I'm on it, though. Remember the scavenger hunt?"

I'd totally forgotten the scavenger hunt. "Of course. The scavenger hunt. How did it work out?"

Snuggles gave a bark of laughter. "It would've been great if we'd been looking for mica chips and tinfoil. We also scored some silver earrings and a couple mirrors in plastic frames and some sharp metal disks with rings on top that smelled like tuna fish. Everything came from Central Park. The other Green Places didn't play."

I sighed. "Well, at least we know it's not here."

"You have any idea how many Green Places there are in New York Between, little mortal?" Snuggles asked.

Of course I knew. When I was very little, Astris sang me to sleep with them: Fort Tryon, Riverside, Gramercy, East River, Inwood, Washington Square, Bryant, Morningside. And those were just the big ones. It was hopeless. Even if the Pooka let me quit school and I spent every minute of the next three months looking, I'd never find the Mermaid's mirror.

"That stupid mirror," the Lady said, "has been more trouble than it's worth. I wish I'd never heard of it."

"Me, too," I said, "seeing how everybody in the Park is going to get poisoned."

The Lady ignored this. "I can never remember how to turn the dumb thing on, and when I get you to fire it up, it won't answer my questions."

I stared at her. This, I thought, was what the Diplomat referred to as a piece of unearned luck. "So you'd be willing to give it back to the Mermaid Queen? If you had it, that is."

The Lady made a sour face. "Yes. No. I dunno. Look— the mirror's mine. Her Fishyness is just a bad loser. But she's threatening my Park, my Folk. I'm the Genius, right? I have to protect them."

Something sparked in my head. It wasn't a plan,

it wasn't even a whole idea, but it was the beginning of one. "So if I go on a quest for the Magic Magnifying Mirror and find it, I have your permission to return it?"

The Lady looked mulish, then thoughtful. "Maybe."

"And you promise you won't try to keep the mirror for any reason expressed or unexpressed?" I wasn't sure what this meant, but I'd heard the Diplomat say it and it sounded official.

The Lady's face puckered like she'd eaten a basket of lemons. "A promise is no fun if I can't mess with it."

"That's the deal," I said. "No backsies."

She exchanged a long look with Councilor Snuggles, then sighed. "Howzabout this. I ever find out you ratted on me about losing the mirror, the deal's off."

It was the best I was going to get. "All right. I wouldn't anyway, but I promise I won't tell anyone you're the one who lost the mirror." I wouldn't have to, I thought. They'd figure it out for themselves. "Let's shake on it."

So we did that, her hand like polished wood in mine, smooth and hard and cool.

When the Lady let go, she said, "You're at that mortal school, now, aren't you? Whose bright idea was that?"

"The Pooka's," Snuggles said.

"Yeah, I remember. He jawed at me until I was ready to blast him."

Councilor Snuggles scratched his ear. "You said yes instead."

"Here's hoping I don't regret it," she said, and melted back among the trees with Councilor Snuggles, leaving me standing in the middle of the Ramble in the dark. I had to cry before a moss woman would show me the way home.

Chapter 9

RULE 400: STUDENTS MUST NOT MAKE BARGAINS WITH
SUPERNATURAL BEINGS WITHOUT PERMISSION.

Miss Van Loon's Big Book of Rules

So now I had permission to return the Mermaid's mirror and save the Park. All I needed was a clue where
to start looking for it.

Astris and the Pooka weren't any help. When I came
back to the Castle and told them about my new quest,
they just nodded. I was a hero; I found things nobody
else could find. It was all part of being official Park
changeling.

They weren't worried about whether I'd find it by the
Solstice deadline, either. Astris laughed when I started
listing all the Parks of Manhattan. "Silly pet. Don't you
worry. It'll be the last place you look. It always is, in
quests."

The Pooka was just as optimistic. "I wouldn't be

questing too hard to begin with. Whatever you do, you'll not be finding it until the very last moment, so there's no use wearing yourself to a thread over it."

"You don't know that," I protested.

"I do so. Can you call to mind a single quest that ended before its set time? Of course not. So stop fretting and go to bed. Unless I'm much mistaken, you've got school tomorrow."

Next day, I skipped lunch to sit on the back stairs and fret without interruption or question. When the horn blew, I went to Diplomacy, where I did my best to pay attention while the Diplomat talked about the difference between bargains you have to keep and bargains you can fudge a little.

When I looked up from taking notes, Tiffany was glaring at me meaningfully.

Obviously, summoning Bloody Mary was a bargain I had to keep.

When the last horn blew, I headed to the library to look for maps of New York Between.

Espresso cornered me on the stairs. "What's happening, man?"

"Nothing. I have to go to the library."

"No, you don't. You have to come with me."

Espresso speaking Village I could ignore. Espresso speaking plain English meant business. I put on my coat and followed her outside.

Fortran was on the swings again, kicking at a maple

branch. Stonewall and Danskin were lounging against the iron fence. Mukuti was playing hopscotch. When she saw us, she ran out of the grid and threw her arms around me.

"You missed lunch," she said into my shoulder. "We were worried."

"I had to do something. No big deal." I wiggled uncomfortably. "Mukuti, you can let go now."

Mukuti stepped back. "Sorry."

Everybody gathered around me. "You think we're not hep to your jive?" Espresso asked. "You're way off-beat, man. We want to know why. Say we're curious. Say we're your friends. They're both true."

I looked around at the circle of faces. Even Fortran looked serious for once. "I can't tell you much," I said apologetically. "There's a kind of geas involved."

Stonewall shrugged. "So tell us what you can. We won't ask questions."

I wanted to believe him. I did believe him. I licked my lips. "Okay. Here it is. I have to find the Mermaid Queen's Magnifying Mirror before the Winter Solstice."

Fortran gave me a grin I could have read by. "Is that all? That's easy. It's in Riverside Park."

I liked Fortran. He was smart, and he put his whole heart into everything he did. But he lied. And this was just the kind of thing he could practically be relied on to lie about.

"I don't believe you," I said. "You've never been inside a Park in your life."

The grin dimmed. "I have so," Fortran protested. "I've been there lots of times. I won an acorn off an oak dryad once. Wanna see?" He unzipped one of Backpack's pockets and produced an acorn. It was battered and worm-eaten. "Wicked, huh?"

Stonewall picked it up, examined it, put it back in Fortran's hand. "So not impressed."

"Okay, I picked it up on Riverside Drive," Fortran admitted. "But I do know where the mirror is. This goblin's been howling. Everybody's heard it that lives on Riverside Drive." He shot me a look. "You can ask anybody. Howl, howl, howl all night, every night. Nobody's got any sleep since before the Equinox."

"What's that got to do with the Mermaid's mirror?" Mukuti asked reasonably.

"Well, a bunch of the guys got fed up and snuck into Riverside Park to shut it up. They heard what the goblin was muttering about between howls."

"'I've got the Mermaid Queen's Magic Mirror, and now I know everything?'" I asked sarcastically.

"No-o. It was something about glass beads and a nymph." He paused. "*And* a magic mirror."

We looked at each other. "That's it?" Danskin said. "That's your big scoop?"

"There couldn't be that many mirrors in the Park," Fortran explained patiently. "What else could the goblin be talking about?"

"I don't believe in coincidences," Stonewall said.

"I do," Espresso said unexpectedly. "Bigger ones go down in fairy tales all the time."

The whole thing sounded like a long shot to me, but it was a place to start. "All right," I said. "I'll check it out tonight."

"Wizard!" said Fortran. "I wish I could help."

As we were leaving the courtyard, Stonewall went to walk by Fortran. "By the way, what happened to the guys? Did they get the goblin to shut up?"

Fortran grinned. "They woke up a kelpie, and it chased them all the way back to the Riverside wall. The goblin's still howling."

Even though she'd never taken me to Riverside Park, Astris had made me learn a lot of facts about it. I knew that it covered 266.791 acres (Central Park covered 840.01) in a kind of long, reedy ruffle along the western shore of Manhattan Island. Nature spirits live there, and most of the Swamp Folk—Jenny Greenteeth, kelpies, Viz-Leany, enchanted frogs. And marsh goblins, of course.

I took the Betweenway from Yorkville to Riverside. As I stepped out of the Riverside station, I was hit by a gust of wind off the river that made my eyes water. I wiped my eyes and searched for a path that looked like it might go to the river. There were several. On the theory that middle ways tend to be lucky, I picked the middle path. It led me through a tangle of rocks and swamp myrtle, then left me at the edge of a swamp. Nearby was a faint trail of matted-down marsh grass. It didn't look inviting, but it was the only path around. I followed it.

I knew if I turned around, I'd see the buildings of Columbia University behind me, but it felt like I was in the middle of nowhere. The wind whistled, the reeds clacked, and the wet grass squelched under my feet, releasing a scent of hay and rot. The path skirted a still, black pond that hinted at saucer eyes and hungry, tooth-rimmed mouths. I kept away from the water's edge and hurried on.

The path ended at a muddy island. It wasn't much of an island: scrub brush and rocks and some tufts of marsh grass. I was going to have to go back and look for another path.

As I turned, I slipped on a patch of green and sank ankle-deep in black ooze.

I grabbed two tufts of marsh grass and hauled myself out of the mud, which released my feet with a slurping pop and a stinky sigh. Liquid mud seeped down inside my sneakers, where I could feel it squelching slimily between my toes. I sat down on roundish gray rock and started to pick at my wet laces.

The rock screamed and bucked, throwing me backwards into a very prickly bush.

I yelped and flailed and wiggled out of the bush, coming face to grainy, gray face with a marsh goblin.

"You sat on me!" it gibbered. "Your posterior, on my *head*! Was that nice? And *then*"—it cranked up the volume—"*you destroyed my house!*"

"I didn't mean to," I said. "I thought you were a rock."

The goblin put its hands over its bat-wing ears, curled its head over its webbed feet, and howled. Even now that I knew it was a goblin, it still looked like a rock to me, dark gray and knobbly, encrusted with lichen and veined with black. Except that rocks don't howl.

"I'm sorry about your house," I shouted. "It was an accident. Really." The goblin's accident, not mine, but I didn't need diplomacy lessons to know I shouldn't say so. "I meant no harm. I was clumsy. I'm really sorry."

The goblin shut up midhowl, uncurled, and pointed a long, curved claw at me. "You're a mortal," it said accusingly.

"Yes."

"I've heard of you. You're the Park changeling. Which means that drowning you or picking out your eyes isn't an option." It sighed unhappily.

"The Lady wouldn't like it. I *said* I was sorry."

"Sorry isn't enough. You have to earn my forgiveness. Let me think." Its claw rasped against its scaly head. "All right. I'll forget about you sitting on my head and turning my house into kindling—if you do me a favor."

"What kind of favor?" I asked cautiously.

"You promise you'll do it?"

"I promise I'll think about it."

The goblin gave me what it probably thought was a friendly smile. "It should be easy for a hero like you. All you have to do is make a nymph give me her green glass beads, and we'll call it even. Otherwise, you owe me a new house. Or maybe an eye. I'm sure the Lady wouldn't object if I took just one."

I blinked. "Green glass beads?"

The goblin pulled its next sigh from the bottom of its webbed feet. "*The* green glass beads. Round, luminous, smooth. On a silver ring. They're beautiful. Gorgeous. Magical. They're better than stars or water, better than voices of winds that sing. They're better than—"

"Sliced bread," I interrupted. "I get it. And the nymph who has them won't give them to you."

"No." The goblin's voice was mournful.

Things were looking up. Even in the middle of a swamp, I was on firm ground, fairy-tale ground, playing by rules I understood. "I don't know," I said thoughtfully. "Getting green glass beads from a nymph who doesn't want to give them up sounds like a very difficult task, maybe even an officially impossible one. You have to give me something just as valuable in return. That's the rule. I'll get you the beads in exchange for your forgiveness and answers to three questions. And that's my final offer."

The goblin sighed some more and chewed its claws.

"Oh, all right," it said irritably. "What's the first question?"

"Have you seen a mirror, about yea big?" I made a cereal-bowl sized circle with my fingers. "It shows you things—if you know how to ask."

The goblin rolled on the ground in another fit of howling. "You're mocking me!" it wailed. "You're in league with the nymph! You know about the mirror!"

"I don't know much," I admitted. "So what's the connection between the mirror and the glass beads?"

The goblin sat up. "There isn't one. That's the problem. When she gave me the mirror, I saw the beads in it, all round and cool and green as grapes. Then she went away, and all I could see was a monster with black teeth and squinchy yellow eyes. It gave me nightmares. Woe," the goblin howled. "Woe, woe, woe, woe—"

"Third question," I shouted. The howling stopped. "Where is the mirror now?"

The goblin showed me its teeth. They were long, black, and pointy. "Not here."

"That's not a good enough answer."

The goblin grinned wider. "It's the only one you're going to get. Homewrecker."

"Fine." I stood up. "If you don't want those beads, I don't care. And I can live without your forgiveness."

"Can you?" The goblin leered at me.

"Of course," I said. "I'm under the protection of the

Green Lady of Central Park, after all. If you hurt me, you'll have a lot more to howl about than some stupid glass beads."

The goblin writhed unhappily. "Oh, all right. I gave the mirror to a dwarf. They're digging up Riverside Drive, apparently. A few days ago, one of them came up here to . . . comment on my howling. He took a fancy to the mirror and we made a deal. He wouldn't push my face in, and I'd give him the mirror and keep the howling down during working hours. He said he was dating a swan maiden at Lincoln Center, and thought she'd like it. And that's all I know.

"Now, about those beads . . ."

The last thing I wanted to do was go chasing a marsh nymph all over a swamp. A bargain's a bargain, but I suspected I could fudge this one, just a little. All I needed to do was display a little creative diplomacy, otherwise known as lying. "I've heard about those glass beads," I said thoughtfully. "They have a special magic that will be broken if a mortal touches them. *However*," I said as the goblin began to growl, "I have a plan so you can win them for yourself."

The goblin stopped growling.

"Okay, here's the plan. Challenge the nymph to the Riddle Game. I'll give you a riddle, a new riddle, a riddle that nobody in the Green Places has ever heard before. You can win the green glass beads, plus prove you're smarter than the nymph. It's way better than if I did it for you."

The goblin shot me a suspicious look. "A new riddle?"

"I made it up myself."

"It's not one of those bogus riddles that don't have a real answer, is it? Because if it is, I'm not interested."

"It has a real answer."

"Promise?"

"Cross my heart and hope to die."

The goblin thought this over, then nodded. "Fair enough. Come whisper the riddle in my ear. I've met Rumplestiltskin. I don't want anybody overhearing and telling the nymph before I see her."

My heart thumped as I leaned close to its bat-wing ear to whisper the riddle I'd stumped the Mermaid Queen with.

"A cat?" it asked. "Are you sure?"

"It's my riddle," I said.

The goblin shook its head. "I hope this works. I'm getting tired of all this howling."

"So why don't you just stop?"

"I promised the nymph I'd lie in the reeds and howl until she gave me the beads," it said. "I'm a goblin of my word."

Chapter

10

**RULE 333: STUDENTS MUST NOT ALLOW THEIR TEMPERS TO
OVERCOME THEIR COMMON SENSE.**

Miss Van Loon's Big Book of Rules

The next day, I could hardly wait for lunch so I could
talk to my friends about my conversation with the
goblin. Astris hadn't been that interested. ("How clever of
you, pet. Now, what would you like for dinner?") I wanted praise. I wanted sympathy. I wanted more information about Lincoln Center.

I'd asked Astris, of course, as soon as I got home. She
knew that Lincoln Center was on Broadway, just north of
the Theater District, and that its Genius was the Artistic
Director. He wore white tie and tails and a white mask
over his one eye. And that was it.

Of course, I hadn't known much about any of the
Neighborhoods I'd quested in last summer, either, and
I'd done just fine. With a lot of help and even more

luck. Not to mention my fairy twin, Changeling, who could use the Mermaid Queen's Magic Mirror probably just as well as the Queen herself. Once Changeling got over thinking New York Between was a dream and freaking out every time something surprised her, we'd made a great team. Now she was back in New York Outside, learning about computers and social skills. I missed her.

Our table was full, but Espresso had saved me a seat across from Danskin and Stonewall.

As I sat down, Fortran leaned around Espresso. "So? How'd it go? I was right, wasn't I? The goblin had the mirror and you're not worried anymore?"

"Actually, I'm still worried," I said. "The goblin gave the mirror away before I got there. To a dwarf."

Espresso giggled. *"Mirror, mirror on the wall, who's the fairest dwarf of all?"*

"You're a nut, Espresso. The dwarf was going to give it to his girlfriend. She's a swan maiden at Lincoln Center."

Danskin looked up from his smoked salmon sandwich. "Swan maiden? Did he say which one?"

"I was hoping you'd help me find out."

Danskin frowned thoughtfully. *"Swan Lake's* in repertory this season," he said. "I'll get us tickets and a backstage pass."

I gaped at him. "Tickets? For the ballet?"

"The best way to approach a swan maiden is to tell

her what a wonderful dancer she is. It works better if you've seen her dance."

I tried to wrap my brain around attending an actual ballet. "Are you sure, Danskin? I'm the Wild Child, re-member—I only know about Folk dancing."

"It's all Folk dancing, Neef. Don't worry. I'll do the flattering part."

"I hate to ruin your lovely plan," Stonewall said, "but does Neef have a quest pass?"

"Quest pass?" I asked blankly.

Mukuti swallowed a mouthful of naan. "*You* know, Neef. Rule 746: 'No student may embark upon a personal quest or journey of discovery without a valid quest pass.'"

"This isn't a personal quest," I said. "It's for the Park."

Mukuti, who was clearly going to be an expert on rules when she grew up, said, "You should have one any-way. A lot of Miss Van Loon's rules are against things you need to do on a quest, like going places without permis-sion. A quest pass lets you break rules without getting in trouble."

Fortran wiped his mouth on the sleeve of his sweater. I was surprised it didn't have a permanent red-orange stain on it, he did it so often. "It's no fun breaking rules if you're allowed to do it."

"She's not doing it for fun, Fortran," Stonewall said. "She's doing it for real."

In fairy tales, quests fall into three parts:

1. Find out about a magical thingummy.
2. Go look for it.
3. Get it away from whoever has it.

There are rules governing each of these parts. Be kind to animals you meet in the forest. If an oven asks you to clean it, get out your rubber gloves and start scrubbing. Ask birds for directions, but not rocks or mysterious little men. If somebody offers you a choice between a box of gold, a box of silver, and a box of lead, take the lead. If you're offered three coffee mugs, take the gold one.

They don't always make sense, but it doesn't matter. They're *rules*, and you have to follow them. If you don't, there are *consequences*.

When a quest begins with the quester not knowing the location of the object she's looking for, the rule is that she should start walking until she meets somebody magical to give her advice. There's nothing, not even in the most obscure fairy tale, about waiting for a quest pass.

The day after the Lincoln Center conversation, I skipped lunch again, went to the Schooljuffrouw's office, and knocked.

"Come in, dear."

It was not the Schooljuffrouw's voice, and it wasn't the Schooljuffrouw's office. Everything in it was pastel and cozily cushioned, including the man who'd called me "dear." When I came in, he removed his glasses and let them dangle against his Inside Sweater, which was a delicate leaf green.

I pulled myself together. "Hi. Um. I'd like to speak to the Schooljuffrouw about a quest pass?"

"A quest pass. Well." The man fiddled with the cord holding the glasses around his neck. "That's not . . . I don't think . . . I'm not *authorized*, you see. I'm just the Secretary. Are you sure you really want a quest pass, dear?"

"I'm positive," I said. "It's very important."

He put the glasses on again. Behind them, his eyes were like fish eyes, big and goggling. "You'll have to talk to the Assistant, then. In there."

He pointed to a door I hadn't noticed before and I went through it into the next room.

The Assistant's office was as spare as the Secretary's had been cluttered. The Assistant was kind of spare, too. She was all angles and bones, with hair scraped back in a painful-looking bun and a nose like an eagle's beak. Her eyes, behind thick square glasses, were like twin gray poached eggs.

I went up to her desk. "I need to talk to the Schooljuffrouw about a quest pass, please."

"No," the Assistant said briskly. "The very idea! You haven't even filled out the paperwork."

"Paperwork?"

"There's always paperwork."

As her poached-egg eyes glared into mine, daring me to argue, I suddenly realized what was going on.

When I was little, one of my favorite stories was "The Magic Cigarette Lighter." It's about this young policeman, down on his luck, who has to get past three dogs, each with progressively huger eyes and huger bodies to keep them in, before he can get to the Magic Cigarette Lighter that will give him his heart's desire. There was a lot more to the story, about the policeman's adventures with the cigarette lighter. But the important point to remember right now was that the guard dogs at the beginning didn't attack the policeman. They just sat and stared at him. All he had to do to get past them was not freak out.

I stared back at the Assistant. After a long moment, she took off her glasses. Without them, her eyes were small and weak. "You'll have to ask the Deputy," she said. "In there."

The Deputy's office was gloomy and brown and smelled of very old sandwiches. The only furniture in it were some bookcases and, in front of the far door, a wheeled chair loaded with what looked a pile of brown blankets.

I squeaked forward a few steps, the hair prickling along my arms.

The blankets stirred and groaned, and the Deputy turned to look at me. His (or possibly her) face was a nest of wrinkles with a bony nose and a narrow, sunken mouth. If she (or possibly he) had eyes, they were invisible under a mop of yellow-white hair.

"I know there's somebody there." The Deputy's voice was creaky and thin, like the wind through bare branches. "Identify yourself immediately."

I reached for a curl. "Neef." My voice came out in an uncertain squeak.

"Beef? Stupid thing to call a changeling. When I was young, the Folk had style. Nonpareil. Dead Rabbit. Four-in-hand. Geegaw. A mortal could answer to names like that with pride. Come here, Beef."

Nervously, I took a step forward. A gnarled hand, all bones and skin, snaked out of the blankets and pulled at my arm. I jumped.

"Stop playing with your hair," said the Deputy. "It's childish. What do you want, Beef?"

"A quest pass," I said, snatching my hand behind my back. "And it's Neef, not Beef. N, as in Nonpareil."

The claw shook as the Deputy made disgusting liquid noises I guessed were laughter. "You think you're pretty smart, don't you? Heard all the fairy tales, learned all the lists, got a magic bag and a pure heart, think you're ready to seek your fortune? Well, it's not that simple, Beef."

It was simple for the policeman: the dogs hadn't argued. I was beginning to lose patience. "I know. I have to pass a bunch of tests first, and this is obviously one of them. So stop trying to scare me off and tell me what I have to do next."

"You're going to be late for your lesson, you know," the old voice warned. "Unless you leave *right now*."

Another test. "So I'll be late," I said.

The Deputy's wrinkles grew more threatening. "You could be banished from Miss Van Loon's."

"I've been banished before," I said. "I survived. Look, I need a quest pass. Can you please just give me one?"

The pile of blankets pulled itself higher in the chair. "You'll have to get by me first," the Deputy said.

It would have been so easy just to shove the wheelchair away from the door. But Astris had dinned it into me that only oldest sons and wicked magicians are mean to old people. Heroes give them their cloaks, or half their lunch. And I was a hero, right?

Well, I didn't have a cloak. And I suspected that toothless mouth wouldn't be able to deal with bread and cheese. I thought a moment, then opened Satchel and wished. A cup nudged into my hand. I pulled it out, steaming fragrantly.

The Deputy sniffed loudly. "Is that hot chocolate? I haven't had hot chocolate in over a hundred years."

"It is. And I'll give it to you when you let me pass."

The Deputy's voice edged into a whine. "I'm not a wicked witch or an evil dwarf. I'm just a poor old mortal, good for scaring away cowards and weeding out bullies. You're obviously neither. Go on in. But give me the chocolate first."

I shoved the cup into the Deputy's bony hands and opened the door.

This time, it really was the Schooljuffrouw's office, complete with books and huge wooden desk, with the Schooljuffrouw behind it, looking into a large crystal ball. When I came in, she covered it with a piece of cloth.

"I understand you want a quest pass," she said.

When the policeman got past the guardian dogs, he'd found a magic treasure. I'd only found another guardian. I took a tight grip on my impatience. "Yes, ma'am."

"A quest pass is a privilege, you know. No student is entitled to one just for the asking. You have to have a good reason."

"I have to find the Mermaid Queen's Magic Mirror," I said. "If I don't, she'll drown Central Park in salt water."

The Schooljuffrouw frowned. "Our policy here at Miss Van Loon's is to avoid taking sides in inter-Neighborhood squabbles and let our graduates handle them."

"I'm the only changeling the Lady's got."

"And whose fault is that?"

I twisted my hands behind my back. "Listen, I know the Green Lady is hard to love. She's unreliable, she's dangerous, and she can't stand mortals. She doesn't even like me very much. But she doesn't deserve to be wiped out. She was the Genius of all Manhattan once. She's been here since the island was covered with swamps and hills and forests of poplar and maple."

"The island has changed since then," the Schooljuf-frouw said. "The Lady has not changed with it."

I was starting to feel desperate. "Well, what about the Park Folk? If the Mermaid Queen poisons the water, a lot of innocent Folk are going to get hurt."

"Innocent? Park Folk? The Wild Hunt's hardly innocent. If they had their way, they'd eat every live thing in New York."

"There are other Folk in Central Park besides the Wild Hunt!" The Schooljuffrouw winced—I was shouting. "What about the giants and wyrms on Wall Street?" I went on more softly. "What about the Scalpers on Broadway and the ogres and the disease spirits and the alligators in the sewers? What about the Mermaid Guard? They're all just as dangerous as the Wild Hunt. Which, by the way, only the Lady can control."

The Schooljuffrouw held up her hand. "Enough. I note your persistence and your affection for the Park. These are points in your favor. You could have been more polite, though, and you need to watch that temper of yours. Thankfully, the final decision is not mine." She reached into a drawer, pulled out a sheaf of papers, and handed them to me. "Fill out these forms and give them to the Secretary."

I took the forms. "I need this quest pass soon,

Schooljuffrouw. I've got to get the mirror to the Mermaid Queen by Midwinter, or it's all over."

"Midwinter? That's months away," the Schooljuffrouw said. "You'll hear when you hear. That's the rule."

The Deputy had been right: I was very late to Diplomacy. The Diplomat didn't even give me a chance to explain, just pointed me toward a bulging sack of feathers. Tiffany almost burst trying not to laugh, and I saw the Harbor changeling Airboy staring at me warily, like a cat watching a beetle. Maybe he knew about the Mermaid Queen's threat. Maybe he thought it was a good idea.

I turned my back on all of them and got to work on the feathers. By the time I finished sorting, the last horn had blown, the last changeling had left the schoolyard, and the sun had set.

I traded my starless Inside Sweater for my coat and took the Betweenway home.

Chapter 11

RULE 4: STUDENTS MUST NEVER VISIT ONE ANOTHER'S
NEIGHBORHOODS WITHOUT PERMISSION OF ALL RELEVANT
GENIUSES, THE SCHOOLJUFFROUW, AND A NATIVE GUIDE.

Miss Van Loon's Big Book of Rules

Not knowing when, or even if, I was going to get my quest pass made me crazy. I wanted to *do* something—find the ballet-loving dwarf, maybe, or even go track down the goblin's nymph and make her tell me where she had found the mirror. Espresso said I should go for it; Stonewall pointed out that champions who go off on side quests usually don't come back.

Mukuti suggested I go to the library and work on the Bloody Mary problem.

This almost counted as a quest. The Librarian had a very Folkish attitude to all the Van Loon's rules on library use. Open your magic bag in the library, turn down the corner of a page, leave a book open on its face, and she'd be on you like a pigeon on a crumb.

I left lunch early and went up to the library. The Librarian was sitting at the checkout desk, reading a book and petting the library cat, which was asleep on her lap.

"Good morning, Librarian," I said in a library-friendly murmur. "Can you please tell me where I can find the books on urban Folk lore? Oh, and exorcism, too."

She fished a pair of glasses on a chain out of the pocket of her scarlet Inside Sweater and peered at my starless sweater. "That's *advanced* material," she said. "I'll need to see a letter of permission or a quest pass before I can—"

I couldn't have this conversation again. I just couldn't. "Never mind," I said. "Thanks anyway."

Back in the hall, I saw a slender shape darting toward the stairs.

Airboy had been listening at the library door.

Ever since the Equinox, I'd been tripping over Airboy everywhere. In Diplomacy and Mortal History, I could feel his black eyes drilling holes in me from the back of the room. In the lunchroom, he'd moved to sit nearer our table. And every time I'd tried to talk to him, he pretended I wasn't there.

This time, I'd make him pay attention.

I bounded up the stairs three at a time, reaching the third floor just in time to see him disappear through a door at the end of the hall. I followed him into a room sporting a row of sinks, marble stalls, and some unfamiliar plumbing against the wall.

I was in the boys' bathroom.

Airboy spun toward me, his cheeks blazing. "Get out!"

Thinking fast, I locked the door. Somebody rattled the knob. I shouted for them to get lost. They yelled. I made retching noises. They went away.

I turned to Airboy. "Why are you following me?"

Airboy turned to the sink, turned on the water, and splashed his face. "I don't talk to liars, cheats, and thieves."

"Who are you calling a thief?"

"You stole the Mermaid Queen's Mirror, didn't you?"

"No, I didn't. I won it in the Riddle Game. If anyone's a cheat, it's the Mermaid Queen. Did you know she tried to drown me?"

"That's her right." Airboy turned off the tap and faced me. "She's a Genius. You're just a mortal land-dweller. And you took her mirror."

"What's the big deal? Champions win talismans from Folk all the time—it's the whole point of questing."

"The big deal," Airboy snarled, "is that the Queen can't run New York Harbor without the mirror. Ships run into each other. The Kraken sank a ferry Outside and ate some of the passengers. The Queen's in a horrible mood. Nobody's safe. When Flotsam reported you hadn't drowned, the Queen turned her into shark bait."

I hadn't known Airboy could even say that many words in a row. "Gosh," I said weakly. "I didn't know."

"I *liked* Flotsam." Airboy's voice wobbled. He took a breath and went on. "Then the Queen drowned Canoe, so Oxygen's the Voice of the Mermaid Queen now, and he's not really ready. She made him threaten to destroy the Park even though he told her it would just make the Green Lady mad."

"That's horrible," I said.

"Like you care," he sneered. "Barbarian."

Coming from a subject of a queen who fed her subjects to sharks, this was totally unfair. "I am not!"

"Are too!"

"Am not!"

"Are!"

"You don't know what you're talking about."

"Everyone knows how the Park Folk enchant Outside mortals to steal pets and leave them for the Wild Hunt, and how the Hunt kills any mortal changeling caught inside the wall after dark and pretends it was an accident, and how it's not even safe for mortals to dance there at Solstice, and—"

"Shut up!" I yelled. "It's not *like* that."

"I knew you'd deny it," he said simply.

I couldn't hit him—that would just make him more sure he was right. I was on the edge of a total fairy fit. And then, suddenly, I wasn't.

I'd had an idea.

There's a story about a girl who was under a spell that

made her speak flowers and jewels. My best ideas feel like that. And this was one of my best ideas.

"You don't have to believe the Park's not a total jungle," I heard myself say. "Come visit, and I'll show you."

Airboy's mouth opened and closed. "That's against Rule Four," he managed at last.

"Do you really care about rules? I don't believe it. I think you're scared."

"Am not," he said.

"Come to the Park, then. I dare you."

He hesitated. "I don't have to. I already know everything I need to know."

"So do I." The words poured glittering out of my mouth. "You're a coward, Airboy, and the thing that scares you most is that you might be wrong and I might be right."

"I'm not wrong. I'm *not*." He looked like he was going to cry.

"I challenge you," I said. "I challenge you to come to the Park with me."

It worked like magic. Airboy's face uncrumpled and his shoulders went back. "Very well. I accept."

When my initial triumph wore off, I realized two things. One, I'd just broken about a million rules without even noticing. Two, getting Airboy into the Park was going to take some help.

It went without saying that I couldn't ask the Pooka and Astris. And my friends would probably freak out about the rules. Which left me only one place to turn.

Instead of going home that evening, I took the Betweenway to the Metropolitan Museum.

I'd spent a lot of time at the Museum while I was growing up. I'd learned things from every exhibit and docent there, but the Old Market Woman and Bastet were special, like extra fairy godparents. But they're not fairies of any kind. The Old Market Woman is a Greco-Roman marble sculpture. Bastet, who swears she's a genuine Egyptian cat goddess, is a hollow bronze statue. And Van Loon's rule against talking school business is about Folk, not art.

Why this should have seemed so important after my afternoon rule-breaking orgy, I don't know. But it did.

I found Bastet and the Old Market Woman in a gallery, watching my mortal friend Fleet copying Hopper's *Portrait of a Woman*.

Last summer, Fleet had been an Executive Assistant-in-Training to the Dragon of Wall Street, dreaming of being an artist and in immediate danger of being eaten for disorganization. In return for her getting me in to see the Dragon, I'd rescued her, and now she was the official changeling of the Metropolitan Museum, with thousands of paintings eager to teach her how to paint.

When I came up, the Woman was complaining that Fleet had her nose all wrong. Fleet looked harried. Bastet looked amused. The Old Market Woman looked furious, but that didn't mean anything. It's the way she's carved.

"Hi, guys," I said. "I've got a problem."

"We missed you, too," Bastet said.

"A problem? Wonderful." Fleet put down her brush. "Let's go to the Fountain Court and talk about it."

I'd only meant to ask them about sneaking Airboy into the Park, but I ended up telling them everything: about school and the *Big Book of Rules* and Espresso talking Village and diplomacy and the goblin and *Swan Lake*. For different reasons, I didn't mention the Lady or Tiffany.

When I was done, I listened to the bronze dolphins spouting water in the fountain and felt peaceful.

The Old Market Woman broke the silence. "The Museum's practically in the Park," she said. "If you bring the Harbor child here, we can sneak him out the back door."

"Great idea!" I said sarcastically. "And how am I supposed to get him here?"

Bastet grinned. "Field trip."

First she had to tell me what a field trip was, and then we had to figure out how to make it work. It took a while, and several dishes of chocolate ice cream from Fleet's Briefcase (Satchel didn't do ice cream), but eventually, we got a plan worked out. It was kind of complicated, and included a truly mind-boggling amount of lying, but we all thought it had a good chance of working.

Over the next couple of days, I set things up. I lied to Astris, to the Curator of the Metropolitan Museum, to the

Mortal Historian, to the Schooljuffrouw and the Diplomat. I lied to my friends, which bothered me more even than lying to Astris. The only person I told the truth to was Airboy, whose only comment was, "Works for me."

It worked for me, too. Three days later, every Van Loon's changeling currently studying Mortal History gathered in the Great Hall of the Metropolitan Museum. Everybody (except Airboy) looked happy and excited. I was as nervous as a mouse at an owl convention, but it must have looked like excitement, because nobody noticed.

I'd proposed a field trip as a way of learning about the development of mortal customs through the ages. Each one of us would pick a custom, research it, and write a report. I'd picked burial systems. Bastet, my docent, was supposed to introduce me to some Egyptian mummies and Roman sarcophagi and Greek funeral steles. Airboy's project was to find out how mortals who didn't have magic bags got food. His docent was—surprise, surprise—the Old Market Woman. Airboy and I had already filled our notebooks with fun facts about funerals and food. All we had to do was get back from the Park in time to hand them in.

The Historian went over the rules and regulations one last time. "Don't wander away from your docent and don't talk to any of the exhibits without permission. Be polite. Don't touch anything. No fairy food from the cafeteria. I'll be in the Frank Lloyd Wright Room. We'll meet in the Great Hall an hour before sunset."

Everyone scattered. I followed Bastet through the

Egyptian Department, down to the Costume Institute, and through some storage rooms to the back entrance. The Old Market Woman and Airboy joined us a minute later.

The kouros on guard duty opened the door.

It was a beautiful day, all crisp and blue and green and gold like a Fra Angelico landscape, perfumed with damp earth and fresh water. Airboy hung back in the shadows, so pale and stiff and blank-eyed he could have been an exhibit himself: Statue of a Frightened Boy. Bright autumn sunshine poured onto the marble floor like honey.

"Race you," I said, and took off into the Park at a run.

I heard footsteps pounding behind me. Grinning, I turned onto the path that led to the Reservoir.

Airboy caught up to me by the Reservoir and we clambered up the steep embankment side by side. It felt so good I had to laugh. To my surprise, Airboy cracked a shy smile.

"Welcome to the Reservoir," I said cheerfully. "You ready to meet some of *my* Water Folk?"

The smile disappeared. Airboy nodded once, stiffly.

I threw some pebbles in the water, breaking the smooth copper-green surface of the water into a million tiny ripples. Shadows moved in the depths. Then Algae the undine, the nixie Pondscum, and two naiads popped their heads out of the water.

"What's up?" Algae asked.

Pondscum glared at Airboy. "Who's that?"

There was a liquid chorus of exclamations and questions, all running into one another like drops of water: "Mortal or City Folk?" and "Is he your boyfriend?" and "Doesn't he look delicious!"

Airboy had retreated into statue mode again. "Cool it, guys," I said. "This is serious. I want you to meet Airboy of New York Harbor. He—"

The water women started yelling. "Traitor" was the nicest thing they said. The nastiest gave me an itch in a place I couldn't scratch.

"What's it going to hurt to hear what he has to say?" I asked. "You know you're curious."

They were, although it took a while to get them to admit it, and a little longer to get Algae to undo the itching spell.

"We're listening, Salt Boy," said Pondscum finally. "Talk."

I bit my lip and waited.

Airboy opened and closed his mouth a few times, looking as much like a fish as a mortal boy can look. The water women laughed.

Airboy took a deep breath. "Salt Water Folk know very little about Fresh Water Folk. I want to learn more."

"So you can poison us better," said Pondscum, obviously unimpressed.

"So I can find a reason not to poison you." His voice was steadier now.

Algae and Pondscum looked at each other and

shrugged. "Seems fair to me," Algae said. "What about you guys?"

The naiads murmured softly to each other. "What if he's all salty, and poisons the water?" one of them asked nervously.

Airboy knelt down and held his hand over the water. "Taste," he said.

I had to admit it: the kid had guts. The water women had pointy little teeth that showed when they talked, teeth that could have stripped his fingers to the bone. He had to know that they were tempted. But he offered them his hand just like he trusted them.

Pondscum gave his forefinger a little lick. "You can relax, ladies," she said. "He's no saltier than Neef here. Okay, young mortal. Show us how they swim in the Harbor."

While I wondered how Pondscum knew what I tasted like, Airboy took off his outer clothes. Underneath he was wearing short, scaly-looking pants and a kind of chest harness with pouches on it. I watched him unbutton a pouch and pull out what looked like an oversized acorn cap, patterned with scales.

"What's that?" I asked.

"My merrow cap."

I added merrow caps to my mental list of Folk lore Astris had never taught me. "I've always wondered what they looked like," I remarked.

Airboy's mouth twitched a little, like Astris's whiskers. "It lets me breathe underwater."

"When I was in the Harbor, they put me in a magic air bubble."

He dunked the cap in the Reservoir and pulled it over his close-cropped hair. "Air bubbles are for tourists," he said. Then he stepped up to the edge of the Reservoir and disappeared into the water. He didn't even make a ripple.

I stood for a while, watching for him to surface. When I got tired, I sat down, took off my sneakers, and dangled my feet in the water.

What if Pondscum changed her mind about Airboy and snatched the cap off his head? What if the other Water Folk hurt him or threatened him? What if someone told Astris? What if someone told the Lady?

A fury of bubbles roiled the water's surface, followed by a swirl of sleek, wet bodies. I saw Airboy leap out of the water, twist, and dive back in, lithe as a fish. Was he playing or swimming for his life? He was too far out for me to see. I pulled a curl into my mouth and chewed it.

The roiling moved closer. Airboy dolphined again. This time I could see he was laughing.

Laughing. Airboy.

I spat out the curl. Airboy liked my friends. He'd be my ally in the court of the Mermaid Queen. Maybe he'd be help me find her stupid mirror.

The game moved to the middle of the Reservoir. The

water surged and boiled like Astris's tub on wash day. It looked like the whole Reservoir had joined in.

Algae's head popped up by my feet. She looked amused. "Trouble. One of the naiads tattled to a vodyanoi. He and his friends are going for the mortal tooth and nail. Your boyfriend's still in one piece, but the girls are starting to lose interest. Just thought you'd want to know."

I panicked. Totally and entirely. On land, there were things I could do, words I could say. I was totally helpless dealing with Water Folk I couldn't talk to. My fingers clumsy with fear, I fumbled in my pocket for the Pooka's tail hair. I wasn't supposed to use it except in case of extreme emergency, but if this wasn't an emergency, I didn't know what was.

The hair was long and black and coarse. I held it in my fingers, blew on it gently, and whispered:

> *"By thy oath and by thy faith,*
> *Come thou quickly by me.*
> *Gallop, gallop to my aid;*
> *Danger draweth nigh me."*

At the third line, I heard the pounding of unshod hooves on the Reservoir path. By the last words, a wild black pony was prancing by my side.

"I'm here," said the Pooka, blowing down his nose. "Where's this danger I'm to save you from? Are you hurt, at all?"

"It's Airboy—a friend of mine from school. He's in the Reservoir, and the vodyanoi are after him. You've got to rescue him."

The yellow eyes fixed on me, their expression far from godfatherly. "I do not so. Your friend is no concern of mine. Why does he not call on his own godparent, for all love?"

"He can't," I wailed. "He's from New York Harbor. And if anything happens to him, it's going to make this whole thing with the Mermaid Queen so much worse I can't even imagine. Plus, I'll get in trouble at school."

"Trouble, is it?" the Pooka's voice was dangerously mild. "I'll show you trouble, my girl. Just as soon as I've fetched your *friend* out of the Reservoir—presuming there's anything left to fetch."

The Pooka leapt into the water. I stuck a big hank of hair into my mouth at once and bit down. It didn't help.

A wave surged up over my feet, closely followed by the Pooka. Airboy was on his back, clutching the Pooka's mane. He was gasping and coughing and retching water down the Pooka's neck, but he was alive and he wasn't bleeding, and he still had his cap and his Harness.

I felt awful.

I can't remember what I babbled at him: how sorry I was, mostly, and was he feeling okay and had I said yet how very, very sorry I was about the vodyanoi, and why hadn't he used the Words of Protection?

"Be silent," the Pooka snapped. "If there's anything to be salvaged from this sorry mess, you must provide the plan. It's far too disgusted with you I am, my girl, to be putting myself to the trouble."

The Pooka is always more Irish when he's angry. I reminded myself crying wouldn't help and took a couple of deep breaths.

"The Historian doesn't expect us until right before sunset," I said. "We'll go back to the Museum, find the Old Market Woman, and let her take Airboy somewhere he can dry out until it's time for the class to leave."

I looked at the Pooka, who blew a gusty sigh. "Very well. I shall deliver this soggy morsel to the Museum, after which he may shift for himself. You, my girl, will wait here until I return."

"But I'll get in trouble," I protested feebly.

"You *are* in trouble," the Pooka said.

"The cat—" Airboy coughed and tried again. "The cat can tell the Historian you went home early."

I'd almost forgotten the actual boy in the process of making plans for him. "That'll work," I said gratefully. "Airboy? They liked you—Algae and Pondscum and that crew. And you were having a good time, right? Until the vodyanoi showed up?"

Airboy coughed again, wetly, and turned his face from me.

Chapter 12

Rule 600: Students must not spread rumors.

Miss Van Loon's Big Book of Rules

The rest of the afternoon and evening were the absolute pits. I tried to explain what I'd been doing, but nobody would listen. The Pooka scolded me in Gaelic and Astris's whiskers drooped in mute disappointment. Satchel gave me dry bread and warm water for dinner. It rained.

Astris even took my silver dress away.

By morning, the rain had stopped, but the sky was gray and the air heavy and chill. My hair was an explosion of frizz and so was my brain. I slipped into Assembly still half awake and definitely grumpy. We were on the second chorus of "It's a Beautiful Day in the Neighborhood" when I felt someone tugging at my Inside Sweater.

Looking down, I saw a tightly folded note sticking

out of my pocket. The kid standing beside me glanced at it significantly, then went back to telling the world he wanted to be its neighbor.

I unfolded the note. *Ding-dong, the witch is gone!* it said. *Pass it on.*

Shrugging, I refolded the note and stuck it in the next kid's pocket. She smiled when she read it. I would have asked her what it meant, but Rule 14 (No talking in Assembly) is one of the harder ones to get away with breaking.

After a reading of Rules 160 (Students must not bully, intimidate, tease, or otherwise provoke other students) through 165 (Students must never curse, ill-wish, or use strong language in the presence of another mortal), Assembly finally came to an end. As we filed out the doors, I heard a clinking noise, like someone rolling in a leprechaun's hoard. It was Mukuti, draped in olive green silk and about a million protective charms.

"What's with all the metal, Mukuti?"

Mukuti rushed up to me, amulets clashing like cymbals. "You don't *know*? Drat. That means I can't tell you."

I remembered the note. "I know the witch is gone, if that's what you're talking about. I don't think it counts as spreading rumors if you just fill in details."

"I guess." Mukuti lowered her voice to an almost inaudible whisper. "Tiffany's disappeared."

"Tiffany's *what?*"

Mukuti winced. "Shh! My fairy godmother heard it on the Grapevine." She glanced down at her magical breast-plate. "She made me wear these, just in case there's a sudden wave of magical kidnappings."

"Don't the East Siders know what happened?"

Mukuti's shrug set her amulets jingling. "East Siders don't talk about stuff that happens at home, even to each other. It's like a geas or something. I think Bergdorf knows though. She looks like the ghost of a ghost."

By this time, we'd reached the Talisman Room. The Magic Tech took one look at Mukuti's amulets and made her take them off. Then he lectured us on how too many charms cancel one another out.

"Most of these are junk," he said. "If they weren't, the humming would drown out the jingling. Enchanted things hum. You just need to learn to listen."

We spent the rest of the lesson listening to each one of Mukuti's amulets and throwing out the duds. By lunch, Mukuti was down to three working amulets and every changeling at Miss Van Loon's knew that Tiffany had disappeared. The lunchroom buzzed with conversations that bent Rule 600, but didn't break it. The East Siders sat in a silent island of gray wool, hunched over their identical quilted leather Shoulder Bags and Briefcases, pretending to eat their salads.

Bergdorf, who was staring into space with a frozen look, didn't even pretend.

I sat down by Espresso and got out my lunch. Bread and dry cheese and water. Satchel was still mad at me.

Fortran cantered up and started talking before he even sat down. "You guys hear what happened to Fish-Face yesterday?"

Stonewall lifted his eyebrows. He'd recently dyed them golden, to match his new hairdo. He looked like a gilded cherub at the Metropolitan Museum—if cherubs were into spiked hair and gray sweaters. "Airboy, too? Miss Van Loon's hasn't seen so much excitement since Tony of the West Side got thrown out for turning magical."

Fortran stopped rummaging in Backpack. "That really happened? Wizard!"

"I don't think he enjoyed it," Stonewall said. "He was bitten by a werewolf."

Espresso punched Fortran on the arm. "What's up with Airboy?"

"Oh, right. Fish-Face threw up on the Betweenways on the way back from the field trip. All over some ogre's feet and everything. It was unbelievably gross—the Historian had a real fairy fit. I can't believe he didn't notice Fish-Face was sick before we left the Museum. He was all kind of droopy and green around the gills." He laughed. "Get it? Fish-Face? Green gills? Hey, maybe he was *landsick*!"

Everyone groaned. I tore off a piece of bread. It was stale.

"Fortran," Espresso said, "you are the living end."

"Thanks," he said. "So, what's up with Tiffany?"

After much discussion, we boiled down our theories about Tiffany's disappearance to three:

1. She'd been banished from Miss Van Loon's because she'd finally broken so many rules that the Tutors couldn't ignore it anymore.
2. She was locked in a tower polishing cockroaches for breaking some rule of the Dowager's—refusing to kiss a frog, maybe, or getting a pimple or eating some actual food.
3. She'd spontaneously turned into the wicked witch she was so obviously destined to be and was learning to make poison apples.

Number 3 was Espresso's idea—and my personal favorite—but I thought number 1 was most likely.

The next day the Schooljuffrouw announced in Assembly that the Hallowe'en Revels were less than a moon away. Anyone interested in helping run the Haunted House should report to the Magic Tech, and the library would be open for people researching their costumes.

"The Librarian has been notified, and will make the relevant books freely accessible to all."

If Fortran changed his mind once about what he was going to be, he changed his mind a million times. Each time, it was going to be the scariest costume ever and he'd win the costume competition for sure. Espresso announced she was going to be a flower child, which didn't sound very scary to me.

"That's 'cause you haven't seen my threads. They're outasight, man. What are you going to be?"

I shrugged. "I've had other things on my mind."

Stonewall grinned. "Remember—no Tiffany, no challenge. No challenge, no being scared out of your mind. Now you can concentrate on the true meaning of Hallowe'en."

"Being scared out of your mind *is* the true meaning of Hallowe'en, Daddy-o," Espresso said.

They'd forgotten about my quest for the mirror. I wished I could.

The days went by. Still no quest pass. I didn't understand. I'd passed the test, I'd filled out the forms, I'd sorted feathers. I hadn't complained. The Schooljuffrouw had said it wasn't her decision. Couldn't she tell whoever's decision it was that I was in a hurry?

I knew I had to be patient, but I couldn't help poking my head in the Secretary's office occasionally to see if there was any news. After a few days, I found the door wouldn't open. I rattled the doorknob, just in case it might be stuck. A folded sheet of pink paper slid under the door.

It had *Neef* written on it in green ink. I picked it up and unfolded it.

Do that again, it said, *and there'll be no quest pass for you, young lady*.

The day before the next full moon, the Diplomat kept me after the final horn. Wondering what I'd done this time, I watched her open her desk drawer and pull out a large white envelope. She put it in my hand. The contents shifted heavily from one corner to the other.

"Your quest pass." The Diplomat's voice was a study in mixed feelings. "I feel I should tell you, Neef, that if there were another changeling available with any working knowledge of Central Park, we wouldn't have given it to you."

Fury rose up inside me like a swarm of bees. I clenched my fists.

"You're volatile," the Diplomat went on, her eyes on my face. "You speak before you think. You jump in without a plan and hope for the best. You can't keep your temper. All this is perfectly natural behavior for a mortal adolescent or even for a Genius, but it's unacceptable in an official Voice." She sighed. "You're turning purple, Neef. Take a deep breath and count to ten. Aloud. Or I'll put this quest pass right back in my drawer."

The breath almost choked me, and the numbers

shook a little at first, but by the time I'd reached ten, I was calmer.

"That's better," the Diplomat said. "There are rules, of course. First, the quest pass is nontransferable. No other student may accompany you or break a school rule to help you. Second, you may not speak to any Genius except your own. Third, a quest pass does not permit you to skip lessons. You must limit your quest to weekends, holidays, and after school."

She paused. I held on to my volatile temper and waited.

"Well, Neef?" she said patiently.

I took another deep, calming breath. "I understand, Diplomat."

"I'm sure you do." I thought she sounded amused. "Good luck with your quest, Neef. I fear you're going to need it."

The quest pass was a medal on a chain. The symbol of New York Between was engraved on one side—a beaver, looking annoyed. The other side bore the familiar profile of Miss Wilhelmina Loes Van Loon. I hung it around my neck, under my jacket and T-shirt, where it pressed against my breastbone.

What had the Diplomat called me? Bad-tempered? Not my fault. Volatile? There wasn't anything wrong with that. Being unpredictable was un-Folklike: a strength, under the circumstances. Jumping in and hoping for the best? It had worked just fine last summer.

The Diplomat might know a lot about contracts and manners, but I'd bet anything she'd never been on a quest in her life.

I went out into the yard, which was full of kids darting around like imps and screaming. The sun was low and golden, the shadows long and black. The wind from the East River was cool on my face.

Autumn was coming.

Hugging my coat around me, I headed for the swing. Fortran was standing on the seat with Espresso sitting between his feet, both of them hanging on to the ivy ropes and pumping for all they were worth. Espresso was kicking at the top branches of a maple, which was dodging.

"I got it," I shouted as they whooshed backwards into the sky. "I got the quest pass."

The swing swooped forward.

"Wiiiiizard!"

"Groooovy!"

As soon as they'd slowed down enough to jump off, they were on either side of me, jittering with excitement and curiosity.

I took off the quest pass and held it out for them to look at.

"This is deeply groovy, Neef," Espresso said. "Dig that crazy beaver!"

Fortran put his ear to the medal and listened. "It's not magic," he said, surprised. "I thought it would be magic."

"It's plenty magic, Number Man," said Stonewall, who'd strolled up with Danskin just in time to hear. "It lets her do what she wants without worrying about the Loonie Rules."

I put the quest pass back around my neck. "I wish it was magic enough to get me out of lessons. I can only quest on weekends and after school."

"Then it's a good thing that the next performance of *Swan Lake* is going to be the night after the Full Moon Gathering," said Danskin. "Do you have anything to wear?"

I smoothed the lapels of my black coat. "What's wrong with what I've got on? I thought you said my coat was dashing."

"Oh, it *is*," Stonewall said. "But it doesn't exactly say 'Evening at Lincoln Center,' does it? What did you wear to Autumn Equinox?"

"A Dress Silver as the Moon."

"You have one of *those*?" Danskin was impressed.

"Excellent!" said Stonewall. "Wear that. And lose the sneakers. You think your fairy godmother can magic up some glass slippers for you?"

"No glass slippers," I said. "I might need to run."

The next night, I was standing in Central Park Central between Astris and Mr. Rat, listening to the Lady hand out prizes for the scavenger hunt. The winner was the silver earring, with a pocket mirror (un-magical) and a shiny quarter as runners-up. The winners got to keep what they found, plus their choice of what everybody else had collected.

It was a beautiful night. The trees were beginning to turn, the ground beneath them scattered with the first of a dragon's hoard of gold and ruby leaves. The moon was gigantic in a sky so clear and black I could see stars. Jack and his chilly relatives had touched the wind with the promise of frost. Astris had given me a new dress made with wool from the Sheep's Meadow flock. I was as happy as a rat in a garbage bag.

And then Astris started chittering. "He's here again. The Mermaid's Voice!"

I looked past a flock of fauns to the Lady's granite throne, where the Lady, crowned with leaves, was glaring at the shiny-vested mortal who had threatened the Park on the last full moon. I remembered Airboy had said that the changeling's name was Oxygen, and he wasn't really ready to be a Voice. Now that I'd been around mortals, I could tell he wasn't grown up yet—maybe Stonewall's age. He was nervous.

"Hail, Green Lady of Central Park," he said. "Have you considered the Queen's offer?"

The Lady laughed angrily. "You call that an offer? Sounded a lot like a threat to me. Yeah, I'm thinking about it, and I'm not done yet. Get lost, Fish Boy."

"That's the Lady," Astris said, voice sad, whiskers admiring. "Proud as the rocks underfoot and twice as hard."

In other words, the Queen was a pigheaded idiot. And I seemed to be the only one who thought it was a problem.

When Oxygen was gone, Astris grabbed Mr. Rat and plunged into the dancing. I ran up to the Castle and climbed into bed, where I shut out the stars with the curtains and the music with my pillow.

Chapter
13

RULE 208: STUDENTS MUST GIVE THEIR FELLOW MORTALS
AID IF ASKED, INCLUDING, BUT NOT LIMITED TO, ADVICE,
HELPFUL FACTS, CUPS OF TEA, AND USEFUL TALISMANS
AND ARTICLES OF CLOTHING SUCH AS CLOAKS, BOOTS,
WOOLLY HATS, AND UMBRELLAS.

Miss Van Loon's Big Book of Rules

I told Astris about Lincoln Center the next morning.

Her whiskers quivered like butterfly wings. "How very exciting," she said. "You'll wear the silver dress, of course, and I'll see if I can fix up Satchel a bit. You'll be needing a carriage. And a cloak. Oh, and a ticket." Her pink nose wrinkled. "I can't magic up a ticket."

"It's all set," I said. "This Lincoln Center changeling said he'd fix it up for me."

The whiskers went into overdrive. "A mortal boy has invited you to the ballet? Oh, dear. Is this a Date?" I could hear the capital letter in her voice. "The Fairy Nurse told me about Dates. Is he going to make you pay him with a kiss?"

I went hot, then cold, then hot again. "It's not a date," I managed at last. "It's a quest. Sheesh, Astris. He's a *friend*. I wish I hadn't said anything. I shouldn't have said anything. It's probably against Rule Three."

The whiskers went still. "Rule Three's very convenient, isn't it?" Astris fixed me with a ruby eye. "You'll be careful, won't you, pet? Oh, dear me. A Quest and a Date. Whatever next?"

When I came down the stairs in the Dress Silver as the Moon, Astris, Mr. Rat, all the mice wintering in the basement, and some of the bolder ghosts were waiting in the kitchen to see me off. Astris had spent the afternoon with the dress and a bottle of polish. It was pale gray now, and patches of it glittered in the lamplight like stars in a cloudy sky.

"Ooh," said the ghosts, who were easily impressed.

"She walks in beauty, like the night," murmured Mr. Rat, who liked poetry.

Astris handed me Satchel, spelled down to half its size and decorated with a silver bow. "You look very nice, pet," she said. "Remember to pay the horse and the driver—Satchel will give you some cheese. Try not to get the cloak wet. And remember that the carriage won't last past midnight." She looked at my sneakered feet. "Oh, dear. Are you sure you don't want me to change those into glass slippers for you?"

"They're fine," I said. "I'll remember about the carriage. You're a peach, Astris."

She patted my skirt fondly and said she'd see me at midnight.

Pumpkins are thin on the ground in Central Park, so Astris had provided me with an apple cart. It had a shiny red body and round, bright green wheels and white velvet upholstery. Astris had recruited one of our mice and a (non-talking) rat and turned them into a cabbie and a dun-colored cab horse, both with buck teeth. The cabbie tucked my silver skirts inside the door, jumped into the driver's seat, squeaked at the horse, and we were off.

In no time at all, we were through the Park and stuck in traffic in Columbus Circle. I saw horseless carriages and chariots pulled by everything from frogs to gigantic dogs, plus coaches made from every kind of fruit I could think of, including a pomegranate. There was even an old-fashioned witch's sulky hitched to a pair of fire-breathing goats.

Then my rat-horse leapt into a gap between two carriages and the apple cart lurched forward, throwing me back against the white velvet seat.

Eventually, we pulled up to Lincoln Center and stopped. Everything—the plaza, the fountain, the three theaters—glittered with fairy lights and jeweled torches, as bright as Broadway but a lot more elegant. It was all I could do to wait for the cabbie to open the door and help me unpack myself from the apple cart. I did, however, remember to give him the cheese before I picked up my silver skirts and marched up the golden steps to the Plaza.

The crowd in the Plaza was dressed to kill. I saw lots of fur—both self-grown and borrowed—and velvet cloaks and lace and fairy dust. Folk with fingers or necks had decorated them lavishly with jewels. Many wore top hats, and not just the vampires, either. I was glad to see my dress fit right in.

Since Danskin had said he'd meet me in the lobby, I stationed myself by a door, where I'd be easy to find. A stream of elves, kitsune, afrits, air spirits of a hundred different nations poured past me. No Danskin.

Maybe I was early. I waited. The stream slowed to a trickle. Still no Danskin.

When I realized he wasn't coming, I was furious. Also, without a ticket or any way of buying one: Satchel didn't do gold.

Well, I'd just jump in and hope for the best.

By now, there was almost nobody in the lobby except a group of East Side fairies and the guardian spirit taking tickets by the stairs. The fairies headed for the stairs in a clump. I slid in behind them.

A muscular arm in a dark blue jacket barred my way. "Ticket, please."

"Oh, dear." I looked up at the uniformed guardian. "Didn't Prince Hyacinthe give you my ticket just now? Maybe you dropped it. Will you check?"

The guardian spirit didn't take his eyes off me. They were a cold, clear blue, like sunlight through thick ice. "One person, one ticket," he said. "If you have no ticket, you go away."

His hair was ice white, hanging in two long braids over the shoulders of his jacket. I guessed he was from Finland or Norway.

I opened my mouth to explain about Danskin and the promised tickets, shut it when I realized he probably wouldn't believe me, not after the lie about "Prince Hyacinthe."

"I have to see the ballet. I'm on a quest. See?" I pulled the quest pass from the neck of my dress. "Here's my pass."

The guardian bent to examine the medal. "Nice metalwork. Pure gold. Very pretty. Not a ticket, though."

"A quest pass is *like* a ticket," I said. "It gets you into places the quest leads you to. Like the Ballet Theater. It's very important."

The guardian chuckled. "You are funny person. Very entertaining. You might should go to Broadway. But not to ballet. Here is high art, not low joking."

"This isn't a joke. You're a guardian spirit, right?"

He proudly tugged his jacket straight. *"Ovenvartija,"* he said. "Door Warden in the Old Country. I come over with my family. Family go west, I stay New York. Now I am Usher at Ballet. Is good job."

"Well, Usher . . ."

"Fred," he corrected me.

"Fred?"

"New country, new job, new name." He leaned down a little. "We talk about you see ballet with no ticket, better you talk to Fred."

"Okay then. Fred. I really have to see this ballet."

The ice-blue eyes narrowed. "You such big fan, why I never see you before?"

"I'm not a fan." Fred frowned. "I told you, I'm on a *quest.* My Neighborhood is in danger and I'm the only one who can save it."

"Swan Lake is ballet," Fred pointed out. "Ballet is beautiful only. I think you are telling mortal thing. What you call it? When story is not true?"

"You mean a lie. And no, I'm not. I really do need to see *Swan Lake.* I'm looking for a swan maiden, you see, and—"

"Swan Lake has plenty swan maidens." Fred thought for a moment. "Is impossible, what you ask. My job is to make sure nobody sees ballet who does not pay."

I pulled the strip of silver moon-cloth out of my hair. "This is silver. Also magic. Will it do?"

Fred made it disappear into his pocket. "Come. I hear overture begin."

He led me up a wide flight of marble stairs to a glass and marble hall you could have fit all of Belvedere Castle into with room to spare. He headed for another, narrower stair, which led to another and another and another. I climbed grimly, thankful I'd held out for my sneakers, getting slower and slower. Fred grabbed a handful of my cloak, dragged me up the last flight of steps, across a carpeted hall, and through a bronze door into a darkness full of beautiful, swoony music.

We stood inside the door while I got my breath back and my eyes adjusted to the dark. We were up by the ceiling of a gigantic cavern filled with rows and rows of well-dressed Folk. About ten miles below was a dazzling stage. On it, a bunch of dancers, tiny as mice, moved in patterns like the figures of a fairy reel, but much more complicated.

I didn't see any swans.

Fred guided me to a velvet-covered rail. "Stand here," he whispered, and slipped away.

Figuring the swans would show up later, I settled down to watch. I knew the dancers had to be Folk—ballet was high art, after all—but they seemed to be pretending to be mortals. Nobody flew, although they jumped around a lot, and there was lots of bowing and touching each other, which isn't usual Folk behavior at all. They were mostly dressed like peasants, too, except for a few elves in tights and velvet jackets that didn't even cover their butts.

One elf, in blue tights and a tiny gold crown, was clearly a handsome prince. After watching everyone dance for a while, he picked up a little golden bow and ran offstage. I guessed he was going hunting. I hoped it was for swans.

At that point, the curtain went down. Everybody got up and wandered around, but I stayed where I was, in case somebody wanted to see my ticket. I wasn't going to risk getting thrown out before the swans showed up.

Finally, everybody came back, the lights dimmed, and the curtain rose again on a fake-looking forest. The handsome prince came on and leapt around the stage, waving his little golden bow in a way the Pooka would have said was very dangerous. Luckily, he didn't have an arrow.

Suddenly, the music rippled, and a large white swan flew onstage and circled the prince, who dropped the bow. The swan touched down lightly and swept off her swanskin in a dramatic, feathery swirl to reveal her maidenself in a floaty white dress. She stood perfectly still while, one by one, the rest of the flock followed her, until maybe two dozen swan maidens were posing gracefully around the startled prince.

There was a little pause, the music changed, and another swan flew onstage. She was too far away to see clearly, but I knew right away she was a princess because of her little gold crown. She had a short, stiff skirt sticking out around her waist like a sparkly wheel. When she lifted her arms, the music soared and twirled and leapt, pulling the swan princess and her court of maidens along with it.

I forgot my feet. I even forgot my quest. I was enchanted.

In the next scene, the handsome prince was throwing a party. An evil wizard in a shiny black cape showed up uninvited with a princess in tow, this one a black swan. She didn't look a thing like the swan princess the prince had danced with in the forest, but the prince couldn't tell the difference. I thought he was pretty stupid, never to have heard of glamours. After a lot of fuss and dancing, it all ended sadly, with the white swan dying and the prince jumping into a lake. I knew it was silly, but I still cried.

After the curtain closed for the last time, the two swan princesses, the handsome prince, and the evil wizard came out in front of the curtain and bowed. I wiped my eyes and clapped until my palms stung.

"Come," someone said in my ear. I jumped. I'd forgotten Fred. "We go backstage now."

There was no marble or red carpet backstage, just twisty passages full of gnomes, brownies, and household spirits of many lands running around holding clothes and ballet shoes and little toy bows and wooden cups and pretend food from the party scene. Fred herded me to a corridor that looked identical to all the others, only some of the doors had stars on them.

"Chorus," he said, pointing. "Principals there: Odette, Odile, Prince, Evil Wizard." He gave me a doubtful look. "You know swans?"

There were swans in the Park—non-magical ones. Pretty from a distance. I'd tried to make friends once, when I was little. It hadn't gone well. "Kind of."

He looked doubtful. "After performance, they are difficult. Artistic temperament." He hesitated. "You are true hero, young mortal, even if you are not blonde."

I told him he was very kind. I didn't even need to count to ten. Maybe my temper was getting less volatile.

At the dressing room door, I listened. Women's voices, laughter, a couple of honks. It didn't sound dangerous. I wasn't sure what Fred meant by artistic temperament, but how bad could it be? It's not like the swan maidens could eat me or anything: swans don't have teeth. I knocked. Nobody said to go away, so I opened the door.

Two dozen swan maidens in various stages of transformation turned their beady black eyes on me and hissed.

"Stranger!"

"Danger!"

"Go away, go away, go away!"

I took a deep breath and started babbling. I don't even

remember exactly what I said. The dancing was magical, the maidens were beautiful, graceful, terrifying. I'd never imagined anything could be that wonderdul, and I just wanted to thank them. Nice things. It helped that I meant every word.

Admiration usually softens Folk up, but the swan maidens must have been too artistically temperamental to even hear me. The more maidenlike ones darted their heads at me on necks longer and more supple than was comfortable to look at. Fully feathered swans beat their powerful wings, whipping the heavy silver skirts of my dress against my legs.

"Shaddup!" a voice screeched behind me. "What's with you ladies? Her Grand High Swanness must have quiet after a performance. You want her in here?"

A silence fell over the dressing room, in which I could hear the soft rustle of settling feathers. The swans dipped their heads sheepishly.

I turned around.

My rescuer was a mortal girl, her hands on her hips, her hair twisted up and skewered with a long white feather. I thought she was definitely older than Tiffany.

"What're you staring at?" she demanded. "And why are you here?"

I curtsied hastily. "I'm on a quest."

"Oh, *you're* Danskin's questing girl. Don't tell me he stood you up."

"As a matter of fact—"

The girl glanced over my shoulder. "Oh, boy," she said. "Don't you know not to turn your back on an angry swan?"

At that point, I found out that a Dress Silver as the Moon is good for more than impressing Folk at Full Moon Gatherings. The swan's bite hurt me, but not nearly as much as getting a beakful of silver cloth hurt the swan. I heard a squawk, then the sound of webbed feet shuffling away.

The girl laughed. "I guess you're not as soft as you look. So you're on a quest, huh? What're you looking for? A swan cloak? A used ballet slipper?"

I pulled myself together. "A mirror." I made a circle with my hands. "About yea big. Silver rim, no stand. I heard that a dwarf gave it to a swan maiden. Have you seen it?"

If it had been quiet when the girl had yelled at the swan maidens, it was even quieter now. The girl smiled. "Snowbell. You're talking about Snowbell."

"Who's Snowbell?"

The girl got a sly look on her face. She looked like a pixie, sharp-faced and skinny, with big eyes and a pointy chin and soft brown hair. "Come and see."

Snowbell, it turned out, was the swan princess—the white swan, Odette. She was sitting in a large, untidy nest in a dressing room crowded with water lilies, irises, and reeds growing in painted china tubs. Her swan skin was spread over a couple of chairs to air out, and she had a fluffy pink jacket draped over her shoulders. She looked crabby.

"Where have you been, Minx?" she complained as my rescuer opened the door. "I've been calling and calling. I can't reach my . . . What on earth is *that*?"

The girl Minx began to take the pins out of Snowbell's hair. "It's a mortal, madame," she said, her voice soft and soothing as honey on a sore throat.

"Why did you bring her here?" Snowbell snapped. "You *know* I need to be alone."

"I thought she might amuse you, madame." Minx softened her voice even more. "Your dancing made her *cry*."

"Is this true?"

Minx wiggled her eyebrows at me. "Yes, madame," I said hastily. "Buckets."

"Do you think you could cry now?" Snowbell asked hopefully.

"I can't do it just like that. It was the music. And your dancing, of course."

Snowbell preened. "Oh. Well. I'm glad you liked it."

"Oh, I *did*," I said, and swept her my best curtsy. "I know you're tired, but would you mind terribly if I asked you a question? I'm on a quest, and you're the only person in New York who might be able to help me."

Minx was brushing Snowbell's hair in long, gentle

strokes. Snowbell's round black eyes began to drift shut. She snuggled deeper into her nest. "You may ask."

"I'm looking for a mirror."

"Lots of mirrors in Lincoln Center." Snowbell still looked relaxed, but the edge was back in her voice.

"This is a special mirror. A magnifying mirror. About yea big."

She opened one eye to watch me do my measuring thing. She stiffened. "I see. And what makes you think I know where this mirror might be?"

Minx, still brushing, waggled her eyebrows frantically. "I heard," I said carefully, "that a certain dwarf gave it to the most beautiful swan maiden at Lincoln Center. I knew it had to be you."

Snowbell relaxed again. "Not Sooty?" she asked languidly. "Odile, that is. The black swan. We're supposed to be exactly alike, you know."

"You *are*?" I was afraid I'd overdone the shocked surprise, but Snowbell smiled lazily. "I thought that was just part of the story. You're way more beautiful than she is."

"I think so, too," Snowbell said simply. Minx rolled her eyes. "Yes, little mortal. A dwarf gave me the mirror you describe."

My heart stared to beat hard. "Do you by any chance still have it?"

Snowbell moved restlessly under Minx's hands. "I'm getting bored," she announced.

It was time to stop beating around the bush. "Where's the mirror now?"

"Not here," Snowbell said. "Now, go away."

And that was that. I tried to flatter her back into a good mood, but she got all temperamental and threw the hairbrush at me. She was reaching for her ballet shoes when Minx hustled me out into the corridor.

"I gotta hand it to you," she said. "You almost did it. I had a bet with myself she'd throw you out as soon as you said the word 'mirror.'"

"Why?"

Minx sniggered. "What would you rather know? Where the mirror is or why mentioning it makes Snowbell go berserk?"

I glared at her. "Is Folkishness catching, or what?"

"It's catching," Minx said. "I know, I know. The Diplomat would have me herding butterflies. Oh, yes, I'm an Old Loonie. I even remember the rule about giving fellow-mortals aid if asked. Number Two-oh-eight, right?" I nodded. "Okay, here's your helpful fact for the day. Snowbell's glamourist has the mirror. You'll find her in the Garment District."

"Aren't there a lot of glamourists in the Garment District?"

"Minx!" Snowbell honked from the dressing room.

Minx put her hand on the door. "She's called Elizabeth Factor." She hesitated. "Watch out for her. She's an ex–fairy godmother, blacklisted by the Bureau of Change-lings. I don't know why, but it can't be anything good."

Something hit the door hard, with a crash and tinkle of breaking glass.

"Good luck, kid," Minx said. "If I see Danskin, I'll tell him you did just fine without him."

Chapter 14

When I left the Ballet Theater, it was raining hard. The red apple cart was gone—no cabbie, no bucktoothed horse, not even an apple core. Instead, there was a black pony standing patiently by the curb with his rear hoof cocked up and rain dripping from his long black mane.

"Pooka!" I ran up to him. "What are you doing here?"

The Pooka tossed his head, flinging an arc of diamond raindrops high in the air. "And a fair night to you, too, even if you cannot tear yourself away from your revels in time to catch the coach your godmother was good enough to enchant for you."

"It was an apple cart. And I never asked her to," I said sulkily.

"You didn't have to," the Pooka said. "Just as you didn't have to ask me to come take you home. Are you going to get up now, or do you enjoy standing in the cold and wet?"

It took me two tries to haul myself, my silver skirts, and the wet and slimy velvet cloak onto the Pooka's back. As we trotted toward the Park with the rain trickling down my neck, I couldn't help thinking the Betweenway would have been dryer.

Overnight, frost spirits turned the rain to sleet. In the morning, Astris magically produced a pair of purple rubber boots and made me wear them to school.

I was not in a good mood. Astris was mad about the cloak and the rain spots on the dress, my schedule held a full day of Diplomacy, I had no idea when the next weekend would allow a trip to the Garment District. And there was the humiliation of Danskin's leaving me standing in the lobby of the Ballet Theater like a wicked stepsister at the ball.

Diplomacy was all about cooperation, and involved putting puzzles together in teams of two. I got Bergdorf. As we compared shapes and colors in frozen silence, I had plenty of time to think about what I would say to Danskin when I saw him at lunch.

I couldn't yell at him (see Rule 1). If I took a page out of Airboy's book and ate by myself, I'd be stuck, well, eating by myself. If I made snide comments about oath breakers, à la the East Siders, Stonewall would be mad at me. And I didn't want that.

"It's a Chinese dragon!" Bergdorf exclaimed, fitting a golden eye into place.

I stared at her, startled. It was just surprise that she'd spoken to me, but her smile hardened into a chilly sneer. I thought of explaining, then decided I'd probably mess that up, too.

Mortals are much harder to deal with than Folk.

When the horn blew, the dragon was finished and I'd decided I'd simply pretend that Danskin didn't even exist. If he tried to talk to me. If he was even there.

When I got to the table, I flashed a diplomatic smile to show that I was perfectly happy, sat down, and opened Satchel.

"Hey, Neef," Danskin said. I pretended I hadn't heard him and wished for macaroni and cheese. Satchel, feeling frisky, shot out a piece of flatbread and a chunk of cheddar.

"Danskin's talking to you, Neef," Stonewall said.

I picked up the flatbread.

"Didn't Backdrop give you my message?" Danskin asked unhappily. "Never mind, I can see she didn't. Drat. I'm sorry."

"Message?" I transferred my gaze from my assembly-required lunch to Danskin's face. His cheek was swollen and bruised, and his right arm was thickly bandaged from wrist to elbow and supported across his chest by a scarf.

"What happened to you?"

"An elf challenged him to a leaping contest," Stonewall said dryly. "Danny-boy thought he meant onstage. He meant up in the flies."

Danskin looked embarrassed. "It was stupid. I'm lucky all I broke was my arm. By the time my fairy godfather found the Company Doctor and he strapped it up, it was too late to meet you. I gave your ticket and the backstage pass to my friend Backdrop. She said she'd take care of you, but I guess she forgot. I'm really sorry."

Danskin looked so pathetic, so *mortal*, with his bandaged hand and his bruised face, I couldn't keep on being mad. "Not your fault," I said. "Besides, I got in by myself."

Espresso gave me a thumbs-up. "Right on, Neefergirl. How'd you swing it?"

"I gave the usher a piece of my silver dress. He was really nice. He even took me backstage."

Mukuti and Fortran, who'd been simmering impatiently, boiled over with questions.

"Did you find the right maiden?

"Did you get the mirror?"

"Some glamourist called Elizabeth Factor has it." I picked up the bread. "I hope. If she doesn't, I'll be chasing it round New York Between all autumn."

I needed something to do so I wouldn't go nuts waiting for the Schooljuffrouw to announce the next weekend. Since all I could think about was the Garment District anyway, I figured I might as well spend some time finding out what it was actually like. I'd read mortal fashion magazines, but things were obviously different Outside. Mortal fashion models? Nonmagic makeup? Bags that didn't give food? Interesting, maybe, but hardly useful.

So I went back to the library.

The quest pass worked like a charm. The Librarian didn't even fuss. She just pointed me toward Fodor's *Guide to the Neighborhoods of New York* and told me not to mark it up or take it out of the library. I carried it to the back of the room and sat down on a window seat overlooking East River Park to read it, with the library cat on my lap.

It was helpful up to a point. I learned that the Garment District's main street was Seventh Avenue, that its Genius was the Wholesaler, that it was populated mostly with kobolds, leprechauns, fairy seamstresses, and the kind of house Folk who help tailors. Native Fashion Folk included models and mannequins. There was a short section on glamourists, with Elizabeth Factor's name prominently mentioned. No hint of where she hung out, though.

The more historical books informed me that sweatshops are always bad and designers are always mortal and agents are guardian spirits who take care of models. Elizabeth Factor didn't come up.

Two days later, the Schooljuffrouw finally declared a weekend. One day, which didn't give me much time.

Next morning, bright and early, I told Astris I was going questing. She tried to make me wear an extra sweater, gave me some Autumn cookies wrapped up in a napkin, put a spell on my laces so I wouldn't trip on them, and reminded me that heroes never played with their hair.

That's Astris for you.

As I rode the Betweenways to the Garment District, I found myself missing my fairy twin, Changeling. She'd been a big part of my last quest. Sure, she melted down every time things got too tense, but she'd fixed the Producer of Broadway's computer and even figured out how the magic mirror worked. I missed her perfect memory, her knack of asking just the right question. But most of all, I missed how we both knew what it was like not to fit in anywhere.

I sure didn't fit in the Garment District.

When I exited the Betweenways station, I shoved through the crowds of chattering Fashion Folk on Seventh Avenue. Huge metal racks stuffed with clothes trundled past me like charging trolls, piloted by teams of kobolds, one pushing and one pulling, neither one looking where he was going. As I watched, a brownie arced through the air, landed on top of a rack, and was swept away downtown, swearing and threatening.

If I was lucky, Elizabeth Factor would be on this side of Seventh Avenue. If I wasn't, I'd just have to cope. Either way, I only had one day to find her, so I had to get started. I turned to an elf standing beside me with a heap of turquoise ruffles boiling out of his arms. "Excuse me. Can you tell me where I can find Elizabeth Factor?"

He stepped into the traffic and disappeared without even looking at me.

It was the same with the other Fashion Folk I approached. It was like I didn't exist. I tried standing in their way, yelling and waving my hands. They just stepped around me.

I decided to try the models. Impossibly tall, skinny as giraffes, they prowled the sidewalk on tiny, tiptoe feet, pouting beautifully. One struck a pose against a lamppost, and a cloud of brownies with black boxes appeared. There was a tiny storm of flashing and clicking, then the model waved her long, pink-tipped fingers, and the brownies disappeared again.

The model was tall and skinny and polished, very like Tiffany. She made me feel dusty and short and fuzzy.

They're just Folk, I told myself. *You can talk to Folk. Plus, you have the Pooka's coat. That's got to count for something.*

I marched up to the nearest model. She was dark-haired for a change, and carrying a hairless dog like an oversized gerbil in a pale lavender tote. The tote matched her fluffy coat and echoed the startling deep amethyst of her huge, shadowy eyes. She was the most beautiful thing I'd ever seen.

I cleared my throat. "Excuse me. I'm a mortal changeling. I'm on a quest for a glamourist. Can you help me?"

The model's eyelashes were long and curly, and her eyelids were smeared with smoky gray. When she blinked, it looked like window shades going up and down. "Huh?"

I tried again. "I'm looking for a glamourist."

The window shades went all the way up. "Duh. I mean, look at you. Ugly, much? I just got myself redone. Whaddya think?"

She gave a practiced twirl, struck a graceful pose. There was a small local lightning storm of brownies and flashbulbs. When it passed over, the model wandered off, her gerbil-dog barking at me from her tote.

Beautiful. And as dumb as a park bench.

"Fashion emergency! Mannequin coming through!"

I spun right into the path of a small, wiry supernatural in a big black hat like a saucer with an upside-down cup on it. He cannoned into me and fell over on top of the strange, stick-like thing he'd been towing. His dog, which looked like a puffball with legs, bounced around my feet, growling like a zipper. Apologizing, I caught the puffball while he disentangled himself from the stick.

"Give me that!" he screeched, grabbing the puffball and tucking it under his arm. "And get out of my way! I have to get this mannequin to a glamourist! Right away!"

Now that he was more or less still, I could see his backward feet. A duende, then. I switched to Spanish. "What a coincidence," I said. "I'm looking for a glamourist too. Elizabeth Factor. Do you know her?"

The duende sneered. "I'm a model's agent, aren't I?" he said in English. "Of course I know Elizabeth Factor. She's strictly Artistes and Debs."

"What?"

The duende stamped his foot. "Don't you understand simple English? Oh, why am I even talking to you?"

He grabbed the mannequin's stick arm and darted around me.

I darted after them.

The duende turned onto a side street. I turned the corner just in time to see him disappearing into a low brick building with LIVING DOLLS painted over the door in swirly silver letters. Through the door were stairs. I leapt up them, two at a time.

When I got to the top, panting and sweating, the agent, his mannequin, and the puffball were standing in front of another door. The duende saw me and sighed. "You're harder to get rid of than a bad dye job," he said. "Okay, you can come with us. But I'm warning you. If you so much as open your mouth before the glamourist's done with my client, I'll turn you into a pair of orthopedic oxfords."

As I nodded, the door opened. I followed the duende and the mannequin into a huge, airy room lit by tall, gauze-draped windows. Half of it was taken up by racks of clothes and the other half by shelves filled with bottles and jars and boxes and trays and tubes and lidded bowls. Between the halves was a narrow strip of carpet and a black leather chair occupied by a floating copy of *Vogue*.

"Oh dear," said a voice from behind the *Vogue*. "Another challenge. Two challenges. Pelo, *darling*. Why do you keep bringing me these no-hope cases?"

"The mortal's not important," Pelo said. "Jacaranda needs a Look."

The *Vogue* dropped and the Glamourist detached himself from the black chair like a solid shadow. I wasn't sure what kind of Folk he was—some minor djinn, maybe. He was all black—not black like Fortran, who was actually very dark brown, but black like a black cat: eyes, teeth, fingernails, clothes, everything. He pulled the sticklike mannequin into a clear space, then started waving his hands and shouting orders at the air.

Jacaranda and the Glamourist disappeared in a swirl of airborne beauty spells and potions.

"A real artist," Pelo said admiringly. "He can copy anything. Watch your head! Here come the clothes."

The racks behind me rustled. I ducked just in time to miss being knocked over by a stream of dresses, skirts, petticoats, and tops. They spun like a bright cyclone around Jacaranda and the Glamourist, then froze.

The Glamourist's head popped out between a blue velvet skirt and a glittery red gown. "Fairy princess?" he asked hopefully.

"Goose girl," said Pelo.

"Retro?"

"For *Fairy Parade*."

"Why didn't you *say* so?"

A few minutes later, the clothes slumped to the floor, revealing Jacaranda's new Look.

Jacaranda didn't look like any goose girl I'd ever heard of. The Glamourist had provided her with just enough flesh to keep the clothes from collapsing, but she still looked kind of like a stick figure. She was wearing an apron made of sky-blue net. Her tiny brown skirt showed off long legs ending in high-heeled wooden shoes with little cream-colored geese painted on the toes. She had pouty red lips, rosy cheeks, and wide blue eyes shadowed with the same brown as her skirt. A silver stick dangled from one slender wrist by a blue ribbon.

Jacaranda twirled. "How do I look?" she said, breathy and high and worried.

"Gorgeous, darling. As always." Pelo shot me a glance. "What do you think, mortal?"

I thought any geese Jacaranda came near would

probably attack her. "Gorgeous," I lied. "But isn't it kind of impractical?"

Pelo laughed. "Are you kidding? This is *glamour*. It's not supposed to be *real*. If you want to talk to the Glamourist, do it quick, before I turn you into an accessory."

I turned to the djinn. "Can you tell me where to find Elizabeth Factor?"

The Glamourist tilted his shadowy head. "Are you sure? I mean, okay, you're a total fashion disaster, but she's—"

"For Artistes and Debs," I interrupted him. "I know. I don't want a makeover." I glanced at Jacaranda and shuddered. "I'm on an official and very important quest." I pulled out my quest pass. "See?"

The Glamourist examined the pass. "Pretty," he said. "The beaver's got style." He turned to the makeup shelves. "You can come out, little boy. I'm ready to tell you what you wanted to know now."

A small figure stepped out from behind the shelves—a pale, skinny figure with a close-clipped fuzz of black hair and slanting black eyes.

Rage boiled up my chest and into my throat. "*What*—"

The Glamourist, the agent, and Jacaranda leaned forward eagerly. I took a deep breath and counted carefully to ten, then fifteen, just to make sure.

"Hi, Airboy," I said stiffly.

He nodded. "Neef."

"I see you two are *old* friends," the Glamourist said.

"Now listen carefully, because I'm only going to say this once."

And then he told us how to get to Elizabeth Factor's Beauty Salon.

Folk can't understand that everybody else isn't familiar with their Neighborhoods. The Glamourist's directions were full of phrases like "turn left where the Button Shop used to be," and "take a right two blocks before the Knitting Factory." When he was done, all I knew for certain was that I was going to have to cross Seventh Avenue after all.

"Cool," I said brightly. "You coming, Airboy?"

Airboy bowed deeply. "Honored sir, you are a master of glamoury and as kind as you are great. I will recommend you to all my friends."

"Paint me white for shock," the Glamourist said. "A mortal with manners. Hold on a tick."

He snapped his fingers and two objects appeared—a small blue jar and a shiny, brightly colored oblong. He plucked them out of the air like fruit and handed them to Airboy.

"Here you are: a map of all the known Neighborhoods of New York. The jar is my special beauty cream. You don't need it now, but you will." He leaned close to Airboy. "A word to the wise: Don't waste it on your girlfriend."

Airboy and I clattered down the stairs in one of those noisy silences that happen when you're really mad and can't yell. It lasted until we got to the street.

"What was *that* all about?" I hissed at him. "What are you even doing here?"

Airboy fixed his eyes on the street. "I'm looking for the Queen's mirror."

"How do you know the Lady doesn't have it? And how did you happen to turn up in the Garment District? Have you been talking to my friends?"

He shot me a look.

It did seem unlikely. "Why are you spying on me?"

He shrugged. "There's no rule against spying on enemies."

"I'm not your enemy. That's really slimy, you know that, Airboy?"

He turned and looked at me. "Slimier than vodyanoi?"

Now I was mad *and* guilty. "I *said* I was sorry. I didn't even know it was going to happen!"

Airboy turned back to the street.

I counted to ten again. "Listen. Hate me if you want. We can still cooperate. You know—like that exercise in Diplomacy?"

Airboy unfolded the map the Glamourist had given him and held it so we could both see it.

It was, of course, a magic map. Fortran would have loved it. Any part you focused on got bigger and so detailed you could see the signs on the buildings. If you kept looking, it burrowed down under the streets to show the shadowy tangle of the Betweenways. Central Park, however, was just a blank green rectangle without even Belvedere Castle or the Reservoir marked.

Eventually, we found ELIZABETH FACTOR'S BEAUTY SALON, uptown and east, not in the Garment District at all. It was, as I had feared, on the other side of Seventh Avenue. Which looked just as impossible to cross as it had when I first saw it this morning.

We walked to the curb. I watched racks zip by, their bright burdens swaying, their kobolds scowling and yelling as they tried to outrace each other. I glanced at Airboy. He was breathing normally. Fine. If he wasn't scared, neither was I.

A rack veered slightly toward me. I jumped backwards.

Airboy sighed. "Focus on the ground a little in front of your feet. Step wherever you see a space. Don't look up, don't run. And don't stop."

He stepped to the curb, stared for a moment like a cat at a mousehole, and walked into the traffic.

A moment passed. No extra screeching or screaming. No Airboy flying through the air. I stared down at the pavement. I saw wheels and gray kobold feet. I saw the rainbow flash of clothes. More wheels. More feet.

Open space.

It was gone before I could react, but now I knew what to look for. Another space appeared. I stepped into it, saw a second open space and beyond it, a third. I walked forward. The rumbling and shouting, the bright clothing and the kobolds' gray faces blurred around the quiet path unfolding at my feet.

The last step delivered me to the other side of Seventh Avenue, where Airboy was waiting.

"That was *wizard*!" I said. "Is it magic?"

Airboy shrugged. "We learned it last year in Questing. Come on." He turned uptown.

It was a long walk. Above 42nd Street, the racks disappeared, as did the leprechauns and sewing elves. I still saw plenty of models, though, complete with tiny dogs. But mostly I saw Midtown Executives, Folk dressed in dark suits and striped ties and snap-brimmed hats, their hands and wrists heavy with gold. Some had models on their arms. Some carried briefcases. All had flint-gray eyes that looked through Airboy and me as though we didn't exist.

Airboy guided us down a side street that came to a dead end, consulted the map, turned and retraced our steps, walked another block uptown, and stopped in front of a smallish town house built of cream-colored stone. Every window sported a window box planted with geraniums and deep purple petunias. The curly gold letters over the front door (red, to match the geraniums) read ELIZABETH FACTOR.

While we were taking this in, the door opened and two fairies came out.

I'm pretty good at identifying fairies. The sidhe from Ireland are redheads with green eyes; the fate of Italy are brunettes with dark eyes; the elle-folk of Denmark are blue-eyed blondes. Peris are cinnamon-skinned; afrits are midnight blue, with scarlet eyes. These fairies could have been just about anything. Their hair was glamoured in streaks of lime and shiny black, and their faces were painted in headache-making swirls of pink and turquoise. One was wearing a wide stiff coat that made her look like a giant bell. The other, in unbendable black pleats, with a wide, pleated hat on her streaky hair, looked exactly like a streetlamp.

I wondered if they were Artistes or Debs.

The bell saw us, clutched her chest, and squeaked. "Gargoyle!"

"It's only a mortal, dear," the streetlamp drawled. "An ugly one in a fatally costumey coat. What it's doing here, I cannot imagine."

"As it happens," I said coldly, "the Ambassador here has an appointment with Madame Factor. On a matter of state." I opened the door and bowed. "After you, Mr. Ambassador."

Airboy gave me a dirty look, then swept past me, holding his head high and looking—I had to admit—pretty impressive for a skinny kid in jeans and a T-shirt and high-top sneakers.

"The Ambassador of the Court of the Mermaid Queen," I announced to the startled model sitting in the front hall. "Here to see Madame Factor. Please announce us."

For a moment, I thought it wasn't going to work. The model was giving me the kind of look beautiful princesses give trolls who want to marry them.

Then Airboy smiled at her and she giggled. "Oh, Mr. *Ambassador*! Go right up. Top of the stairs, the red door."

At this point, I spotted the flaw in my otherwise flawless plan. If Airboy was an Ambassador, then I was just an aide. A nobody. A sidekick. Somebody Elizabeth Factor wouldn't listen to. Which was really a shame, since Airboy couldn't talk his way out of a wet paper bag.

Clearly, Airboy was having the same thoughts. He eyed the red door with loathing. "I don't like this," he announced.

I tried to look sympathetic. "You want me to take over as Ambassador? I know you don't talk much."

"That's because I think before I say something."

"What's that supposed to mean?"

"That you've just told some random Glamourist that the Mermaid Queen's Magic Mirror is missing."

"No, I haven't."

"What other mirror would the Mermaid Queen's Ambassador be looking for?"

I was trying to think of an answer when the red door swung open and a voice said, "Come in. I'm just *dying* to hear what would bring the Mermaid Queen's Ambassador to Madam Elizabeth Factor's Beauty Salon."

It was not the kind of voice I wanted to hear a lot of— loud and flat and harsh, with a rasp to it like a bad cold. Airboy stiffened, then took a deep breath and walked forward, with me a half step behind him.

I'd half expected Elizabeth Factor's salon to look like the LIVING DOLLS loft, full of clothes and shelves and beauty products. Instead, all I saw were mirrors.

There were hundreds of them, hung floor to ceiling on the walls and set up on stands and tables in a glittering maze. There were pier mirrors and wall mirrors; hand, table, and compact mirrors; mirrors round, rectangular, oval, and heart shaped; mirrors framed in metal and tile and carved wood; and mirrors with no frames at all.

And then I noticed the humming.

It was more a feeling in my back teeth and breastbone than a sound, uncomfortable and exciting at once. It was the sound of magic, and it came from the mirrors.

Interesting.

"So you're the Mermaid Queen's Ambassador?" Thinking the voice came from behind a tall mirror in a gold frame, I looked behind it and saw—another mirror. The voice went on. "Please tell me she's ready to get rid of that faux punk pirate look. It's so . . . last century."

"He's not really an Ambassador," I said, when Airboy didn't answer. "I just said that so you'd see us."

The invisible Madame Factor laughed—a loud *hnya, hnya*, like a donkey braying. "A lie, eh? How human. I never thought *you* belonged to the Mermaid Queen, little girl. You're too ugly. The boy, on the other hand, has a certain waterlogged charm."

"Do you think so? He's my sidekick." Airboy glared at me. "I'm a hero. I'm on a quest."

"A quest?" Madame Factor sounded amused. "Quests

are Out, you know—too Olde Countrye for words. Still, I could use a laugh."

The humming changed pitch, and the mirrors began to move. I stood very still as they slid around me, tossing me fractured glimpses of my startled face and Airboy's frozen stare. When they stopped, we were standing in a solid oval of mirrors.

The humming intensified. The air shimmered unsteadily, then thickened into a glittering mist that twisted and flickered and solidified into the figure of a woman.

I stared at her, open-mouthed. Madame Elizabeth Factor was sun-haired and emerald-eyed, graceful as a young birch in spring, divinely tall, and stunningly, awesomely beautiful.

She stretched out her white arms and smiled into my eyes. It suddenly became clear to me that Elizabeth Factor was the most important person in New York Between. Her love and approval were like air and water. I was willing to do anything if only she'd let me stay and look at her forever and ever.

"You, ugly girl." Her voice was still harsh, but somehow I didn't care. "Close your mouth before something flies in, *hnya, hnya*. You look like a perfect pig. Or do I mean a toad? Take a look and tell me what you think."

A mirror appeared, cutting off my view of Madame

Factor's beauty and replacing it with a spreading, lumpy horror. I moaned and covered my eyes.

"What's wrong, ugly girl? Are you afraid to face the truth? You know magic can't lie. Look, I said."

I dragged my eyes open and gazed at the toad. It was wearing my jeans, my sneakers, even beat-up old Satchel and the stupid black coat I'd thought was so cool. The expression on its wide, lumpy face was the same disgusted horror I felt pulling at my own. And the worst thing of all? It wasn't even scary, which might have been bearable. It was just pathetic.

"Does that look like a hero to you?" Madame Factor went on. "Of course it doesn't. Heroes are tall and strong and as beautiful as a summer's morning. You're more like a wet November afternoon, *hnya, hnya.*" She and all her gorgeous reflections smiled happily. "Lucky for you, I used to be a fairy godmother. I'll grant you a wish, and in return, you'll serve me for a year and a day."

"Madame," I breathed, "I'd *love—*"

"Shut up, Neef!" Airboy's shout jerked me out of my rosy dream. I glared at him. He glared back.

"Little boys," Madame Factor said, "should be seen and not heard." She waved her slender hand. The magical humming rose. Two mirrors trundled forward to stand on each side of Airboy, reflecting him back and forth between them down an infinite tunnel of frightened boy statues. He didn't move. I didn't think he could, even if he'd wanted to.

"That'll keep him quiet," she said. "Now, ugly girl, if you keep my mirrors polished and do everything I tell you, in a year and a day, you could look like this."

The gargoyle-me in the mirror shimmered and morphed into a beautiful maiden. Her—my—hair was straight and shiny, her—my—skin was pale and smooth, her eyebrows perfectly arched, her mouth perfectly full and pink. She was tall and slender and graceful.

In fact, except for her brown hair and hazel eyes, the mirror-me looked exactly like Tiffany or Bergdorf or Best. She didn't look like a hero at all. She looked like someone the hero rescued.

"What do you say?" Madame Factor asked eagerly.

My beautiful self gazed out at me pitifully. "I don't know."

Madame Factor's perfect eyebrows rose. "You aren't thinking clearly. It's that boy, isn't it? You're jealous because he's better-looking than you are. Shall I turn him into a real fish? We could watch him drown in the air."

The hunger in her voice reminded me of Peg Powler and the Wild Hunt. Clearly, Madame Factor wasn't nearly as good as she was beautiful. I began to be very frightened.

"Or I could make you uglier," Madame Factor said. "Or I could turn my mirrors on that stupid bag of yours and burn it to a crisp."

I moaned and clutched Satchel to my chest. Something inside it nudged me sharply. I reached inside, grabbed the first thing I felt, and flourished it over my head. "But you won't," I said. "You'll let me go. *And* you'll tell me what I want to know. Because if you don't, I'll break all your mirrors."

Madame Factor burst into a storm of scornful *hnya, hnya*s. "With one little apple? I don't think so. I can turn it into applesauce."

"Then why don't you?" I said, and threw the apple as hard as I could at the nearest mirror.

The apple hit the glass with a dull thud and rolled away. The mirror wasn't even cracked. My heart sank.

Madame Factor gave a horrible screech. "You broke it!" she wailed. "You broke my mirror!"

I turned around and gasped. Elizabeth Factor had changed. Oh, she was still tall and slender, but her golden hair was more like wisps of dry grass, her teeth like steel chisels, and her sparkling green eyes like bulging, malevolent grapes in a face that would have sent a demon screaming.

I reached into Satchel again, groped around hopefully, and pulled out a giant drumstick, too big for even a turkey leg. Ostrich, maybe? It didn't matter. It was big and heavy and shone with grease. I started to feel somewhat less frightened. "There's just something knocked loose," I said. "Maybe this will fix it."

"You're an ungrateful, selfish little girl," Madame Factor wailed, "and nobody likes you. I could have made you beautiful. I could have made you *popular*."

I raised the drumstick threateningly. "I didn't come here to be made beautiful. I came here to ask you some questions. You can answer them or I can destroy your mirror. You choose."

Madame Factor writhed. "I'll answer, I'll answer. Next time an ugly girl wants to see me, though, poof. She's a toad before she opens her mouth."

I ignored this. "I want to know about the magnifying mirror you got from Snowbell the Swan Maiden in Lincoln Center. The whole story. Every detail."

Madame Factor took me literally. I got *far* too much information about what Snowbell was wearing and what Madame Factor was wearing and the magic mirror shades that allowed her to leave her Salon, and what kind of spell she used to give Snowbell's hair that otherworldly shimmer. Finally she got to the part about seeing a fine mirror in Snowbell's nest, and taking it as payment for her services.

"So the mirror's here?"

"I couldn't do a thing with it," she said disgustedly. "All it would do was show me my real face, in extreme close-up. I couldn't wait to get rid of it."

"Who did you give it to?"

"I don't know," said Madame. "*Hnya, hnya.*"

I stepped up to the closest mirror and swung the drumstick threateningly.

"Don't!" she screeched. "It's true. Every Equinox, the Dowager starts sending me the latest crop of debs so I can make them beautiful for the Solstice Ball. I never pay attention to their names."

"Was one of them blonde?"

"My dear." Madame Factor shrugged. "When I'm done with them, they're all blonde. One was almost *elfin*—there really wasn't much to do. But she thought there was. You ought to have seen what she thought she looked like. Yes, I have a mirror for that, too. She thought she was too fat—that type always does—and her nose was too big. I said I'd grant her wish if she'd get rid of Snowbell's mirror for me." She glanced at my drumstick and licked her lips. Her tongue was pointed, and an unpleasant shade of gray. "Can you put that thing away?"

Tiffany was a member of the Dowager's court, and she was going to be presented at Midwinter. But so were a couple of the other girls. "When did all this happen?" I asked.

"How should I know?" Madame Factor said, honestly surprised. "I'm not a mortal. That's all I can tell you. Now will you go away?"

As I was about to put the drumstick back into Satchel, I caught sight of Airboy, still frozen between two mirrors.

I'd totally forgotten him. "You have to release my side-kick first," I said hastily.

Elizabeth Factor growled and waved her hand, now tipped with scarlet claws. The imprisoning mirrors rolled away and Airboy staggered forward, looking furious.

"You okay?" I asked.

Ignoring me, he stalked toward the mirrors in front of the door, which slid aside to let us through. As we left her salon and ran down the steps, the last thing I heard was Madame Factor neighing after us. "You are ugly, you know. You're fat and sloppy and your hair's a disaster. You'll never look like a hero. Never."

"Well!" I said as the geranium red door of Elizabeth Factor's Beauty Salon closed behind us. "I think that went pretty well, considering."

Airboy glared at me. "Considering you made a total mess of it?"

"What are you talking about?"

"You. Bombing around without a plan or telling me what you were going to do next. One minute I'm an Ambassador; the next, I'm a sidekick. What happened to co-operating?"

"That's not fair," I said. "You were the one who said being an Ambassador was a bad idea. I was just trying to divert her attention."

"You were taking over." Airboy's eyes burned like black

coals. "I cooperated. I saved you. If I hadn't stopped you, you'd have ended up being her slave."

This was true, but I was in no mood to admit it. "I got her to release you from those mirrors," I pointed out.

"Once you remembered I existed." And he stomped off, taking the magic map with him.

I had to ask a brownie the way to the nearest Betweenway station.

Back at school after the weekend, I went looking for Airboy.

After an evening spent on the window seat in my room staring out over the Park, I'd come to the conclusion that Airboy had a point. I *had* kind of taken over. Ad he had definitely saved me from becoming Elizabeth Factor's slave.

His reaction had been kind of extreme, though. And it had been truly un-groovy of him to leave me in Midtown without a map.

Still, I was ready to apologize if he was.

I didn't see Airboy until lunch. He was sitting as far from our table as he could get, hunched over his usual sushi. When he looked up, I gave him a friendly nod. He looked right past me.

Cooperation. Right. I should have let Madame Factor turn him into a fish.

When I got to our table, Espresso waved me to a seat

next to her. "Hey, Neefer-girl! How's the questing gig?"

I sat down and launched into the exciting tale of my adventures in the Garment District. I skipped over the part where Airboy appeared, and then of course I had to slide over how I learned to cross Seventh Avenue and pretend I'd left the magic map at home and leave out the whole thing with the Ugly Mirror because, well, because. But I told them all the important stuff.

When I finished, Stonewall looked thoughtful. "Tiffany, huh? You know, there are a lot of blonde debs in New York Between. Aren't you jumping to conclusions?"

"I'm not jumping to anything. I thought about it all day yesterday. Tiffany *has* to have the mirror. Why else would she disappear?"

"If the other deb was Bergdorf, she could have it," Mukuti pointed out.

"It makes more sense the other way," Fortran said. "Besides, Bergdorf's a total minion. Can you see anybody giving her a magic mirror when Tiffany was around?"

There was a thoughtful silence. Danskin said, "Well, if Tiffany had the mirror, wouldn't we know? I mean, I can't see her taking one of the great talismans of New York and not using it."

"Tiffany, Queen of New York!" Mukuti chortled. "She'd like that."

Fortran laughed. "I bet she's lurking on top of the Woolworth Building, planning to take over the world!"

"Then why is Bergdorf so freaked out?" Danskin asked.

Espresso shrugged. "Minion, remember? Maybe Tiffany left the mirror with her, stashed in a bag of last season's lip gloss."

"Ha-ha, very funny," I said. "Here's something I never thought I'd hear myself say: I want to find Tiffany."

Stonewall groaned. "Oh, yeah," he said sarcastically. "You're the hardest-working mortal changeling in New York Between. Boo-hoo." I looked at him hard. He didn't seem to be teasing. "Can we talk about something other than Neef's quest for a while? Everybody got their Hallowe'en costumes? Fortran, you still set on that monkey-warrior thing?"

Fortran glanced at me. I shrugged. Stonewall was in a mood. It happened.

"Nah. Too much trouble." Fortran hesitated. "What do you think about a troll?"

Stonewall narrowed his eyes thoughtfully. "Well, you're approximately the right color, so that's a start."

I watched Fortran decide this was supposed to be funny. "Good one," he said doubtfully. "Should be easy, then. What about you, Mukuti?"

"I'm tired of always being something Indian," she said. "Miss Van Loon's is all about diversity, right? So I was thinking about one of those nasty Russian water nymphs. You know, a rusalka. I could get my hair all wet."

"Oh, your godmother's going to love *that*," Stonewall said. "Dripping all over your clothes *and* shorting out all her nifty amulets. The ones that actually work, that is."

Danskin gave his friend the kind of look you'd give someone who was turning into a toad. "Hey, lighten up, Stoney—or should I call you 'Too-Much-Coffee Man'?"

Espresso giggled nervously.

"What about you, Neef?"

I glanced at Stonewall. His eyes were hard and unfriendly under his golden eyebrows. If this was just a mood, it was certainly a foul one. Even if I'd decided about my costume, I wouldn't have necessarily wanted to say anything.

I gave a noncommittal shrug.

"How about somebody from the Wild Hunt?" Fortran asked helpfully. "That gives you lots of scary choices."

"It's obvious," Stonewall said. "Peg Powler."

"What's that supposed to mean?" I asked.

"Well, you're not exactly skinny, are you? And there's the hair—definitely fly-away. A few weeds, a little green paint, and you'll be ugly enough to scare the little kids into fits." He stood up and slung his red leather Shoulder Bag across his back. "I've lost my appetite. I'm outta here. You coming, Danskin?"

Danskin shook his head slowly. "I don't think so."

"Whatever," Stonewall said, and sauntered away.

We all looked at each other.

"Better wash your face, man," Espresso told me.

I hadn't even known I was crying.

That night, I spent a long time in front of the mirror on the Castle stairs, trying to figure out how ugly I actually was. I'd never really thought about it, but Stonewall obviously had. I'd considered asking Astris or the Pooka, but decided I probably didn't want to listen to them trying to tell me the truth without hurting my feelings.

The mirror didn't care about my feelings. Its magic was to show me what was real.

In fact, I hadn't turned into a monster or a toad. I was still plain ordinary-looking. Being ordinary might make me a monster to someone like Madame Factor—or Stonewall—but it shouldn't matter to a hero. Maybe a real hero didn't have to be as beautiful as the day, as long as she was as sharp as a drawerful of knives.

What I couldn't decide was whether or not I actually believed that.

Next day, Stonewall had lunch with the Downtown artists and Danskin sat with the Lincoln Center crowd. The rest of us talked about school stuff. Nobody mentioned Tiffany or Hallowe'en costumes. The day after that, I walked into the lunchroom and saw Stonewall sitting at the East Siders' table, next to Bergdorf.

I felt weird. More mad than hurt, disgusted that he'd

turned out to be such a jerk. I felt like an idiot, too, because I'd liked him.

I sat where I didn't have to look at Stonewall making up to Bergdorf, but I could still hear him saying things like "Ooh, sweetie. How sick-making!" and "What was she thinking? Blue is *not* your color" and "Of course I'll help you with your Hallowe'en costume. Ugly stepsister, you said? We can do a lot with that."

"Neef," Fortran said crabbily, "are you listening to me at all? Because I've been working on your mirror thing, and it would be nice if you even pretended to be interested."

"Sorry," I said. "I am interested. It's just—"

Fortran gave an impatient bounce. "Forget it, Neef. Stonebrain's under an evil spell or something. Nobody cares what you look like."

"Way to go, Talis-man," Espresso said. "Now she feels a *lot* better."

I resisted the impulse to kick Fortran under the table. "It's okay," I said. "So. What do you have?"

Fortran zipped open one of Backpack's tiny pockets, pulled out a palm-sized magic tablet, and laid it on the table. Espresso, Mukuti, and I scooched around so we could see better.

Fortran fiddled with the tablet. It filled with numbers and symbols.

"Very cool, Fortran," I said. "What is it?"

"It's a magic formula. Magic Techs use them to design new magic talismans for the Folk to make. I think I've figured out a new use for them. You wanna hear?"

"You know we won't dig it like you want us to," Espresso said. "Just lay the bottom line on us."

Fortran called up another screen, headed "The Mirror's Travels." On it was a list of names:

1. nymph
2. goblin
3. dwarf
4. Snowbell
5. Elizabeth Factor
6. Tiffany

I tapped Tiffany's name. "How can you be sure? I mean, it *could* be Bergdorf or Best, or even some random blonde Deb we don't even know."

"I've checked everything a billion times," Fortran said, "and it always comes out Tiffany. You gotta believe me. Tech doesn't lie."

"Fair enough." I looked back at the tablet. "Can that thing tell us what happened to her?"

Fortran deflated slightly. "Not as such," he said. "But it does say that there's a 99.98 percent chance that Bergdorf knows."

"Which means I have to talk to Bergdorf." I sighed. "At least I know where to find her."

Knowing where to find Bergdorf didn't make talking to her any easier. She avoided me like I was some kind of disease demon, making sure I never caught her alone. But I kept shadowing her, and late on the third day after Stonewall's personality change, after the final horn, I saw her go into the library.

I waited a moment, then slipped in the door. At the checkout desk, the Librarian was asleep in her comfy chair with the library cat draped around her shoulders like a furry neck pillow. Both of them were snoring like whistles.

I looked around. Bergdorf must have gone to the hidden window seat at the back of the room.

I padded carefully through the stacks until I heard Bergdorf's voice, soft and low, so as not to wake the Librarian. "I don't know," she murmured. "Tiffany liked the blue striped dress with the ruffles. She said I'd look delicious."

A second voice gave a low chortle. "Honey, *food* is delicious. You want to come as an ugly stepsister or an iced cake?"

I froze. Why was Stonewall hiding in the library with Bergdorf? Why was he talking to her like he used to talk to us? I leaned my forehead against *The Mortal's Guide to Immortal Beings* and listened.

"I'm thinking black and red," Stonewall went on, "with a black wig and lots of makeup. The point is to look scary, not ridiculous."

"But Tiffany said—"

"And Tiffany is your best friend ever, isn't she?" Stonewall murmured understandingly.

"Yes." Bergdorf's voice was sad.

"And always gives you good advice?"

A little pause. "Ye-es," Bergdorf said, a little doubtfully.

"And never, never gets you into trouble or asks you to do something you don't want to do?"

This pause was longer, ending in a soft noise that sounded a lot like crying.

I thought Stonewall would laugh, but he didn't. "Here, take my handkerchief," I heard him say.

I couldn't stand it anymore. I peered around the edge of the bookcase.

Bergdorf was blowing her nose into Stonewall's white handkerchief. He was patting her shoulder. He looked almost as miserable as she did. Sympathy was one mortal custom none of us was very good at.

I delurked.

"Where's Tiffany, Bergdorf?"

It came out louder than I'd intended. Bergdorf stared up at me like a cornered rabbit, Stonewall's handkerchief pressed to her lips. Stonewall frowned and held up one finger. We all waited, but nothing happened.

I lowered my voice to a whisper. "Answer me!"

"I don't know?" Bergdorf wavered.

I snorted. Quietly.

"If you were made of wood, your nose would be three feet long," I said nastily. "Tiffany didn't even go to the girls' room without you. She needs you to tell her how clever and brave and cool she is."

Bergdorf's eyes narrowed angrily. "I *don't* know where she is, as it happens. But I wouldn't tell you if I did, Wild Child, not even if you tortured me, which I wouldn't put past you. It's all your fault anyway." Her voice started to break up again. "Ever since you made Tiffany fall off that beam, she's been like a crazy person. Well, you know what? I hope you get eaten by ogres and Central Park withers away and all its Folk have to go live in New Jersey!"

Her voice was definitely entering the Librarian danger zone. Stonewall put his hand over her mouth. Silence. Stonewall lowered his hand. Bergdorf crossed her arms across her stomach, curled up like an armadillo, and made painful little mewing noises.

Oddly enough, I didn't find this even remotely funny.

Stonewall gave me a strange half smile. "Is this Park diplomacy, Wild Child? A little heavy-handed, don't you think? If I were you, I'd leave before the Librarian wakes up and makes us reshelve all the books."

I would have liked to snap him a cool line to show how little I cared. But I couldn't think of anything to say. So I slunk back to the front of the room and peered around a shelf to see if the coast was clear.

The library cat looked straight at me with clear amber eyes. My heart stopped. It yawned, then sank its chin back onto the sleeping Librarian's shoulder.

As I crept out the door, I could just hear Bergdorf's sobbing.

I hated her. I hated everybody. I especially hated me.

RULE 125: STUDENTS MUST TREAT ONE ANOTHER AS THEY WOULD WISH TO BE TREATED THEMSELVES.

Miss Van Loon's Big Book of Rules

That night at the Castle, I announced to Astris that I was going to Miss Van Loon's Hallowe'en Revels dressed as Peg Powler.

She freaked, as Espresso would say, far out.

"Oh, no, no, *no*, pet! What can you be thinking? Peg Powler rides with the Wild Hunt. She's mean and ugly and hungry all the time. Wouldn't you rather be something sweet and pretty?" Her whiskers twitched thoughtfully. "A wood nymph, maybe."

"Mean and ugly is what Hallowe'en's about," I said. "We learned about it at school. When you make fun of scary things, you make them less scary."

Astris's whiskers trembled with distress. "Oh, dear," she said. "Is that what they're teaching you? I'm not sure

I approve. It seems, well, *human*. It's certainly dangerous. What if you get hit by a stray spell and get stuck that
way?"

I rolled my eyes. "Like *that's* going to happen! First
of all, I'm under double protection—the Lady's *and* the
school's. Second of all, I'm a mortal. Changing how I look
doesn't change who I am. Third of all, I'm already mean
and ugly, so I might as well go with it."

Then I ran upstairs to my room, slammed the
door, crawled into bed, and drew the curtains closed
around me.

Unfortunately, Folk aren't good at taking hints. And
being my fairy godmother made Astris even more hint-
deaf than she was naturally. I hardly had time for one
good sob before I heard the hinges creak and her claws
scurrying across the stone floor. I hastily wiped my face
on the pillow.

Her whiskers brushed my cheek. "You're not ugly,
pet," Astris said in my ear. "And you're not really mean.
You're just at an awkward age."

"Thanks," I said. "That makes me feel a *lot* better."

I put all the sarcasm I could into it, but Astris is also
sarcasm-deaf. "Good," she said briskly. "How would you
like to attend the Hallowe'en Revels as a Swedish troll
maiden? They're scary, but in a good way. I'll glamour
you a tail and a false nose, and Pepperkaka can lend you
her apron and her felt hat."

I buried my face in the pillow. "Glamours are against the rules," I mumbled.

"We'll use rope." Astris jumped off the bed, leaving me feeling worse than ever.

During Basic Manners next morning, I kept my head down, answering when the Diplomat asked me something, but otherwise focusing my attention on not breaking Rules 132 (Students must not be snarky) and 386 (Students must be polite at all times). As a result, I got yelled at for breaking Rule 242 (The very difficult Students must not play with their hair—although I was actually chewing on it) and failing to cultivate a pleasant expression. Also for not paying attention to the lesson, but that was getting to be a chronic condition.

I spent most of the lesson sorting beans and rice.

The big news at lunch was that Stonewall had talked to Espresso.

She'd been on the Chinatown bus as usual, reading up on dryads, when Stonewall squeezed into the seat beside her. Which was way weird, because Stonewall never took the bus.

"It was jive, man," Espresso said. "No 'How are you' or 'Sorry I was such a jerk' or anything like that. Just, 'We gotta talk.' I told him to am-scray."

Fortran's eyes were round black marbles. "Did he go away?"

"He just kept on pitching me all this hype about meeting everybody at the Mansion after school."

My stomach clenched. "Everybody except me, right?"

"He said you in particular. And Airboy, which blew my mind. Anyway, I said I'd rather have tea with King Kong. He was glum, chum. Like, what did he expect?"

Since nobody had an answer to this, we took out our lunches and swapped around. Nobody wanted any of my pease porridge, but Mukuti gave me some *saag paneer* anyway. Fortran tried to cheer up Espresso by describing all the wizard things the Magic Tech was planning for the Haunted House. I poked at my food and wondered what was up with Stonewall.

Maybe he was sorry he'd been such a troll. I hoped he was sorry. I almost wished Espresso hadn't blown him off so I could listen to him apologize and then tell him to go turn into a frog. If he apologized. Which he wouldn't. Like I'd never apologized to Airboy. Not that he'd given me a chance.

I might as well have skipped Mortal History for all I learned about the Dead Rabbit Riots in the Bowery. The Historian reminded me, sharply, that a quest pass was a privilege, not a right, and could be revoked at any time on the recommendation of my tutors. In the end, he didn't punish me, although he did say I was skating on thin ice.

It felt like I'd already fallen through.

When the last horn finally ended my torture, I headed downstairs, intending to go straight home.

In the front hall, Airboy appeared at my elbow. "Hi."

I stared at him. He stared back, waiting. "Um, hi," I said. "Listen. About the whole Elizabeth Factor thing. You're right. You saved my butt, and I acted like a jerk. I'm sorry."

Airboy blinked. "It's okay," he said. A tiny smile pulled at his mouth. "That makes this easier. Your friends know about you-know-what, right?"

I nodded, feeling better than I had for a while. "Yeah. We're kind of stuck, though. There's too much we don't know."

"I found out something that might help," he said. "You guys going to the Mansion?"

"We could," I said.

It took me a while to find Espresso and Fortran and Mukuti and Danskin, and then I had to persuade them. We hadn't been to the Mansion since Stonewall had gone all East Side.

"It'll be fine," I told Danskin. "Stonewall probably won't even be there. Besides, it's important. Airboy's got news about the mirror."

Danskin rolled his eyes. "Oh, the *mirror*! Well, that's certainly more important than my feelings, isn't it?"

I didn't want to be mad at Danskin. I really didn't

want him to be mad at me. I counted to ten and said, "No, it's not. You don't have to come. I understand. Really."

After that, he said he might as well tag along. We walked the few blocks to the Mansion together, squeezed into our old booth, and ordered a pitcher of milk.

It was weird being there without Stonewall.

Danskin wormed a finger down inside his bandage and scratched. Someone, I noticed, had drawn feathers on it, like a wing. "So where's Airboy?" he asked.

"He just swam in," said Espresso, sounding grim. "With a couple of sharks. Did you know about this, Neef?"

I turned around and saw Airboy standing in the door. Behind him, like some kind of dishonor guard, were Stonewall and Bergdorf.

My first impulse was to jump up and run away. Of all the beings in New York Between I didn't want to see right now, Stonewall and Bergdorf were right up there with the Mermaid Queen.

Except that Bergdorf probably knew where Tiffany was. And I'd have to go past her if I ran away, and how lame would that be?

Before he even reached us, Stonewall started to apologize. "I'm sorry, I'm sorry, I'm sorry. I was horrible, I know. I did it because I needed to get in with the East Siders. The whole plan just came to me, like a flash of lightning."

Stonewall looked embarrassed. "I guess I was afraid if I explained, it wouldn't work right. So I just went with it."

"You *went with it*," Danskin said. "Then go with this. What you did was mean, low down, and hurtful. It was like you'd suddenly turned into some kind of evil wizard or demon prince. You freaked us *out*."

I got the impression Stonewall was counting to ten. "I'm *sorry*," he said at last. "Really and truly. I don't remember exactly what I said, but I didn't mean any of it. Please believe me. It was totally Folk-like, and I deserve to be turned into a cockroach." He took a deep breath. "Is everything copacetic? Neef?"

The kobold stumped over with our pitcher of milk, slapped it down on the table, and stumped away.

I looked at Stonewall. "I'm too mad to get over it just like that. But I'll work on it."

Danskin adjusted his sling. "What she said."

"I'm not mad at you," Fortran said. "But I do wonder what *she's* doing here."

Through all this, Bergdorf had been glaring at the painting of the bowling dwarfs as if it offended her. Now she looked at Fortran, her eyes as big and blue as Tiffany's—the result of Elizabeth Factor's makeover, I guessed. "Since you ask, Geek Boy, *she* is wishing you'd turn into the frogs you so gigantically resemble."

Stonewall rolled his eyes. "Bergdorf, we've *talked* about this. You said you'd cooperate."

Bergdorf shrugged. "I'm here, aren't I? Not that anybody seems gigantically excited about it."

She obviously meant to sound snotty, but she only managed pathetic. Bergdorf was scared. And from the way she wasn't looking at me, I figured it was me she was scared of.

I decided to show her the Wild Child could be nice—when she wanted to be. "We're delighted you decided to join us, Bergdorf," I said in my best Astris tea-party voice. "Please sit down and have some milk."

Bergdorf glared at me. I smiled as warmly as I could and offered her my seat. While I was getting another chair, I reminded myself of the Diplomat's handy hints for negotiators. Listen more than you talk. Smile a lot. Let someone else ask the questions.

Everybody else must have been remembering, too, because the silence went on for a long time. Finally, Bergdorf said, "I promised Tiffany I wouldn't tell. But I so can't deal anymore, and Stonewall said you might be able to help."

Mukuti the Kindhearted gave her a sympathetic smile. "We'll do our best."

"When we've got the skinny," Espresso added practically.

"So tell us everything," said Fortran.

"Okay," said Bergdorf. "So Tiff and I go to Madame Elizabeth Factor for makeovers. She's got all these magic mirrors, and they show what's wrong with you, and then she fixes it? So we do the makeovers, and it's horrible but totally worth it, and then Madame Factor asks Tiff if she'll do her a gigantic favor, and Tiffany's like, Duh, of course. Then Madame Factor gives Tiff this package and says it's a mirror with a curse on it and Tiff has to get rid of it for her. And then we go to her house and unwrap it, and, OMG, it's the Magic Magnifying Mirror of the Mermaid Queen!"

"So she recognized it right away?" Fortran asked.

Bergdorf looked insulted. "Hello? Gold star in Talismans? Tiff was like, Great Talisman, I can know everything in the world, I can even control the Dragon of Wall Street, gigantic power, I'll show everybody, blah, blah, blah. I was like, do you even know how to use it? And she was like, I'm so smart I'll figure it out."

We exchanged glances. Espresso spoke for all of us. "So did she?"

"Not so much. But she wouldn't quit trying. I got all bored and started looking through her closet to see if there was anything I wanted to borrow. And then I heard her saying it." Bergdorf stopped short.

"Saying what?" Fortran asked eagerly.

"*You* know. The thing you say to mirrors."

"'Mirror, mirror on the wall'?" Mukuti asked, puzzled.

Bergdorf's face was as white as her untouched milk. "No! The other thing. The incantation that summons *her*."

"Her?" I asked.

Espresso suddenly looked sick. "She means the one she challenged you to summon at Hallowe'en, Neef."

Mukuti gasped. "The Angry One?"

There was a moment of horrified silence. Then Danskin said what I was thinking. "That wasn't too bright, was it?"

Bergdorf glared at him. "Well, she paid for it." Her voice teetered, and she bit her bottom lip. "I don't want to talk about it."

"You don't have to," Stonewall said gently.

"Yes, she does," Fortran objected. "I want to hear. Did Old Five-Inch Nails rip her into strips? Ow, Espresso. That *hurt*."

Bergdorf's chin came up. "I saved her, as it happens. I said the genie spell."

Everyone looked even more shocked than they had before. I didn't know what she was talking about. "What?"

"The genie spell," Bergdorf said, sounding defiant. "The thing that puts genies in bottles or lamps or whatever and keeps them there. They teach it in Advanced Talismans, for emergencies. This was an emergency, so I said it. And it worked: the Angry One disappeared."

There was a long silence, broken by Stonewall. "So what you're saying is, you bound a wild urban power, who doesn't belong to any Neighborhood or accept any authority, in one of the Great Talismans of New York Between?"

Bergdorf's eyes widened. "Yeah. I guess I did."

"Whoa," Fortran said.

The kobold appeared with a fresh pitcher of milk. He traded it for the old one and stomped off again.

"Okay," Stonewall said to Bergdorf. "What else didn't you tell me?"

She shrugged. "You wanted to know about Tiffany."

"So, what *about* Tiffany?" I asked.

Tiffany had been a gigantic mess. Her face was all bloody and she was moaning and there was blood on the white wall-to-wall carpet and her new designer sweater was totally ruined.

"I was this close to a meltdown," Bergdorf said, "and then I hear her fairy godmother knocking, and she's like, Is everything all right, girls? And I'm all, Everything's fine, Mother Carey, thanks for asking. Like she was going to believe *that*. So Tiff quick stuffs the mirror down her jeans and Mother Carey comes in and starts screaming that Tiff's totally ruined and all her hard work's gone for nothing. I get out before she decides it's all my fault, and that's all I know. Cross my heart and hope to die."

"So where's Tiffany?" Airboy burst out impatiently.

I sighed. "New York's a big city. She could be anywhere."

Stonewall shook his head. "She's ugly now, remember? Mother Carey would send her where nobody would care what she looks like."

Mukuti gasped. "You mean, she sent her *Outside*?"

Bergdorf looked shocked. "Even Mother Carey's not *that* evil. No, she's got to be in the other place, where changelings go when they lose their looks."

"There's a *place* for that?"

Bergdorf shot me a disbelieving look. "Like your fairy godmother isn't threatening you with it all day and night? I almost ended up there when I got zits. I swear, I have nightmares about it."

"Me, too," Danskin said. "The Artistic Director wanted to send me there when I broke my arm, but my fairy godfather persuaded him that I could be fixed."

Airboy said, "The Mermaid Queen doesn't care what you look like. On the other hand, when she gets mad at you, she drowns you, so I guess it all evens out."

And I'd felt sorry for myself for being thrown out of the Park.

"Right," Stonewall said. "Different strokes, I guess. In City Neighborhoods, they mostly send their unwanted changelings to the Bowery."

Even in the Park, we knew that the Bowery was all about junk. The Bowery Bum collected it: broken talismans, outgrown bogeymen, worn-out spells, out-of-work hobgoblins, cracked mirrors, bad-luck demons, nicked swords, lost hopes, bad fairies of many lands.

And broken-down changelings, apparently.

"The Bowery," I said. "Great. The worst Neighborhood in New York Between. Anybody got a magic sword I can borrow? A Helmet of Invisibility? A Horse Swifter Than the Wind?"

Nobody laughed.

Espresso burst out, "That rule about flying solo, that's just off-time jive. I'm going with you."

I was trying to think of some way of saying no without hurting her feelings when Airboy beat me to it. "I'm Neef's sidekick," he said. "I'll go."

I opened my mouth to ask if he had a quest pass, then closed it again. Some questions it's better not to ask.

Chapter 18

There's always a three-day weekend around Hallowe'en, so at least I knew exactly when I'd be going to the Bowery. In the meantime, all I had to do was at least pretend to pay attention to my lessons. Questing? Piece of cake. Mortal History? Not so much.

When I wasn't trying to sit still, I was drinking dirty milk at the Mansion and trying to make plans. What made this difficult was that nobody really knew much about the actual Bowery. Espresso, who was turning into a Folk lorist Astris would have been proud of, was full of fun facts about roving gangs of snappily dressed Bowery Boys and their little silver knives, and rogue vampires who drank fairy blood even though they were allergic to it because it gave them beautiful dreams. But not even

Stonewall knew where changelings went once they'd been banished there.

The whole thing was starting to give *me* nightmares.

Airboy finally lost patience.

"The Bowery runs into the Canal," he said. "The Canal runs into the East River on the Lower East Side. I'll meet you on the Grand Street pier two hours after dawn. Then we'll play it by ear."

"I'll be there," I said.

The next morning, I paced the dock at the south end of Grand Street, watching the water for Airboy.

It was frost spirit weather, touched with a chill wind and the promise of rain. I dug my hands into the pockets of my black coat and wished I'd asked Astris for an umbrella.

The pier was busy. Two trollish longshoremen in homburgs staggered by, carrying a huge wooden crate between them. "Out of the way, *maidele*," one grunted. "You want you should be squished flat like a bug?"

I wandered away from the water to the foot of Grand Street, where peddlers hawked pickles and potato knishes and old clothes from pushcarts. A fiddler perched on a roof played a lively mazurka. I'd just bought a bag of roasted chestnuts when I heard a terrified shout.

"Help! A sea demon! *Gevalt!*"

I bet I knew that sea demon.

Everybody in earshot rushed to the end of the pier. I elbowed and shoved and wiggled my way through the crowd. When I finally made it to the front, I saw two giant longshoremen advancing threateningly on a small, scrawny, dripping black figure with a many-pocketed Harness strapped across its chest.

"Stop!" I yelled. "*Hert oyf!* He's not a demon! He's a mortal changeling, like me."

The longshoreman eyed me doubtfully. "He don't look like you, *maidele*."

"We're in school together," I said. "Miss Van Loon's. We're on a quest."

The longshoreman shook his head stubbornly. "Mortals have hair. He don't have hair. And how come he don't say the Words?"

Airboy yanked off his merrow cap and recited the Words of Protection proper to the Lower East Side. The crowd laughed and agreed that anybody who spoke Yiddish that badly was probably harmless. An old *alte-zachin hendler* popped a bright blue sweater from her pushcart over Airboy's head. It hung down past his knees and hid his hands.

"So the *boychik* shouldn't freeze," she said. "You want I should find you some shoes? It's not so healthy to walk *borves* on the city street."

"I have shoes." Airboy snaked his hands inside the sweater. The *alte-zachin hendler* and I watched as the sweater bulged and wriggled like a sackful of gremlins. When the hands reappeared, flourishing sneakers and the glamourist's magic map of New York, the peddler applauded.

Airboy flushed and handed me the map. "Figure out where we're going, will you?"

I studied the map while the *alte-zachin hendler* watched, probably to see if we'd do something else amusing. Unfamiliar names and buildings popped out at me. "Krimhild's Garden," I read. "The Oompa-pa Music Garden. Woden's Flophouse. CBGB. Do you know what any of this means?"

"Nope." Airboy stood up. "What now?"

I refolded the map. "We walk to the Bowery."

The *alte-zachin hendler* tsked. "Such a long way, you'll walk your feet to the bones. Better you should take a cab."

A cab? "What's that?"

"Some city girl, doesn't even know what a cab is! Never mind, I'll tell you. Any carriage or coach or cart you see yellow like a canary, that's a cab. Stick your hand out and it'll stop, take you where you need to go. For a price, but nothing comes for free. You understand?"

I thanked the *alte-zachin hendler*, then herded a reluctant Airboy to the street to look for a cab. I didn't see anything yellow—anything with wheels, anyway—but I stuck my hand out just in case.

A scarlet kirin with neat golden hooves and a stormy

golden mane stopped in front of us. It was pulling a two-wheeled sulky, painted bright yellow.

"Where to?" it asked as we climbed onto the bench.

"Bowery," I said.

The kirin tossed its horn. "Bums in the Bowery. No pay, no ride. One mackerel. Fresh."

Airboy produced the mackerel from his Harness and the kirin trotted off—slowly, because of the crowds. Everywhere I looked, unfamiliar Folk argued and bargained and leaned out the windows of the low brick tenement buildings. In the Canal, fat little tugs chugged companionably beside triangle-sailed junks. Then I saw a fox girl in a padded silk coat, bright as a flower among the Lower East Siders' gray and brown, and suddenly we were in Chinatown, where the buildings were roofed in green tile and the Canal was lined with flat-bottomed barges manned by shinseën with wispy beards selling knobby fruit and bright silk and strange spices.

The kirin stopped. "Bowery," it said. "Another mackerel, maybe?"

I looked up a wide street lined with tumbledown buildings. It looked cold and dark and unfriendly. "Can't you take us inside?"

The kirin shivered head to tail. "Bad place. *Bums*."

"No more mackerel, then," I said. "Come on, Airboy. Let's go find some bums."

We climbed down from the sulky and entered the

Bowery. A nasty wind crept up the sleeves of my jacket and attacked my nose with the stink of smoke and garbage and beer. The buildings, the street, even the air, were smeared with soot. I groped for my jade frog. I knew it wasn't very powerful, but holding it made me feel better.

"What now?" Airboy asked.

"We find somebody who looks helpful and ask if they know a mortal changeling girl with a scratched face."

"What if they don't?"

"How many blonde, scratched-up former debutantes could there be in the Bowery?"

Airboy shrugged. "I don't know. But there sure are a lot of bums."

Once Airboy pointed them out, I wondered why I hadn't noticed them right away. In rags or fine clothes, in cloth caps or heavy jackets, in filthy parkas or stocking caps or their own mangy fur, bums of every sort, shape, and size wandered down the street or propped up sooty walls, picking their teeth, coughing, muttering to themselves. They didn't look very helpful. Or friendly.

A door opened down the block and a short, stocky figure staggered into the street, singing unmusically:

> *"The Bow'ry! the Bow'ry!*
> *They say such things and they do*
> *   strange things*

> *On the Bow'ry! the Bow'ry!*
> *I'll never go there any more."*

"You could ask him," Airboy said.

"Did you see his beard?" It was hard to miss—so thick and wiry he looked like he was eating a porcupine. "That's a duerg. I'm not messing with him."

"Don't you know the Words of Protection in Norwegian?"

I clutched my frog nervously. "Of course I do. It's just I've got a feeling the Words of Protection aren't going to protect us here."

The door opened again, and one of the Bowery Boy dandies Espresso had told us about swaggered out, a swart-alfr in a red shirt, a long black coat, and a tall shiny hat tilted tipsily to one side.

He pointed a long, white finger at me. "Will you look at that, Thekk. What's the world coming to, I ask you, when infants like these here is found loitering outside a dive like Sifrit's Saloon? Ain'tcha kids kinda young to be on the skids?"

There was nowhere to run to. The bums were crowding around us like pigeons looking for crumbs. I eyed the Bowery Boy. "I'm not on the skids. I'm under the protection of the Genius of Central Park."

The swart-alfr laughed. "That and two bits'll buy you a beer, girlie."

I swallowed. *Show no fear*. "Listen, we're looking for a changeling girl, blonde. Her face is probably kind of scratched up. Have you seen her?"

The Bowery Boy laughed so hard he had to steady himself on the duerg's head. "All the goils here is scratched up. If they ain't that way when they gets here, somebody generally takes care of it right away."

I ignored this. "Have you seen her?"

The Bowery Boy's laughter stopped short. "Mortals brings down the tone of the Neighborhood. They's like bedbugs, see? When you see 'em, you gotta stick 'em." He slid his hand into the pocket of his coat, drew out a gleaming silver knife. "Hold 'em, Thekk!"

And then we did run, dodging Thekk's clumsy grab and ducking under the Bowery Boy's arm, straight into the crowd of bums.

They were all ghosts.

I'm used to ghosts. I *live* with ghosts. But the Castle ghosts are shy and float out of the way when I try to touch them. The Bowery ghosts clung to my face and arms, wrapping me in a thick, chill, damp cloud of misery. I struggled with them for a long, heart-pounding moment and then burst through, freezing cold and scared half out of my mind. Behind us, the Bowery Boy was giggling madly, and the duerg was staggering around in circles, shouting, "Where'd they go? Where'd they go?"

I spied what looked like an empty doorway and darted into it, pulling Airboy with me.

"Well!" Airboy said shakily. "I think that went pretty well, considering."

We both started giggling like maniacs.

"Youse shut up youse faces," a raspy voice complained from the shadows. "Some of us is trying to pass out."

We left the doorway like we'd been shot from a bow. At some point I realized that I was holding Airboy's hand, but I didn't let go. We ran until I got a stitch in my side and stumbled to a halt, gasping.

"You kids lost?"

I froze with terror.

"It's just a dog," Airboy said. "A big dog."

I couldn't believe there was such thing in the Bowery as "just as dog." It had to be something horrible: a black dog, a kelpie, even a Gabriel hound. I was cold and I was scared and I was tired of being a hero. I wanted my godfather.

I slipped my hand into my pocket, grabbed the Pooka's tail hair, and turned around slowly.

A shaggy brown-and-white dog the size of a small bear examined me with sad amber eyes.

"Don't be afraid," it said. "I'm a Saint Bernard, from the Bowery Mission. It's my job to rescue anyone who gets lost here. Are you lost?"

I hesitated, then let the tail hair go. "Yes," I said.

The Saint Bernard bent his head and snuffled at me. "Lower East Side. I don't suppose you happen to have a half-sour pickle on you?"

"We're not from the Lower East Side," I said. "And we're not *lost*, exactly. We're looking for somebody."

"That's not really part of my job description."

"*She's* lost," Airboy said helpfully.

The Saint Bernard scratched itself thoughtfully. "Oh. Well. In that case, maybe—"

"That's great," I said before it could change its mind. "She's a mortal changeling—a girl, bigger than us, blonde, scratched-up face. She hasn't been here long."

"That's not a lot to go on," the Saint Bernard said. "Not for someone who looks with his nose. Where'd she come from?"

"The Upper East Side," Airboy said.

"Fifth Avenue? Park? Madison? Third? Is she Chanel No. 5 or Calvin, designer jeans or pinstripes?"

Airboy and I looked at each other blankly. "I'm not sure," I said.

The Saint Bernard stood up. "I'll just have to use my head, then. Grab hold of my collar. We're going for a run." And he raced off down the street, baying: *"Excelsior! Excelsior!"*

The baying, while embarrassing, cleared the bums and Bowery Boys out of our way. It didn't stop them from yelling insults after us and laughing like storm drains when one of us stumbled or stepped in something nasty. Soon I was out of breath and my stitch was back. "Can we slow down?" I panted.

The Saint Bernard skidded to a halt. "Take a sip of this." He lifted his chin, displaying a small wooden barrel and a little tin cup tied to his neck with a thick leather strap. "It will give you the strength to go on."

I unhooked the cup and turned a wooden tap. A dark liquid poured out, fizzing. I took a cautious sip. Bubbles tickled my nose and filled my mouth with a bittersweet explosion. "What's *that*?"

"Cola," said the Saint Bernard. "In the old days, I carried brandy for the lost explorers and mountain climbers—because of the cold and snow, you know, to warm them up. It wouldn't be smart to carry brandy in the Bowery, though. Do you want some, changeling boy?"

"I want to find Tiffany," Airboy said.

The Saint Bernard shrugged. "Suit yourself. Over there, across the street, is the Wannabe. Mortal changelings only, no Folk allowed. Without knowing her scent, it's the best I can do. Good luck, changelings." And he lolloped off, baying.

The building housing the Wannabe had been fancy once, with big glass windows—now boarded over—and rusty iron pillars crowned with iron leaves. As we walked up, a man in a filthy raincoat pushed away from the wall and flicked out a long, wicked-looking blade.

"Mortals only," he growled.

"We are mortal," I said. "I'm Neef of Central Park, under the protection of the Green Lady. And this is Airboy, under the protection of the Mermaid Queen."

The knife disappeared back into the man's pocket. "Slumming, eh? Well, come in if you want."

"*Excelsior,*" Airboy said, and we went inside.

The Wannabe was a gloomy cavern, uncertainly lit with candles and smoky lanterns. At the far end, a band of scrawny changelings in black leather and big boots were rocking and rolling over two guitars, a keyboard, and drums. As my eyes got used to the gloom, I saw the room was about half full of mortals of all sizes, some in Village black with berets, some in ragged coats, ratty hats, and layers of scarves.

Nobody looked like they'd even heard of the Court of the Dowager of Park Avenue.

"I don't think she's here," I said.

"You could ask that guy at the counter," Airboy said.

"Why do I have to do all the asking? You have a mouth, don't you?"

He smiled. "It doesn't work as well as yours."

The guy at the counter was actually a woman in a shapeless tweed coat, polishing a glass with a dirty towel. She glared down at me. "You think I'm going to pull you a beer, Short Stuff, you've got another think coming."

"I'm looking for a girl. Mortal, blonde. Her face is all scratched up. She hasn't been here long."

The woman jerked her chin toward the band. "Woolworth's down by the stage, last table on the left," she said. "Ugly girl, and I ain't talking about the bandage. You sure you want to find her?"

Woolworth?

We made our way forward. The guitars dropped out and the drummer started banging on the drums like he was trying to break them to pieces. Airboy tugged at my sleeve and pointed.

At first I didn't recognize her. Big dark coat, fingerless gloves, a dirty turban wound over long, lank hair. But the profile was familiar.

I sat down. "Hi, Tiffany."

Tiffany turned to me and I winced. The whole left side of her face was wrapped with layers of cloth, like a mummy. The tail of a red, scabby scratch crawled down her neck and into the collar of her coat. She bared her still perfect teeth in a sarcastic grin, turned away, and went back to banging her fist rhythmically on the table.

I tapped her arm. She answered with a gesture I'd never seen before. I guessed it meant "no."

The singer started to screech like a banshee. The music thudded angrily in my skull. My heart was beating so hard it felt like it was going to tear through my chest. I grabbed my jade frog.

It was breathing.

Startled, I pulled it out and squinted at it. The candle caught its ruby eye, and for the second time, it winked at me.

I knew what I was supposed to do next, of course. I just didn't want to. The frog was *my* frog—my present from Fleet, the only thing I got on last summer's quest that I could keep. I wouldn't even give it to Espresso or Fortran, let alone my enemy, that wicked-witch-in-training, Tiffany of Park Avenue.

Which was just exactly why I had to.

I clung to it, ignoring my throbbing ears and Airboy's puzzled black eyes. Then I lifted the black silk cord over my head, caught Tiffany's pounding hand, and laid the frog into it.

Tiffany brought the frog up to her good eye and examined it. She looked at me, the still beautiful half of her face expressionless. Then she hung the frog around her neck, got up, and marched up to the bar, with Airboy and me scrambling after.

"Back room empty, Rummy?" she asked the massive woman.

"Sure thing. Just clean up after yourself, and remember—blood attracts vampires."

I didn't think this was funny, but Tiffany did. She was still chuckling as she led us down a dirty corridor to a tiny, dark room furnished with a lamp, a sofa, and a desk.

She flung herself down on the sofa, one booted foot on the cushion. "Congratulations," she said. "You found me. What can I do to make you go away?"

Getting half killed and booted out of her Neighborhood had not made Tiffany any nicer. "You can tell us what happened to the Mermaid Queen's mirror."

"Bergdorf!" Tiffany spat the word out like a curse. "Some freaking friend she is."

Airboy shrugged. "Well, she did save your life."

"Big whoop. Anything else? Because if there isn't, I want to go back and catch the rest of Mortal Coil's set."

There weren't enough numbers in New York Between to calm me down enough to deal with Tiffany. I'd barely started counting when Airboy went into his gremlins-in-a-sack act.

Tiffany sneered. "Your boyfriend's got cooties."

I stopped myself from telling her Airboy wasn't my boyfriend.

Airboy's hands reemerged from the sweater. He was holding a blue jar. "Beauty cream. Very highest quality, from one of the best glamourists in the Garment District. Guaranteed to clear the complexion, brighten the skin, and smooth superficial scars."

Tiffany's visible eye widened, then narrowed. "These scars aren't superficial."

Airboy shrugged. "So you'll have small scars instead of big ones."

Tiffany reached for the jar.

"Hold on," I said. "What's to keep you from taking the cream and then refusing to talk, or even just making up some lie?"

"Same thing that's keeping you from sticking me with a jar of Harbor mud." She hesitated. "You're not, are you?"

"No," said Airboy. He put the jar in her hand, and she stashed it in the pocket of her coat.

"The mirror," I said.

She hesitated, then went through her pockets. She seemed to have an awful lot of them—in the jacket she wore under the coat, in her shirt, even in the legs of her baggy pants. She didn't look in her sleek leather Designer Bag, though. She didn't have one.

"What happened to your magic bag?" I asked.

"My ex-fairy godmother took it away," she said, still patting and groping. "Changelings without a Neighborhood don't have them."

"Then how do you—?"

Tiffany fixed me with her one blue eye, wild and angry as a were-cat's. "You want the Mermaid's mirror, Wild Child, or the story of my life?"

She had the mirror. She actually had the mirror. I couldn't believe it. And she was going to give it to me, just like that.

There had to be a catch.

"Ta-da!" She produced a thick wad of cloth and laid it on the desk. "Check it out."

Gingerly, I picked it up and unwrapped about a

million layers of grimy cloth. At the final layer, I hesitated.

"Scared, Wild Child?" Tiffany grinned. "Old Scratchy's in there, all right, but she can't get out unless you call her."

"I'm not scared."

The mirror I uncovered was the same size as the Mermaid's mirror I remembered, and had the same plain silver rim. The mirror itself was cloudy and dark, with a storm of red and black lurking in its depths. I held it in the special way Changeling had taught me and felt for the special grooves.

Tiffany snatched at the mirror. "Stop, you moron! What do you think you're doing?"

"Checking it out."

"I meant look at it, not turn it on." She said some words I'd never heard before. "You don't want Old Scratchy loose in the Bowery, do you?"

"Is that what would happen?"

"Do you really want to find out?"

I rewrapped the mirror and laid it on the desk.

"So," said Tiffany, all casual. "You still want it?"

"Of course," I said. "I'm going to give it back to the Mermaid Queen."

"No!" Airboy burst out, horrified. "We can't. It's . . . *infested.*"

"So what? She's the Genius of New York Harbor. She can un-infest it."

He shook his head. "Bad things would happen. Worse than salt water in the Park. You have to believe me."

I did. Airboy wasn't a liar. "Well, we'll just have to exorcise it ourselves."

"She'll eat you alive," Tiffany said.

"I didn't say me. I said us."

Tiffany laughed. "*Us?* A fish boy and a country girl who hasn't been in school for two minutes, and a Neighborhoodless monster? What do you think this is, a fairy tale? You're out of your freaking mind."

Airboy nodded. "What she said."

"No, not just *us*." I had no idea what I was about to say, but I suspected it was going to be brilliant. "*All* of us: Fortran and Espresso and Stonewall and Mukuti and Danskin. And Bergdorf, because she was the one who did the binding in the first place."

Tiffany snorted. "That collection of goody two-shoes would fall over dead if you even suggested they come to the Bowery."

"Not the Bowery," I said. "Miss Van Loon's, tomorrow night."

There was a long silence, and then Tiffany burst out laughing. "You're even crazier than I am. All right. I'll be there." She stuffed the mirror back in her pocket. "Looks like we'll have our little Hallowe'en challenge, after all."

Chapter 19

RULE 46: STUDENTS MUST ATTEND ALL SCHOOL RITUALS.

Miss Van Loon's Big Book of Rules

It was Hallowe'en night at Miss Van Loon's. The stairwell was dark as we groped up the steps. Stonewall went first, with Danskin. Fortran was next, followed by Bergdorf, Espresso, Mukuti, Airboy, and Tiffany. I brought up the rear.

The sounds of the Hallowe'en Revels filtered up from below, shrieks of laughter and fake fear bouncing up the stairwell from the group of little kids playing Ghost Brother with an old sheet in the front hall. The assembly room was full of pretend goblins, fake were-animals, and carefully researched demons of many lands bobbing for apples, telling ghost stories, grilling pounded rice *dango* and popping corn over the Magic Tech's bunsen burner. In the Questing Room, the bigger kids were braving the

Haunted House's peeled grape eyeballs and cold spaghetti entrails and hollow voices rising out of cardboard coffins.

There weren't any Haunted Mirrors, though.

The day had started back home in Central Park, getting into my troll maiden outfit with Astris fussing over the hang of my rope tail and Pepperkaka telling me exactly what she'd do to me if I messed up her embroidered apron and her red felt hat from Finland. If I hadn't been thinking about how I was going to be facing Bloody Mary's iron claws in a few hours, it might have made me nervous.

The celebration began at Assembly. Everybody wore their costumes to school, so instead of silent mortal kids in star-spangled gray sweaters, we were a colorful selection of goblins and demons and ghosts and bogeymen and ghouls from seven continents, all breaking the no-talking rule into bite-sized pieces.

After the School Song, the Schooljuffrouw—dressed as a wicked witch, complete with warts, pointy hat, and cackle—led us in a group scream. She didn't read from the *Big Book of Rules*.

There were no lessons, but we all had to pitch in and decorate the school, following the plan the Art Tutor and the Magic Tech had been working on. As we hammered, pinned, draped, and painted, Miss Van Loon's began to look less like a school for changelings and more like a playground for nightmares.

Lunch was even more chaotic than usual, as if the Wild Hunt had taken over Miss Van Loon's. Demons screamed, goblins threw food, and bogles ran from table to table, begging for treats. In the middle of it all, my friends and I sat around a table disguised as a poisonous toadstool and admired one another's costumes.

Espresso made a truly terrifying flower child in huge bellbottoms and beads and a vest with fringes down to her knees. Fortran, who'd changed his mind again, was a mad scientist in a white lab coat, heavy black glasses, and wild white wig like a dandelion clock. Mukuti was a rather shy rusalka in a flowing white dress, crocheted green hair, a wooden comb, and a totally un-Russian breastplate of protective charms. Stonewall had opted for the classic vampire look: pointy teeth, black tail-suit, and red-lined cape. He'd even dyed his hair black, which made him look weirdly normal.

We all agreed, though, that Danskin's costume was the best. In direct defiance of Rules 305 (Students must not wear glamours or alter their appearance magically) and 306 (Students must not carry or use magic talismans without written permission from their Neighborhood Genius), he'd stolen a feather cloak from Lincoln Center and turned himself into an actual swan, with a long snaky neck and snowy feathers. Or most of one, anyway: his broken arm hadn't transformed.

To my total astonishment, Airboy was sitting between

Espresso and Mukuti, wearing the *alte-zachin hendler*'s fuzzy blue sweater, a blue wig, and big, ducklike feet. When Mukuti asked what he was, he shot me a hunted look.

"A Blue Meanie," I improvised. "They don't speak, you know."

"Oh," said Mukuti. "Right. Um, Neef? Do you know where we're supposed to meet Tiffany?"

I shrugged and ate my bread and cheese. Today was a day for comfort food. I didn't even want coffee.

"She'll show when she shows," Danskin said.

"With any luck," Fortran muttered, "she won't show at all."

"She's got the mirror," I reminded him.

Espresso looked up from her tabouli and wheatberry salad. "Do you have an actual playlist for this gig, Neef?"

I shrugged. "I thought we'd play it by ear."

"No way." Stonewall was firm. "The Angry One is *dangerous*, people. We need a *plan*."

An apple whizzed by my head and splatted against the wall. "We can't talk here."

"Library?" Mukuti suggested.

Stonewall stood up. "It's worth a try. Come on, Danny. I'll carry you up the stairs."

In the library, we found the quiet we were looking for. We also found Tiffany, cross-legged on the checkout desk with the library cat draped over her knees.

She dumped the cat and stood up. I watched

everyone who hadn't yet caught her Bowery act take in the torn fishnet stockings, short black skirt, coat with silver buttons, and the black bandage covering half her face.

Fortran whistled. "Wizard costume! Who are you supposed to be?"

"The punk pirate queen," Tiffany growled. "You got a problem with that?"

Nobody did.

Mukuti disappeared among the shelves. A moment later, we heard a cry of triumph. "Look what I found!" she crowed, reappearing with a book in her arms. "*101 Easy Exorcisms*. And the Angry One's in the index."

"Groovy," Espresso said.

Mukuti sat on the floor, propped the book open on her knees, and flicked over a few pages. "'Urban legend, wild power, iron claws, yadda yadda.' Here it is: 'Avoiding and Escaping: While she is killing her victim, run away as fast as you can, avoiding all mirrors in the future.'"

Fortran laughed. "You're making that up."

"I am not." Mukuti showed him the book. "See? Right there, between 'Black Dog' and 'Brownie.'"

"That's no help," Tiffany said. "She'd still be bound to the mirror."

"And one of us would be dead," Fortran pointed out. "Probably you."

Tiffany shrugged. "That's probably going to happen anyway."

"Don't be such a drama queen," Stonewall said. "She's bound to the mirror. She can't hurt us as long as her mistress is there."

Nobody seemed to remember that I was still in Basic Talismans. "Her mistress?"

Danskin preened his wing. "The one who bound her, of course—Bergdorf."

"Who isn't here," Stonewall said, and sighed. "I knew I'd forgotten something."

I don't know how he got Bergdorf to come to the library. I do know he didn't tell her about Tiffany, because when Bergdorf saw her, she screamed.

Fortran giggled. Espresso kicked him. Tiffany jumped off the desk, grabbed Bergdorf, and shook her. "Shut up, you moron!"

Bergdorf choked. "Oh, Tiff. I thought you were dead."

"*Tiffany* is dead," Tiffany said. "I'm Woolworth of the Bowery, and I don't give a fart in a high wind what you think. Once this mirror thing's settled, I'm blowing this pop stand. *Capisce?*"

Bergdorf opened and closed her mouth a couple of times, then nodded. "Okay. *Woolworth.* What do you want me to do?"

"You bound her," Tiffany said. "You have to banish her."

Bergdorf swallowed. "By myself?"

"We'll help you," Mukuti said soothingly.

"How?"

We all looked at one another. "We're working on a plan," Stonewall said loftily.

Bergdorf rolled her eyes. "How typical is that? I bet you haven't even thought about the iron claws issue."

"The rule with genies is, they can't hurt the person who summons them," Mukuti said.

"Hello? The Angry One's not a genie? Who knows what her rules are? You dorks can do what you want, but I'm not going in there without a mask—preferably one made out of something sturdier than construction paper. Why are you all looking at me like that? Do you think I'm, like, *stupid*?"

Stonewall cranked his jaw shut. "Masks. Of course. *I* should have thought of that."

"What Stoney means," said Danskin, "is, 'That's brilliant, Bergdorf!'"

Tiffany snorted. "Let's not go overboard. She's just not as dumb as she looks."

"I like masks," Mukuti said. "Where do we get the stuff to make them?"

Airboy smiled slyly. "Art Tutor. Magic Tech."

"Now we're cooking!" Espresso high-fived him. "Groovy."

"And," I added, not wanting to be left out, "if anybody wants to know what we want it for, we'll just sing out, 'Decorations!'"

It worked like a charm. Before long we were back in

the library with a roll of strong, flexible wire mesh and papier-mâché to make the masks and some paint and ribbon and glitter to decorate them with.

Much to my surprise, I enjoyed putting my mask together, even if the final product was kind of lame. I was a troll maiden, after all, not a beautiful princess. It didn't matter if my eyeholes were even.

While we snipped, molded, glued, and tied, Mukuti and I got a crash course on genie management.

Once a genie was summoned, it had to grant the summoner's wishes, with a preference for doing exactly what you asked rather than what you really wanted. If you wished for a genie to be free, it was usually grateful to you for life.

Except, as Bergdorf had pointed out, Bloody Mary wasn't really a genie. She was just bound like one.

"She's *wild*," Stonewall said. "She's got her own rules. We can't be sure the binding will keep her from attacking us when we summon her."

Mukuti offered to share her protective charms. Fortran said they were a load of junk. Tiffany suggested we break into the talisman closet and steal some real heavy-duty protection. Stonewall suggested we make a protective circle before we did the summoning.

We added a protective circle to our plan.

"So we just wish her into the bathroom mirror, right?" Bergdorf asked.

"That don't play," Espresso said. "We gotta cut her loose from the Mermaid's mirror before she can hit another one."

"And if we cut her loose," Mukuti said, "she can hit anything she wants. Like us."

"Plus," Bergdorf said, "if she's free, she'll be totally all over Miss Van Loon's."

Fortran raised a finger. "Except, she needs to be in a mirror, and the bathroom mirror is the only one in the school. And we'll be protected by the circle."

"We hope," Bergdorf said gloomily.

Tiffany laughed. "Total suicide. Sounds like a plan."

"It's the beginning of one, anyway," said Stonewall.

We talked a lot more, but basically, that was it. That afternoon, in the brightly lit library, it sounded totally doable.

That night, in the dark stairwell, I wasn't so sure.

The third-floor swinging doors squealed when they opened, like a tortured mouse. Bergdorf gasped. Someone—Fortran, probably—snorted. Laughter fizzed up in my throat.

"Shut up!" Tiffany hissed.

"Welcome to Spookville," Espresso murmured. "Population, uncertain." Which set us all off. Snorting and giggling, we groped our way along the wall to the girls' bathroom.

I heard a click as someone turned the knob and a creak as the door opened. Nobody moved.

"I can't go in there," Fortran said.

"It's all right," Stonewall said kindly. "We're all nervous."

"I'm not *nervous*." Fortran sounded indignant. "It's just . . . it's the *girls' bathroom!*"

Tiffany treated us to one of her new vocabulary words. "You dorks coming?" she added. "Or am I doing this all by myself?"

We trooped into the bathroom, leaving Danskin outside so he could run (or fly) for help if things got really out of hand.

The door creaked shut, leaving us, if possible, more in the dark than ever. "Now we make a circle," Mukuti reminded us nervously. We shuffled around. There was a certain amount of stepping on feet and bumping our hips on sinks and our elbows on stall doors. When we'd all found places to stand and each other's hands, I had the edge of a sink digging into my butt.

I wished I was with the kids downstairs, pretending to be frightened.

Our plan called for Bergdorf and Tiffany to set up the summoning. A match flared, illuminating a white mask with red circles on the cheeks and huge red lips—Wicked Stepsister Bergdorf. Pirate Tiffany lit two red candles at the trembling flame and stuck them on the shelf under the bathroom mirror.

I looked around the circle. Reflected candlelight glinted off Fortran's big black-framed glasses, Stonewall's vampire teeth, and the sequins Espresso had glued to the flowers covering her mask. Airboy had fur over his whole face except where his eyes glittered through two narrow slits. Tiffany's mask was nothing but a blank white oval scored down one side with parallel red lines.

I took a steadying breath. "Ready, Tiffany?"

"*Woolworth*," she corrected angrily, and pulled the bundled mirror out of her pocket.

Layer by layer she unwrapped it, stuffing the rags back into her pocket as she went. When the silver disk of the Mermaid Queen's Magic Mirror lay naked in her hand, she put it on the floor. Then she stepped into the circle between Bergdorf and Stonewall and reluctantly took their hands. She was shaking so hard I could see the shadow of her coat trembling.

"One, two, three," Fortran counted.

"*Bloody Mary, Bloody Mary, Bloody Mary.*" We chanted it three times, and then kept on chanting, not keeping count because you forget to count when you're staring at a mirror as hard as you can, hoping and dreading to see something appear.

The chant was interrupted by a wail that would have made a banshee wet its pants. I wanted to put my hands over my ears, but that would break the circle.

I gritted my teeth and hung on.

The wail swelled. A pale mist appeared above the mirror, a sickly glow that grew and shifted—now bruise-green, now rot-yellow, now the scarlet of fresh blood. Louder and louder grew the wailing, then cut off abruptly with a deep, painful gurgle that made me think of slit throats.

Bloody Mary floated above the Mermaid's mirror, swept our pathetic circle with mad, red-rimmed eyes, opened her terrible mouth, and cackled like a cageful of hyenas.

We couldn't agree, later, on what she'd looked like. Espresso saw a girl with blood-stiff black hair and a gashed throat. Stonewall saw a blood-drenched woman holding a horribly smeared knife. Mukuti saw a child veiled with blood. Fortran saw a woman with knife-tipped fingers and more teeth than any mouth should hold. She was bloody, too.

Tiffany and Bergdorf wouldn't tell us what they saw.

The Bloody Mary I saw reminded me of the Bowery. She wore layers of filthy, ragged clothes, and her wild white hair escaped from a shapeless man's cap, jammed down over a face that sank away from her knife-blade nose and the blood-smeared cliffs of her cheekbones.

Near me, someone whimpered. My ears were full of hoarse, shallow panting. When I realized it was mine, I dragged a lungful of air into my chest. It didn't make me less terrified, but the effort made me think of something besides how much those long, iron nails would hurt when she dug them into my face.

Then Bloody Mary raised her hard, gray claws and lashed out at Bergdorf.

Bergdorf screamed, ducked, and kept on screaming, even when the nails raked through the air a good two inches from her face. Fortran whooped, which was a mistake. Bloody Mary came after him next, with the same non-bloody results. By the time she got to me, I was pretty sure she couldn't touch me. I still jerked back and maybe even screamed, just a little. Her nails were extremely thick and pointy. I thought I could see the dried blood on them.

And then she was going for Stonewall and I was wishing I could wipe my sweaty hands.

Airboy laced his fingers in mine so our hands wouldn't slip. I did the same with Espresso.

The wailing rose to a scream of frustration. Bloody Mary began to hurl herself randomly against the invisible barrier. At one point, her face was an inch from mine, her bottomless eyes staring, her thin lips stretching painfully away from her broken, yellowed teeth. Her breath stank of rotting meat.

I coughed and gagged and held on.

She spun, rags trailing, matted hair flying, to scrabble at the air in front of Tiffany.

Maybe if Stonewall and Bergdorf had been expecting it, they might have held her, but I doubt it. One moment, our circle was complete. The next, Tiffany had shaken herself free, snatched a large and glittering knife from her coat, and was attacking Bloody Mary with it.

I watched, terrified, as they struggled knife against claw, fury against fury, both of them shrieking so loud I was sure the whole school would come running. Mary's shrieks took on a triumphant note. Tiffany staggered.

And what did the big hero and champion of Central Park do?

I could have grabbed a candle and set fire to Mary's rags or kicked the Mermaid's mirror under the radiator or something, but I didn't. I just stood there screaming something lame like "No, no, no!" while Stonewall and Fortran knocked the knife out of Tiffany's hand, grabbed her wrists, and dragged her back into the circle, struggling and swearing.

I sobbed in a breath and let it out slowly.

Bloody Mary's wail sank into a horrible moaning. I heard fear in it, and a horrible, hopeless sadness. It made me feel like life was nothing but betrayal and terror, that I'd never be happy or safe or full or warm, that it would be like this forever and ever and nothing I could do would ever change it.

I looked around the circle. Everyone was standing like they'd been frozen as stiff as Airboy in a panic. All except one not-very-scary rusalka, who was kneeling on the floor with her knitted green hair falling over her mask, sobbing as only a mortal can.

Then Bergdorf broke down, whooping and sniffling in a way that should have been funny, but wasn't. I saw Espresso's shoulders start to heave, and Stonewall bow his head. Fortran gulped and roared like a little kid. Beside me, Airboy began to moan softly.

I didn't get it. If they were trying to make Bloody

Mary laugh and disappear, it wasn't working. In fact, she sounded sadder than ever, sadder than a banshee, sadder than anything I'd ever imagined. As I listened, my throat began to tighten and my eyes stung. I realized, to my horror, that I was about to cry. I tried to suppress it, but I couldn't. Soon, I was crying almost as hard as Bergdorf.

Airboy squeezed my hand. Looking up, I saw Tiffany half crouched between Stonewall and Fortran. Her head was down and her shoulders shaking. Tiffany the ice queen, Tiffany the most Folk-like student at Miss Van Loon's. Tiffany was crying.

Alone in the middle of the circle, Bloody Mary floated. She wasn't trying to kill us anymore, but she wasn't offering to grant our wishes, either. If we were even in any shape to make one. The furious grief pouring off her made it impossible to think, let alone come up with a clever idea. Maybe she couldn't reach us, but we couldn't reach her, either.

Stalemate.

Suddenly, Espresso started to speak.

> *"Bloody Mary, bogeywoman,*
> *Queen of Mirrors, Lady of Terror,*
> *Cut us a break."*

Bloody Mary screamed. The blood froze in my veins, but Espresso kept speaking. She didn't scream to compete, she didn't even shout, but I could hear every word.

Her voice was more like singing than talking, and the way the words sounded was part of what they meant.

> "*Bloody Mary, we see you.*
> *We see the blood on your hands and clothes.*
> *We hear you mourn your lost children.*
> *You want us to sigh with you?*
> *We've sighed.*
> *You want us to cry with you?*
> *We've cried.*
> *But it's over now.*
> *Mother of Fear, we're not your children.*
> *Sister of Death, our blood's not yours to shed.*
> *Child of Violence, we have better weapons*
>   *than a knife.*
> *We have knowledge, we have heart, we*
>   *have courage.*
> *We have each other.*
> *Go back into your mirror-world.*
> *Leave us in peace.*"

Bloody Mary stopped moaning and quivered. Tiffany rolled her eyes at Espresso, who grimaced. And I saw for the first time the thick scarlet rope of the genie spell binding Bloody Mary to the Mermaid's mirror.

I had an idea.

I took a step forward, tugging at Airboy and Espresso. They hesitated, then shuffled forward beside me, pulling Fortran and Mukuti, who pulled Bergdorf and Tiffany and Stonewall, closing the circle tighter around the bound bogeywoman.

Another two steps, and we were all squished together like a human wall. Bloody Mary had gone all thin and shadowy, her hands down by her sides, her head thrown back, her black eyes white-rimmed with panic.

I dropped Airboy's and Espresso's hands, quickly grabbed Fortran's and Mukuti's. The circle tightened.

Tiffany shot me a hard smile, shoved Stonewall behind her, and grabbed Bergdorf's hand.

We squeezed closer.

Bloody Mary oozed toward the ceiling and hovered there uncomfortably, the scarlet spell-rope stretched tight and thin. Behind me, everyone took hands to make a second circle.

Bergdorf dropped back, then Mukuti. The spell's rope was a string now.

Then Fortran dropped my hand and it was just Tiffany and me, our hands joined around a pulsing scarlet thread. Bloody Mary was a thunderous mist above us, the mirror a bright disk between our feet. I focused on where I thought Tiffany's eye was.

Tiffany shrugged and pulled me into her arms and hugged me.

The thread snapped.

Bloody Mary gathered herself in a reddish swirl and

arrowed straight into the bathroom mirror. She hung there for a moment, a vision of reflected horror that filled the mirror from edge to edge. Slowly at first, then faster and faster, she shrank and dimmed until finally there was nothing in the mirror but the reflections of two guttering candle flames and our own masked faces floating above the sinks like ghosts.

Fortran broke the silence. "We sure kicked *her* butt."

Tiffany snorted. "You think? I didn't see much butt-kicking. Just a lot of snot-nosed mortals, crying like babies."

Stonewall whipped a white handkerchief out of the pocket of his classic vampire tail-coat and handed it to her with a flourish. "For your snot nose, Mademoiselle Pirate Queen."

"Oh, go bite yourself."

Mukuti threw herself at me and clung like a spider-web. She was still shaking. Feeling a little strange, I put my arms around her. "It's okay," I said. "It's over. She's gone. You helped."

"I *cried*." Her voice was thick with tears.

"Yeah. Fast thinking," I said. "Um. You want to wash your face?"

Airboy had already peeled off his furry blue mask, turned on the tap, and dunked his face and hands into the sink. As soon as Mukuti let go of me, I did the same. The water felt wonderful. I scrubbed my face hard, then stood up, dripping.

"The mirror?" Airboy asked.

I wiped water from my eyes. "It's in my pocket. Airboy? We did it, right? She's really gone?"

He looked up from the sink into the bathroom mirror. "I guess so," he said.

Espresso's unmasked face appeared over my shoulder, grinning in the fading candlelight like a jack-o'-lantern. She gave me a quick, awkward hug. "Way to go, Neefer-bear!"

"You, too," I said, and returned the hug. I felt like I might be getting the hang of it. "Your poem was far out."

"You think? It just came to me. I thought the last lines were kind of lame."

"No. It was"—I thought for a moment—"outta sight and in the groove."

Espresso's cheeks turned pink. "You were the one who got rid of Miss Scratchy. You and the Tiffster, grooving to the beautiful music of love and harmony!"

"Oh, spare me!" Tiffany's voice came out of the gloom, more East Side than Bowery. I heard the door creak open. "All this Hallmark cheer is making me sick. Let's boogie."

Nobody was in the mood for pretending to be grossed out by a bowl of peeled grapes or talking to anybody who'd been bobbing for apples all night. So we went back to the library. We were totally starving.

Over a cooperative feast of sushi, bean sprouts, hamburger, cheese, bread, apples, sparkling water, chocolate, and lattes, we relived our triumph for Danskin. There was a lot of giggling and toasts with sparkling water to the Lady Poetess and the Banshee Twins (that would be Tiffany and me), the Grand High Weeper of Crysville (Mukuti) and the Queen of the Masks (Bergdorf), and (last but not least) the Grand Vizier Count Stoneywall and his magical swan, Danster.

Through all this, Tiffany sat cross-legged on the checkout desk, swigging from a bottle of green energy drink from Fortran's Backpack, and scowling like a gargoyle.

"Lighten up, Tiff," Bergdorf said. "Have some chocolate. It's over? Bloody Mary's gone. Maybe your face isn't so bad, and you can come home and it'll all be okay."

"Woolworth," Tiffany said through gritted teeth. "I'm Woolworth, remember? And nothing's okay. Even if my face weren't totally trashed, I wouldn't go back. The Upper East Side is garbage. Mother Carey is garbage. I'm Woolworth of the Bowery now. Whatever that means."

There was an uncomfortable silence, and then Mukuti asked, "Do you want to talk about it?"

While Tiffany—or Woolworth, I guess—was telling her just exactly why that was the most stupid idea in the universe, Airboy got up and walked off. I scrambled up and joined him on the window seat where Bergdorf had talked to Stonewall.

"I want to see the mirror," he said.

I pulled it out of my apron pocket. It had lost its gold chain, and the place where the chain had been attached was broken off, but it was in pretty good shape for a mirror with so many adventures behind it.

"Does it still work?" he asked anxiously.

I felt for the grooves in the rim and pressed. After a tense moment, I heard a clear, low chime. The mirror clouded, then cleared to show a familiar gold trident pulsing gently against a pale-blue field.

We puffed out twin sighs of relief. "It works," I said.

"So ask it what we should do next."

I turned the mirror off. "I only know how to make it show me the weather forecast and the answers to one thousand and one common riddles. Besides, I already know what to do next. Take it back to the Mermaid Queen."

"I could do that for you," Airboy said.

I held the mirror to my chest. "It's my job, Airboy," I said, a little more forcefully than I had to.

"It's my job, too."

Suddenly, we were glaring at each other, enemies again. I imagined Airboy plotting to take the mirror and all the credit for finding it. I imagined the Mermaid Queen salting the waters of Central Park because he'd brought it back instead of me. I imagined yelling at him. I imagined hitting him, hard.

Airboy looked away and sighed. He sounded almost as sad as Bloody Mary.

I laid the mirror in my lap. "It's *our* job," I said finally.

There was a little silence. Then Airboy said, "You're right, I guess."

For some reason, I wanted to laugh. "As usual," I said.

Airboy gave me a look of pure shock. I waggled my eyebrows. His expression morphed from annoyed to puzzled, then, slowly and reluctantly, settled into a smile.

"Allies?" he asked, holding out his hand.

"Friends," I said, shaking it.

He didn't argue with me.

Chapter 20

RULE 306: STUDENTS MUST NOT CARRY OR USE MAGIC TALISMANS WITHOUT WRITTEN PERMISSION FROM THEIR NEIGHBORHOOD GENIUS.

Miss Van Loon's Big Book of Rules

In Battery Park, the ghosts were waiting patiently in front of Castle Clinton, surrounded by bundles and baskets and ghostly children.

I'd seen them last summer, with Changeling. I hadn't known, then, who they were or anything about them. Now I knew they were the ghosts of immigrants, waiting to be allowed into New York City so that they could get a job or catch a train out west. Some had brought Folk with them, invisible stowaways who eventually found their way Between and founded the New York I live in.

Airboy and I were sitting on the pier with our backs to the ghosts, dangling our feet in the water, listening to the oily waves lapping at the pilings, watching the lights of the Harbor islands glimmering like sequins on the water, and smelling the tart, salty perfume of the Harbor. We were arguing.

"For the millionth time," I said, "*I'm* the official Voice of the Genius of Central Park. I get to talk first. "

"You'll be official shark food before you can open your mouth."

"I know she's really mad at me, but even the Mermaid Queen wouldn't kill the Lady's Voice."

Airboy kicked at the water viciously.

"You know I'm right," I said.

"I know you like being important. Well, guess what? You *are* important. You're the official Park changeling, Voice of the Genius of Central Park. Nobody there would dare hurt you. I'm the one who has to earn the right to keep my merrow cap."

I stared at him. "You're kidding. Without your merrow cap, you'd—"

"Drown?" Airboy shrugged. "Life is hard in the Harbor."

I was going to say that life was hard in the Park, too, but stopped myself. Sure, I'd faced the Wild Hunt, but I'd escaped. And I'd had help. A lot of help.

"Fine," I said. "We found the mirror as a team, right? Park and Harbor working together toward a common goal? Why not take the next step and give it to the Queen together, too?"

There was a long silence. "Okay," Airboy said.

"Wizard!" I got up. "Let's get this show on the road."

"Just like that?"

"Sure. Why not?"

He tugged at my skirt. I looked down at the delicate embroidered apron. "Oh. Yeah. Pepperkaka would kill me, wouldn't she?"

"So take it off. The skirt, too. In fact, take off everything." He opened one of his Harness's pouches and pulled out something shiny and black. "Extra swim skin. One size fits all."

I found a relatively ghost-free spot behind the Castle and changed into the swim skin. It was like putting on wet jeans, only worse because it was too dark to see what I was doing. When I'd finally managed it, I stuffed the troll maiden gear into Satchel and went back to Airboy. I felt like a shiny black sausage.

The water looked black and cold and thick. "Um, Airboy? How am I supposed to breathe?"

"I've got a bubble wand," Airboy said impatiently. "Come *on*." And he jumped into the Harbor, pulling me with him.

Sputtering, I scrambled for the surface. Airboy surfaced beside me, the lights of Battery Park reflecting off his eyes and his half-moon grin. "It's *cold*!" I gasped.

"You'll warm up as you swim. Ready for your air bubble, tourist?"

"Can't wait," I said sarcastically.

I ducked under the surface. Freezing water stroked my face and ran icy currents through my hair. Airboy, his Harness glowing faintly green through the murk, produced a wand with a circle on top and blew a bubble around my head. I blinked water from my eyes and took a shallow lungful of air. It smelled of fish and stale magic.

"Okay?" Airboy asked.

"I guess."

"Follow me." And he darted off.

I'd learned to swim from nixies, but Airboy had grown up underwater. Within six strokes, I knew I couldn't keep up with him, not swimming in the dark with a bubble of air around my head and Satchel bumping and dragging at my back.

Airboy darted back to me, grinning. "I'll get help," he said. "Just keep swimming."

Alone in the dark, I grimly forced my arms and legs to stroke and kick, stroke and kick. I was moving, but I couldn't tell whether it was forward or up or down or around in circles. Maybe, I thought, I've swum farther than I think. Maybe I'm heading out to sea. Maybe Airboy won't be able to find me, and I'll just keep bumbling along until a sea monster gets me. Maybe—

"Your Diplomatic Honor Guard, Madame Ambassador!"

A sleek black streak with a grin on top flashed past me: Airboy, followed by a pod of sleek, black bodies, their Harnesses glowing faintly green. They twisted and darted above and below, calling out cheerfully to each other and me.

"Hello, Airboy's land girl!"

"Look at her swim! I didn't know landies could swim."

"She looks like a seal maiden. Don't you think she looks like a seal maiden, Godfather Robbie?"

A broad, whiskered seal face popped up close beside me and examined me with dark, mournful, long-lashed eyes. "Not at all," the selkie said. "Canna you see yon great bubble on her heid? And no more meat on her than a sea otter." One of the sad eyes winked at me. "Still, she's fair enough, for a wee skellington."

I went stiff with embarrassment and I started to sink. Two of Airboy's friends grabbed my arms.

"It's like towing an oar," one changeling said. "Relax, landie, and let your legs trail."

The other changeling laughed a trail of brownish bubbles. "Yeah, relax. The sharks won't chase you if you're relaxed."

Which was useful information, but not particularly relaxing.

As we zigged and zagged through the water, faint lights stitched the darkness: a kappa, its head-bowl glowing blue, a merman with a lantern, a magic fish with star-bright bobbing antenna. Once a school of lantern fish darted by, their white glare illuminating mer garbage collectors with yellow vests and nets and a pod of police selkies and a small, horse-faced sea monster.

The Mermaid Queen's Court is in a huge cavern under Staten Island. On Airboy's magic map, it looked pretty close to Battery Park. Swimming, it seemed a lot farther. Still, when Airboy's "honor guard" said good-bye, I wished the trip had been longer.

We floated in front of the deep rift in the foundation of Staten Island that was the entrance to the Queen's court.

Airboy nudged me. "Allies?"

"Right. Allies."

We swam into the rift side by side.

The last time I was here, I'd found the rift uncomfortably narrow, but I'd been all squished up with Changeling in a huge bubble towed by a team of merguards. It was actually plenty wide for all but the biggest sea monsters. It was also dark with the kind of darkness that presses down on you. As I followed the ghostly green glow of Airboy's Harness, I could hear my heart beating in my ears and a deep whooshing that sounded like the breathing of an immense animal.

My hand brushed against something that swayed and clattered and scattered beads of blinding light. I gave a yelp and back-finned.

"I'm going inside," Airboy breathed. "Wait here."

I poked at the clattering thing, catching my finger

on the edge of something sharp. A tin can. More careful exploration revealed metal fragments, more cans, bits of plastic, and a strong, thin line stringing it all together. A curtain of junk.

Not far away, Airboy was talking to a merguard. I steadied myself against the slimy rock wall and tried to listen, but they were speaking some sea language I didn't know. I was starting to get really bored when a sliver of light appeared at the bottom of the curtain.

"Come *on*," Airboy hissed.

I glided through the gap as quietly as I could. After the black, black rift, the cavern was dazzlingly bright. Airboy caught my groping hands and pulled me forward. A moment later, we drifted to a stop.

"You can open your eyes now."

We were in a dim corridor between a rocky wall and a row of rough stone pillars. I remembered from my last visit that there was another row of pillars across the hall.

I peered around the nearest pillar. A thousand lantern fish twinkled in the roof of the cavern like scaly stars, bathing everything in soft, green light. The court itself was surprisingly empty. No nereids, no mermen, no brightly colored magic fish, just a few grim merguards and selkies with HARBOR POLICE medallions around their necks.

Down at the end of the hall, I saw a giant pink scallop shell with a mermaid lounging in it like an oversized black pearl. The Mermaid Queen was In.

I couldn't see her tattoos from this distance, but I didn't have to: I remembered them just fine. She had fish on her cheeks, a trident on her forehead, anchors and ships on her arms, and a nuclear submarine down the whole right side of her tail. Her nose and fins and ears were pierced and her hair spiked out from her head like an orange anemone. Woolworth the punk pirate queen could only dream of being as tough as the Mermaid Queen of New York Harbor.

Two torpedo-shaped shadows crossed behind the throne, turned, and crossed again. Sharks. My mouth went dry.

Airboy tugged impatiently on my hand. It was time to go.

We swam down the dim corridor, keeping close to the floor. We were six pillars from the front. Five. Four. When we reached the last pillar, we'd dart out and announce ourselves, take the Queen by surprise.

At the second pillar, Airboy dropped my hand and whooshed out into the hall like he was jet-propelled.

"Hail, great Queen!" he said. "I bring you good news!"

I floundered out after him, blind with fury.

"No he doesn't!" I shouted. "I do! I'm the Voice of the Green Lady of Central Park, who—"

"You!" The Mermaid Queen roared, rearing up on her tail like an angry sea lion. "Land girl! Mirror thief!

Guards! Feed her to the sharks! Quick—before she makes up another riddle!"

Two muscular merguards twisted my arms behind my back and tangled my legs in seaweed. I wiggled and jack-knifed and shouted that I was an Ambassador, that I had rights, that they better let me go, or there'd be trouble.

"Trouble for you," the merguards snickered. They towed me toward the shadows, where the Queen's sharks circled lazily, grinning their U-shaped grins.

Now, I thought, would be a good time for my brain to come up with a clever escape plan. Maybe if my ears stopped buzzing. Maybe if I could just take a breath that didn't taste of fish.

Airboy yelled, "You can't *do* that!"

The merguards wheeled, pulling me with them. I floated between them woozily and listened to Airboy scold the Mermaid Queen. He was right up in her face, hands and feet finning to keep him there, explaining things firmly and clearly. The Diplomat would have been proud of him.

"Neef isn't just some random landie you can drown now and apologize for later," he said. "She's the Voice of the Genius of Central Park. Okay, you're mad because she tricked you, and you and the Green Lady hate each other because of something that happened before the Genius Wars. But the Green Lady still didn't kill your Voice, and you can't kill hers. You have to listen to her and then you have to let her go home. That's the *rule*. "

The Mermaid Queen flipped her tail, sending Airboy tumbling in a cloud of little bubbles. "Nuts to that. The last time I listened to that kid, I lost my mirror."

Airboy recovered himself and swam back to the throne. "You don't have to listen to her yourself. Your Voice can do it for you."

"Yeah? Oh, *yeah*! I knew there was something I was forgetting." She raised her voice to a screech. "Ox-y-gen!"

"Here, Majesty." The Voice of the Mermaid Queen darted from behind a handy pillar and made a complicated floating gesture of respect.

The Mermaid Queen waved a royal hand. "Find out what that pesky land girl over there wants and then get rid of her. She makes my scales itch. And if she says anything about riddles or cats, I don't care who she is, I'm throwing her to the sharks." She pulled a large metal rasp out of the depths of the Shelly Throne and began to sharpen her claws.

Oxygen swam over to me. I could see that he was nervous and angry. Not a good combination.

"Greetings, Voice of the Mermaid Queen," I began. "The Green Lady—"

Oxygen held up a silencing hand. "Shut up, kid. Boy, are you in over your head. Tell me, have you even gotten to Diplomacy yet, or are you still in Basic Manners?"

He reminded me of Abercrombie. I glared at him. "Both, if it's any of your business. What—"

Airboy wiggled his fingers over Oxygen's shoulder and folded them down one by one.

"—I was going to tell you," I went on slowly, "is that if those sharks eat me, your Genius will definitely never get her mirror back."

Oxygen thought this over. "All right," he said. "Talk."

"Make them let me go first."

Oxygen glanced toward the Shelly Throne, where the Mermaid Queen was filing away, pretending she hadn't heard every word. "No tricks," he said threateningly.

"No tricks."

"Release her," he told the merguards. They looked at the Queen, who shrugged. Then they let go of my arms and drifted back just far enough so they could grab me if I showed any signs of asking a riddle.

Basic Manners, huh? I'd show him Basic Manners. "The Green Lady of Central Park," I said, "greets the Queen of New York Harbor and bids me say that she wishes to return the talisman known as the Magic Magnifying Mirror, which her champion won in fair challenge—"

"Ha!" the Mermaid Queen burst out, filing viciously.

"—*fair challenge*, last summer. Recognizing that the talisman is necessary to the smooth running of New York Harbor, the Green Lady has decided, of her own free will—"

"Double ha!"

"—to return the talisman to its traditional owner, so that the inhabitants of both Park and Harbor can continue to live in safety and comfort."

Oxygen opened his mouth to answer, but the Mermaid Queen was there before him. "Who ever heard of a champion returning a Talisman before the deadline? She's doing that thing mortals do, isn't she, Oxygen?"

Oxygen studied my face. He wasn't sneering anymore. "Maybe not. Neef of Central Park, do you have the Queen's mirror? Tell me the truth."

"I do." I touched Satchel. "It's in here, safe and sound."

"Loonie's honor?"

I fought a giggle and won. "Loonie's honor."

The Queen whooped happily and dropped the rasp. "Gimme," she said.

Airboy was drifting behind Oxygen, looking miserable. He'd tried to take the credit for finding the mirror himself, after we'd promised to be allies. But then he'd saved my life. And he had to earn his merrow cap. I took a fish-flavored breath. "I'll give it to you, just as soon as you hear the proposition Airboy and I wish to put before you."

"Airboy?" said Oxygen.

"Proposition?" said the Queen.

"Yes." I stared into Airboy's eyes, willing him to read my mind. "Airboy and I are a team. Without his cooperation and natural diplomatic skills, I could never return your mirror, certainly not now, maybe not ever."

Airboy winked at me. "Great Queen," he said, "our proposition is this: That you and the Green Lady make an alliance between the Park and the Harbor."

The Mermaid Queen's mouth opened and closed soundlessly, like a fish out of water. And then she screamed. "Not in a million, trillion, gazillion years! What's with you, Oxygen? Do your job! Threaten the land girl! Torture her! Search her bag! I want my mirror! *Now!*"

Oxygen threw Airboy an unreadable look, then turned to the Queen. "With respect, Majesty, an alliance is not a bad idea."

I expected a quick trip to the sharks for all of us, or a fairy fit at the very least, but the Queen sank down in the throne. "I don't make deals with Land Folk," she said sullenly.

This, somehow, was the last straw. "Well, that's just peachy," I snapped. "You don't make deals; the Lady doesn't make deals. All the other Geniuses make deals with each other all the time. That's what we learn at Miss Van Loon's, isn't it, Oxygen?"

Oxygen chewed his lip.

"That's what changelings are for," I went on, "to make alliances. You know why the East Siders run practically the whole City? It's because they make alliances. Yorktown, Fifth Avenue, Madison, Upper East Side, Midtown—they all have each other. Who does the Harbor have?"

"Nobody," Airboy answered, just as if we'd practiced

it. "The Harbor has nobody and nothing. They don't even respect us, the East Siders, I mean. They think we're stupid and violent and old-fashioned."

"Wild," I added. "Like the Park. That's an insult, by the way."

The Mermaid Queen flashed her pointed teeth. "Who cares what a bunch of dry-skins think? It's not like they can hurt me."

"How much garbage have they dumped in the Harbor?" Airboy asked. "How much bigger did the Harbor used to be, before they tore down all the hills and made Manhattan bigger?"

"You're *talking* garbage," the Queen snarled.

Oxygen swallowed nervously. "It's true, Majesty. Don't you remember? Castle Clinton used to be an island. Now it's part of Manhattan. The Dragon did that."

"Don't believe us," I said. "Ask the mirror. Which we solemnly vow and swear to give you the minute you agree to an alliance."

The Queen's trident pleated in a furious scowl. "Okay, okay. I promise I won't salt Old Lady Tree-Hugger's precious water. Now can I have my mirror back?"

Oxygen was silent. Airboy seemed to have used up all his words. I licked my lips. "The alliance," I said. "Or no mirror."

"Fish poop," the Queen said. "What does an alliance mean, anyway? That the Lady says 'jump' and I say 'how high?' I don't jump for nobody."

Diplomacy is all about not letting Geniuses know how stupid you think they are. "It means," I said, "that if the Harbor's in trouble, she helps you out, and vice versa."

"And you promise Her Leafiness won't wiggle out of it if I need her?"

"Yes," I said. "I promise." Which was definitely a rash thing to do, given the Lady's attitude toward the Mermaid Queen. But it was what I had to say, so I said it, and hoped I could make it stick.

The Mermaid Queen waved her tail fin thoughtfully. I watched slow ripples travel up the nuclear submarine tattooed on her tail, and reached nervously for my hair. When my fingers hit my air bubble, I heard a soft snort. I was glad Airboy could laugh. I was about ready to scream.

"I accept the alliance," she said at last. "As long as Old Mud-Face watches my back, I'll watch hers. But no funny stuff. And no riddles. Now, give me back my mirror."

My fingers were shaking so hard with relief, I'd never have found the mirror if Satchel hadn't pushed it into my hand.

As soon as I pulled it out, the Mermaid Queen grabbed it and began to examine it like a flower fairy searching a rosebud for signs of black spot. She grumbled over every ding and nearly pitched a fairy fit over the missing chain. But as soon as she turned it on, a smile rearranged the tattoos on her face.

Everybody relaxed, even the merguards.

Oxygen turned to us. "Not bad for a couple of youngsters," he said. "We'll work out the details later. Somewhere watery, I think. Bethesda Fountain?"

I nodded.

"Now I think you'd better get out of here. You, too, Airboy. I'll talk to the Queen later about making you an official Junior Attaché to the Embassy. Let's hope you get longer than I did to learn about being an official Voice."

We went. Somehow, the swim back to Battery Park seemed much easier than the swim out.

Epilogue

Three days after Hallowe'en, I was sitting in Advanced Diplomacy, listening to the Diplomat's latest made-up problem.

"A leprechaun has entered into a contract to provide two pairs of dancing slippers for each of the twelve daughters of a Chief Executive Officer. When he delivers the two dozen pairs of shoes, the CEO's assistant informs him of two things: his contract obliges him to repair the shoes; the CEO's daughters dance through the soles of their shoes every night.

"To whom should the leprechaun complain?"

In real life, I figured the leprechaun would probably keep his mouth shut and repair the slippers until there was no more upper to attach the soles to, while planning how to trick the CEO out of every gold piece in his coffers. But I was pretty sure that wasn't the answer the Diplomat was looking for.

I raised my hand. "He's got a couple of choices. He could wait until a Full Moon Gathering and take his complaint to the Genius of whatever Neighborhood he lives in—although if it's the Wholesaler of the Garment District, probably all he'll get is a review of his shoe designs."

The corners of the Diplomat's mouth twitched slightly. "And his second choice?"

"He can track down the Voice of the Wholesaler and get him or her to work things out with the Voice of whatever neighborhood the CEO lives in."

The Diplomat nodded. "What do the rest of you think?"

They thought a lot of things. I didn't listen.

It was weird being back in school, sitting in lessons and answering questions like everything was just as it had been. My quest for the Mermaid's mirror felt like it had happened a hundred years ago, to somebody else. I had changed. Everything had changed.

For instance, Airboy was sitting next to me.

We'd been seeing a lot of each other over the past three days. Apparently, being Junior Attaché to the Embassy of the Mermaid Queen meant that Airboy was responsible for setting everything up for the alliance. I'd helped things along by talking Astris into inviting him to tea with the Pooka and Councilor Snuggles. It was a little awkward at first, but by the time the Autumn cookies were gone, Snuggles had promised to arrange an "accidental" encounter with the Lady by Bethesda Fountain.

The meeting itself had been kind of fraught. There wasn't going to be a moon, so it had to happen in the afternoon, when the Lady is never at her best. As soon as she saw Oxygen and Airboy, she totally snaked out, scales and twirling eyeballs and everything. Airboy told me later he thought it was pretty impressive, but not as bad as the Mermaid Queen's rages. "She isn't really going to bite anybody. She just wants you to think she might."

Which was pretty much what I thought, too.

Once she'd recovered from her fairy fit, the Lady listened quietly to our proposal.

"The Wild Places Alliance," she said thoughtfully. "Okay, I'm in. As long as Old Fish-Face keeps her scales clean."

There was a ceremony, of course. Oxygen presented the Lady with a huge pearl that would turn red when the Harbor was threatened. After some thought, the Lady produced an acorn enclosed in a hollow stone that would split when the Park was in danger. Then she disappeared, and Councilor Snuggles went off to present Oxygen to the rest of the Lady's council, leaving Airboy, the Pooka, and me alone by the fountain.

"That's that, then," the Pooka said. "You look dead

beat, the pair of you. Home to bed, my heart, and may a blessing of sleep be upon you for four-and-twenty hours. And where are you off to, boyo?"

Airboy was climbing the steps that led to the street. "Home," he threw over his shoulder. "Like you said."

"You'll be long enough getting there by that road." The Pooka shifted from man to pony, shaking back the inky forelock that fell over his eyes. "Hop up and I'll carry you to the Hudson."

Airboy kept climbing. "That's okay," he said. "I can walk."

The Pooka arched his neck proudly. "It's hurt to the soul I am, to think you'd not trust me to carry the Mermaid Queen's Junior Attaché safely on his way."

Airboy stopped, but he didn't turn around. There was a long pause. "No wild rides," the Pooka said. "By the sacred peace between our Neighborhoods, I swear it."

Then Airboy came down the steps. "I accept," he said. "Sorry."

The Pooka shook his mane. "Pish, boy. No need to apologize. It's perfectly reasonable to doubt a trickster such as myself."

Back in Advanced Diplomacy, the discussion of the leprechaun and his shoe problem was going strong. Abercrombie was arguing that dancing slippers with no soles couldn't really be repaired.

With Tiffany out of the scene, Abercrombie had pretty much taken over as the new leader of the East Siders. Bergdorf had been busted from debutante to personal-assistant-in-training. She blamed Mother Carey, Tiffany's godmother. To get back at her, she told the East Siders just exactly what had happened to Tiffany and what we'd done about it. Now nobody would go near the third-floor bathroom, even though someone had hung a curtain over the mirror.

I still had my quest pass. I was planning to return it to the Diplomat after lessons were over, along with the report—on parchment in my best handwriting— of what Neighborhoods I'd visited in the course of my quest, what magical objects I'd gained (if any) and what I'd accomplished (if anything). It was weird seeing it all written down, ending with "An Alliance formalized between the Mermaid Queen of New York Harbor and the Green Lady of Central Park." It made me feel like a real diplomat.

Airboy's elbow in my ribs let me know my lack of attention was in danger of being noticed.

The Diplomat was making an announcement. ". . . a new student to introduce to you. It is not usually school policy to admit new students between the Equinox and the Solstice, but the Bowery has not sponsored a change-ling at Miss Van Loon's in a very long time. Ladies and gentlemen, I give you Woolworth of the Bowery."

I felt Airboy jerk upright beside me. Advanced Diplomacy students are far too self-possessed to react out loud, but for a second, it was like all the air had been sucked from the room.

Woolworth marched forward and stood beside the Diplomat's desk. Her Inside Sweater, empty of gold stars, was ripped at the shoulder and along one pocket, which was pinned on with safety pins. Under it, she wore a low-cut black top and baggy gray pants stuffed into heavy black lace-up boots. Her nails were painted black and her blonde hair was hacked short and pulled back from her forehead to display what Bloody Mary had done to her.

Five long scars scored the left side of her face from hairline to chin, with one extending all the way down her neck and across her chest. I wondered whether she'd even used the Glamourist's beauty cream. Then I realized it would look a lot worse if she hadn't.

"What're you chumps looking at?" she asked the room at large. "Do I have a smudge on my cheek?" She rubbed at the deepest scar. "Whaddya know? It doesn't come off."

"Woolworth," the Diplomat said warningly. "Do you think this is the most useful attitude to take?"

Woolworth glared at her fiercely. "It's *Bowery* attitude. Get used to it." Then she honored the Diplomat with a graceful and perfectly executed bow, stomped to the back of the room, and sat down. The air quivered with everybody's desire to turn and stare at her, but nobody moved a muscle.

"One more announcement," the Diplomat said. "Today, I have the honor of presenting two gold stars. Neef, Airboy, if you would care to step forward?"

Airboy looked ready to crawl under the desk. I gave him a poke and herded him to the front of the room. His neck and ears were a painful, deep red. I had a feeling mine weren't much better. We stood there, glowing like beacons, while the Diplomat made an endless speech about City Harmony and Diplomatic Initiative and Grace Under Pressure that made me squirm. What saved me was the sight of Woolworth slouching in the back row, tapping a pencil noisily on the desk and sneering furiously.

And then the Diplomat handed us each a gold star.

I'd never really noticed that gold stars were beautiful. Maybe it was because this one was new. Maybe it was because this one was mine. It shone with a glory of pure and golden light around a tiny, intense, five-pointed center. It was magic—not the kind of magic that does anything, just the kind of magic that is wonderful and mysterious and, well, magical.

I looked up at the Diplomat. "This is a greater honor than I can ever deserve."

"Your modesty does you credit, Neef. But you do deserve it, or I wouldn't give it to you. Be careful, though. One quest's diplomatic initiative can be another quest's diplomatic incident. Do you understand me?"

I did. And suddenly, I understood Rule 0, too. "I do, Diplomat."

"Airboy, Neef, these gold stars mean that you need not attend Diplomacy anymore. But I hope that you will continue your lessons, at least until Winter Solstice."

"Certainly, Diplomat," I said. And I meant it, too. There was a lot I wanted to learn, especially about crisis management.

And that was that.

Our table picked up a bunch of new lunchers that day. Some Tech-heads, eager to geek out about the Mermaid's mirror. Fortran was in his element. Mukuti made nice to a couple of renegade East Siders, while Espresso talked Folk lore and poetry with a mixed group of West Siders, Spanish Harlemites, and Villagers. Woolworth sat glowering at the end of the table, bracketed by Danskin and Stonewall, who were sparkling at everyone, planting the seeds, I realized, of future alliances.

I opened Satchel and pulled out my lunch: white cheese, black bread, an apple. Across the table Airboy grinned and offered me a piece of fish.

RULE 0: STUDENTS MAY BREAK ANY RULE IN THE BOOK IF, AFTER CAREFUL CONSIDERATION OF ALL THE ALTERNATIVES AND POSSIBLE CONSEQUENCES, THEY DECIDE THAT THEY REALLY, REALLY HAVE TO.

Neef's Guide to
Supernatural Beings

Arranged in alphabetical order, with country of origin, where known. All the Folk in this list are traditional, except the ones marked "Literary Characters" or "New York Between," who don't appear in any of the old lists but exist anyway. Astris says it's important to remember that there are non-traditional Folk all over the world, not just in New York Between, but the New York ones are the only ones I've met.

Apopa (*Inuit*): A kind of dwarf. They're supposed to be truly hideous and misshapen and deformed, but I've never seen one, so who knows? Maybe it's just bad press related to their habit of playing nasty tricks on people.

Banshee (*Ireland*): A spirit who flies around wailing when someone important is going to die. Think nails across a blackboard. Now turn up the volume. Now think of the saddest sound you ever heard. That's what a banshee's wail sounds like.

Black Dog/Gabriel Hound (*England*): Bad dogs. Very, very bad dogs. They lead you astray, they attack you with their foot-long teeth, they foretell your death. They tend to show up at intersections and on bridges, and they have glowing red eyes.

Brownie/Kobold (*Europe*): Household spirits. They're all about cleaning and helping around the house. They'll do anything: laundry, mending, scrubbing the stove. They'll even wash windows. They're all pretty small (about knee-high) and skinny. There are differences, though. The Brownies (from England) are brown (duh) and shaggy-haired and have webbed hands. You can make them go away by giving them new clothes and saying "Thank you." Kobolds (from Germany) are gray and bald and much crabbier than brownies. They take their milk with dirt, and think everybody else should, too.

Centaur (*Greece*): Half man, half horse, with the man part at the front. Chiron, the Green Lady's Councilor, is a Literary Character. Back in the Old Country, he was a healer and an astronomer and a teacher of heroes. He tried to teach me astronomy once, but we decided it would be better to wait until I was bigger, and maybe knew some math.

Demon (*Everywhere*): A kind of general term for bad

guys of all sizes, shapes, and places of origin. A demon can have anywhere between no and twelve heads, and as many arms as will fit on its body. It's usually a good idea to keep as far away from them as possible.

Djinn/Afrit (*Middle East*): Djinns are wind spirits. Afrits are fire spirits. Both are big, powerful, mean, and smart. When you make a bargain with a djinn or an afrit, be sure you get it in writing and read all the fine print before you sign.

Dryad (*Greece*): A guardian spirit of trees, groves, and woods. Dryads look like wispy girls, and basically, they're only interested in trees. And dancing.

Duende (*Spain*): Duendes are related to brownies, but not as single-minded about cleaning. They do guardian-spiriting, too, and make excellent fairy godparents and artists' agents. Their feet are turned around the wrong way, and they like hats with really wide brims, which make them look kind of like walking mushrooms.

Dwarf (*Europe*): Dwarfs are short, stocky Folk with long beards and axes. Mostly, they mind their own business, which is digging, building, magic technology, and gold. They can be nice or they can be nasty, depending on their mood. Duergs (*Germany* and *Scandinavia*) are pretty much always in a nasty mood.

Elf/Fate/Fay (singular) Alfar/Elle-folk/Sidhe/Peris/Daoine Sidhe (plural) (*Europe*): Different names for the mortal-shaped, tall, gorgeous Folk that show up most often in fairy tales. They tend to be as proud as they are beautiful, and kind of self-centered. They like music and the arts, treasure and beautiful things. And breaking mortal hearts.

Fairy (*Europe*): This is a general term that can refer to any kind of Folk. But most self-identified fairies are tiny, winged, mischievous, and have very short attention spans.

Faun (*Greece*): Half boy, half goat, with the goat half on the bottom. Fauns are nature spirits, basically, although there are a few who live in Lincoln Center, playing their pipes in the orchestra or dancing in the chorus.

Fox Maidens (*Japan* and *China*): Sometimes they're girls and sometimes they're foxes. They like mortal men, even going so far as to marry and live Outside for years and years. Sometimes this even works out. In Japan, they're called kitsune.

Gnomes (*Germany*): Short, stocky, technophile, underground Folk, kind of like bald dwarfs. They make excellent Magic Technicians and Building Superintendents.

Goblin (*Europe*): Any small, ugly, beardless, mischievous spirit with a taste for practical jokes, frequently nasty. Hobgoblins come from England. Puck is a hobgoblin. He's also a Literary Character.

Gremlins (*England*): Little devils who get into machinery of all kinds and gum up the works. They started out specializing in British airplanes, but soon spread to cars, trucks, telephones, and computer networks all over the world.

Iolanthe (*Literary Character*): A peri, one of fairy-kind, and the heroine of *Iolanthe*, an operetta by the mortals Gilbert and Sullivan. In Central Park, she's a dancing teacher.

Jenny Greenteeth (*England*): A bogeywoman who hangs out in ponds covered with duckweed and slime, waiting for unsuspecting children to come too close so she can pull them into the pond and eat them. In New York Between, Jenny hangs out in Riverside Park and rides with the Wild Hunt. She's tight with Peg Powler. They have a lot in common.

Kappa (*Japan*): Demon with webbed fingers, a head like an open bowl, and a gold star in manners. It likes drowning mortals. If you meet a kappa, remember to bow so its strength will pour out of its head when it bows back. Works every time.

Kazna Peri (*Russia*): On the steppes of Russia, it cooked gold over its magic fire in the spring. In New York Between, it brews really strong coffee.

Kelpie (*Scotland*): A nasty, hungry, mortal-drowning, shape-shifting water spirit. If you see a pretty black horse near any body of water, with flaming eyes and weeds in its mane, stay away from it. If it's not a kelpie, it's probably a pooka or a water horse, and none of them are really safe to ride. Unless it's your fairy godfather, of course.

Kirin (*Japan*): A kind of dragon/deer/lion hybrid. Kirin are gentle and pure-hearted and only appear in places ruled by kind and just rulers.

Kouros (*Greece*): "Kouros" is Greek for "young man." There are many, many ancient statues of young men in the Metropolitan Museum, and each of them is called "Kouros." They have long, stony curls and mysterious little smiles, and they'll never tell you what the joke is.

Moss Women (*Germany*): Tiny nature nymphs. They're all about moss: making it, decorating trees with it, taking care of it. They wear moss. Their hair looks like moss. They can also grant small wishes and reorient mortals lost in the woods, but don't step on any moss, or you'll be sorry.

Naiad/Nixie/Undine (*Europe*): Different kinds of fresh-water nymphs. Naiads (*Greece*) and undines (*Germany*) have legs. Nixies (*Germany* and *Switzerland*) have fish tails. Like mermaids, nixies enjoy drowning mortals for fun. Naiads and undines are more likely to fall in love with them.

Nymph (*Everywhere*): Essentially, any female nature spirit is a nymph, no matter what she was called in the Old Country. Moss women are forest nymphs; nixies are water nymphs. The marsh goblin's nymph could have been a helead (nymph of the marshes). Or she could have been visiting.

Ogres (*France* and *Italy*): Big, ugly Folk with a taste for mortal flesh and really bad manners. There aren't many in New York Between, luckily, but you never know when one might show up.

Rusalka (*Russia*): A water nymph of the "come and be drowned" variety. Unlike nixies, she leaves the water to look for victims, carrying a magic comb to keep her hair from drying out, which would kill her. The rusalkas in Central Park mostly live in Harlem Meer with the vodyanoi.

Selkie (*British Isles*): A mortal on the land; a seal in the sea. They are strong, gentle, and patient and make excellent fairy godparents.

Shinseën (*China*): Nature spirits, oddly enough. There might be a few lurking up in Inwood or somewhere, but most of them seem to be down in Chinatown, selling spices and vegetables. New York is like that.

Tanuki (*Japan*): Badger/man shapeshifter. They like rice wine, good food, and simple practical jokes, and are usually almost as wide as they are tall.

Troll (*Scandinavia*): Big, ugly, hairy, and short-tempered. Trolls like treasure and solitude and biting people's heads off. They turn to stone in the sun.

Viz-Leany (*Hungary*): A kind of water maiden. Descended from a goddess, back in the Old Country.

Vodyanoi (*Russia*): Nasty, mean, dangerous water spirits who hate mortals (except to eat . . . raw). They can shift shape—old men with scales and/or green beards, big fish, frogs. Green is a theme. Also horns and big teeth.

Wild Hunt (*Northern Europe*): In the Old Country, a host of evil spirits who hunt souls on windy, stormy nights. In New York Between, a loose alliance of nasty, carnivorous

Folk who are always petitioning the Green Lady to up their quota of fresh meat.

Will-o'-the-wisps/*feux follet/ignis fatuus***: Different names for nature spirits who exist to mislead travelers. They look like little lights, twinkling off in the trees (or down a side street). If you follow them, thinking you've found somebody with a flashlight or a restaurant or an off-duty taxi, you'll get a lot more lost than you were to begin with, probably in a really bad section of town.

Acknowledgments

As always, I have many people to thank.

The Fabulous Genrettes—Laurie J. Marks, Rosemary Kirstein, and Didi Stewart—for helping me make it all make sense.

Ellen Klages, for Friday pages and inexhaustible patience with my early-draft experiments.

Sarah Smith, Elizabeth Bear, Eve Sweetser, Kelly Link, Gavin Grant, Holly Black, Chiara Azzaretti, Shweta Narayan, Nathaniel Smith, Veronica Schanoes, and Liran Bromberg for reading assorted drafts and being honest and helpful about what they found there.

Josepha Sherman and Jerome Chanes, for checking over my folklore and my Yiddish so I shouldn't make a fool of myself. If I have, it's entirely my fault.

Davey Snyder and Chip Hitchcock, for compiling the glossary and noting the inconsistencies.

Eleanor and Leigh Hoagland, for once more opening their Maine home for a much-needed writing retreat, with fireflies.

Christopher Schelling and Sharyn November, for being such a wonderful and supportive agent and editor team.

Jon Keller, Frederick Schjang, and Dr. George Russell, for helping me keep my back supple and my mind clear.

Ellen Kushner, who has read this book almost as many times as I have and still laughs at the jokes. If it weren't for her, this train never would have gotten into the station at all, let alone on time.

Author Bio

Delia Sherman was born in Tokyo, Japan, and grew up in New York City, where she now lives. She is the author of numerous short stories, including three set in a magical New York: "Grand Central Park" (*The Green Man*), "CATNYP" (*The Faery Reel*), and "Cotillion" (*Firebirds*). In addition, she has published three adult fantasy novels, has been nominated for the Nebula and World Fantasy Awards, and has won the Mythopoeic Award. She is one of the founders of the Interstitial Arts Foundation. She is currently working on a third novel about Neef.

Her Web site at www.deliasherman.com has lots more information about New York Between and the Fairy Folk. Also cool pictures.